Come Back To Me

J.R. Barrett

COME BACK TO ME

Cover Design: Winterheart Designs

Interior Design: JW Manus

Also by J. R. Barrett

Novels

Beauty and the Feast
My Everything

The Soul Series
Book I: Incorporeal
Book II: In the Flesh
Book III: Stay
The Soul Series: Special Edition

Daughters of Persephone
Book I: Exile
Book II: Return
Book III: Reborn
Book IV: The Red Demon
The Daughters of Persephone (Complete Collection)

Short Stories

"You Might Just Get It"
"The Artist"
"Is It Spicy"
"Liz and Me"

Poetry

Poems of Love and Hate

Writing As Julia Rachel Barrett

Captured
Anytime Darlin'
Pushing Her Boundaries
One Four All (a ménage)

This book is dedicated to my husband, my own personal James Mackie.

The author wishes to thank JW Manus for her invaluable and shiny assistance.

To my dear readers:

Thank you so much for buying and reading *Come Back To Me.* The book has a long, interesting history. It's *come back to me* twice now, once when my first publisher closed an imprint and a second time at my request. I longed for the opportunity to make Cara's story a little more concise, which is not so easy when one is writing a story that spans ten years.

As you can probably tell, Cara is very dear to me. She and I have a great deal in common. I remember one reviewer asking this question—*How can so many bad things happen to one person*? Well, here's the short answer, they did. To be frank, Cara's life was even worse than portrayed in the book. In any case, I changed the details to protect both the innocent and the guilty alike, but the bones of the story are true. If you've read my earlier work, *Anytime Darlin',* you know I touched on some of these issues.

Chapter 1

May 1967

"Hey, Cara, come over here. There's something I want to show you. C'mere."

A hand on the door knob, Cara whirled around, startled at the unexpected sound of a male voice. She spotted her neighbor, Mr. Walker, her best friend Karen's father, standing at the edge of his driveway. He motioned to her.

"C'mere and take a look." He disappeared beyond the far side of his house.

Wondering why Mr. Walker was home, Cara set her schoolbooks on her front porch and slipped off her shoes and socks. If her mother was there she'd fuss about Cara's tomboy ways, but her mom spent every Tuesday afternoon at her club playing bridge. She wouldn't be home for several hours.

Comfortably barefoot, Cara walked through the cool spring grass, cutting over the low picket fence that separated the two properties.

Karen wasn't around. Cara had seen her friend before she'd left school. Every Tuesday and Thursday, Karen's mom drove her straight to dance class and then to gymnastics. Cara figured Mr. Walker had the afternoon off. He was her dad's law partner and it was rare for either man to leave work before suppertime.

Karen's father was always working on some project or another. He probably had something interesting to show her. They were the only family on the block to have a model train set. Mr. Walker added to it every Christmas. The train ran through three rooms of their large finished basement. One room was meant to be the desert, one the mountains, one the plains. The train traveled through caves and over bridges. Cara wondered if he'd added a new section, maybe that was what he wanted to show her.

Cara had been thrilled when the Walkers moved in three years before. She and Karen quickly became inseparable. They sat together in Mrs. Hughes' fourth grade class, Miss Benson's fifth grade class and in another month they'd graduate together from Miss White's sixth grade class. Everyone at the school teased them about being twins even though they looked nothing alike. Karen was blonde and bubbly, always giggling. She had pale skin, blue eyes, a perfect rosebud mouth, cute freckles and what Cara's dad called a button nose. And she was tiny. Cara's mother described her as petite. In contrast, Cara was a quiet girl and a serious student. She felt awkward standing next to Karen, like she was a galumphing elephant in comparison to a fragile butterfly.

Cara had experienced a growth spurt this year and at five feet, seven inches, she was the tallest girl in the school. Her ungainly long legs and arms didn't necessarily work in tandem and that didn't help her feel any less self-conscious.

Karen took dance lessons and gymnastics and everyone talked about how graceful she was. Cara, much to her mother's chagrin, hated dance and gymnastics and instead played basketball and touch football with the boys. Her hair was a deep auburn, not blonde, and unlike Karen's perfectly straight hair, Cara's curled so tightly in the Iowa humidity that it was nearly impossible to tame. For simplicity's sake she kept it pulled back in a ponytail. Her skin tanned quickly in the summer and she never managed to stay out of the sun like she was supposed to. Her eyes were a weird color, not brown, not green, not gray, but something in-between. And they changed color depending upon the weather and the lighting in a room.

Cara thought her mouth was too big, her feet too long, her legs too skinny. She was embarrassed by the fact that some of the girls in her class, including Karen, were already wearing bras while she still wore undershirts like a little kid. Her mother said she should be glad she didn't have to bother about that. Cara wasn't quite certain why girls even grew breasts. She knew adult women had them, but whenever she asked her mother why, she was told that nice girls didn't talk about it. Nice girls didn't talk about a lot of things, like why her mother bled every month and where on earth the blood came from. After asking numerous times and getting no answer, Cara knew better than to ask again. Her mother would shoot her one of those looks. The only explanation she received was that something happened to grown up women, something unpleasant, and if she was lucky it wouldn't happen to her for a long time.

Cara jogged around the corner and found Mr. Walker waiting by the back door.

"Come downstairs, Cara," he said. "You have to see this."

He turned and vanished through the doorway. Cara could hear him trotting down the basement stairs. Now she was sure he'd bought a new section for his train. Cara trailed after him. He waited for her at the bottom of the stairs, surprising Cara by grabbing her hand as she walked past him. She drew back, but he smiled reassuringly and tugged her towards the far end of the basement.

"Did you get a new section for your train, Mr. Walker?"

"Yes, I did. I want to show it to someone and you're the first one home."

They entered the backroom and Cara immediately noticed the new landscape.

"It's Vermont." He kept hold of her hand, giving it a squeeze. "Do you like it?"

Cara felt a little uncomfortable about the way he held tight to her hand, but she'd known him for three years so she figured maybe it was okay.

"Yes, it's very pretty. I like the pine trees. They look very realistic." She was proud of the fact that she'd used an adult word.

Mr. Walker tugged her closer until she pressed up against his side. "Look over there." he pointed. "See that mountain?" That's supposed to be Stowe, the ski resort."

"Oh." Cara didn't know what else to say. She had no idea what Stowe was. Mr. Walker smelled like aftershave. She felt his other hand tug on her ponytail.

"You've certainly sprouted this year."

"Yeah, I guess."

Mr. Walker was breathing in her ear. He sounded winded, like he'd been playing basketball.

"Um, I better go." Cara felt a little odd.

"No, no," he said. "Stay. Keep me company for a few minutes."

"I have some schoolwork to do, Mr. Walker." Cara tried to politely disengage her hand from his. He gripped hers tighter, pulling her along with him to an old couch. He sat down and grabbed her hips, forcing her onto his lap.

Cara was shocked. She didn't think she was supposed to be sitting on Mr. Walker's lap. She hadn't even sat on her dad's lap since she was little. It just didn't feel right and she began to squirm. He laughed in response, his laughter soft against her ear.

"Mr. Walker, I really think I should go."

"No, Cara. I'd really like you to stay. Has anyone ever told you how pretty you are? How pretty your mouth is? And your eyes, they're a very unusual color. I bet the boys tell you all the time how pretty you are."

Cara felt cold and hot at the same time. She wanted to get off his lap, but she didn't want to be rude and she couldn't understand why he was talking to her like this. Maybe he thought he was being nice, but Cara didn't like it. It didn't feel good. It felt strange. She didn't think Karen would like to find her sitting on her dad's lap. Cara tried to stand up, but Mr. Walker grabbed her arm and squeezed.

"Ow! You're hurting me. Please let me get up. I really have to go home."

"Not yet." He pushed her down onto the couch and lay over her.

"Stop, Mr. Walker. Please, stop. Let me go home." She began to cry. "I want go home."

No matter how hard she pleaded with him, Mr. Walker didn't stop. His voice grew cruel and rough, and he held her down despite her struggles and her tears.

When he had finished with her, Cara felt sick to her stomach.

"You hurt me." She sobbed. "You hurt me."

Mr. Walker smoothed her hair, as if trying to make the caress tender. He kissed her cheek. "I would never hurt you. I love you like my own daughter."

A thought flitted through Cara's mind. *Do you do what you just did to me, to Karen? Do you shove Karen down on the couch and do that? My dad doesn't do this to me.* But she shut it up as soon as she heard herself think it.

"I want to go home now." She reached for her underwear, pulling it on before he could stop her. What would her mother say when she saw blood on her underwear? Is that why her mother bled every month, because her father did this? Cara felt like throwing up.

"Cara, honey, listen, uh, don't tell your mom and dad about this. It's kind of a secret thing, between the two of us. I mean, it's a pretty special way to show you how much I care about you. You're Karen's best friend and I don't want that to change. I think if Karen knew we did this, she might not want to be friends with you anymore. She might be kind of mad at you."

"Mr. Walker, I don't want to do that again." Cara couldn't seem to stop crying.

"It's okay, honey. I understand. We'll see. It doesn't always hurt you know. Sometimes it feels good. One day you might like it."

"I don't want to do it again, Mr. Walker. I feel sick. I want to go home."

"You go on home then, Cara. I'm sure you'll feel better. I didn't mean to hurt you. Just remember, it's our secret. I wouldn't want to upset Karen. You come and see her later. She'll be home in a couple of hours."

He let her go. Cara stumbled up the stairs, feeling sore and sticky between her legs. She jogged stiffly across the lawn and up the porch steps; grateful nobody was at her home. She used the key hidden in the flowerpot to open the door, picked up her discarded books and shoes and ran to her room. How would she get rid of the telltale panties? She couldn't throw them in the laundry. Her mom would know. Her mom would know what she'd done. She undressed quickly, stuffing them into one of her snow boots in the back of her closet. Next time she was home alone, she'd put them in the trash burner in the basement, but all she could think of right now was taking a bath. She had to wash Mr. Walker's smell off her. The sweet smell of his aftershave and the smell of something else, something she couldn't put a name to.

Cara grabbed some clean clothes and locked herself in the bathroom. She sat on the edge of the tub as it filled with hot water. Suddenly the lunch she'd eaten hours ago felt like lead in her stomach and she vomited into the toilet.

Cara had no appetite for supper that evening.

"Are you sick?" Her mom looked her up and down.

"Maybe a little."

Her mom touched her forehead. "No fever. You probably just had too much sun today. What did you do after school?"

"Nothing." Cara's voice shook. "I got kind of sweaty playing basketball at lunch so I took a bath and then I did my homework."

"Basketball. . .? Really? Must you be such a tomboy?"

"She could be coming down with something," said her dad. "Dave didn't come in to work today. He wasn't feeling well."

"Should I give them a call? I saw Marcia pull into their driveway about an hour ago."

"No, I'll walk over and check on him." He turned to Cara. "Do you want to come to the Walker's with me?"

"N-No," she stuttered. "I still have some schoolwork."

"Suit yourself." He turned back to his meal. "Louise, did you get a bill yet for the new lawnmower?"

Their conversation barely registered.

"Cara, Cara. . .? Are you listening to me?" Her mother sounded as irritated as ever. "If you're just going to sit there like a bump on a log you may as well go to your room. You already took your bath so if you're not feeling well put yourself to bed. I'll be up later to say good night."

Cara excused herself and went to brush her teeth. Despite the fact that it was way before her bedtime, she climbed into bed. The sheets slid over her, smooth and soft against her legs. She felt as if her very presence soiled them. She wanted to cry again, but then her mother would want to know why she was crying and Cara knew she could never tell her. It was impossible. Her mother would never forgive such behavior. Besides, Cara didn't even have the words to explain what had happened.

Uncomfortable, Cara tossed and turned. The place between her legs burned, but she didn't know what to do about it. At least the bleeding had stopped. She wondered how she could ever face Karen again. What if Karen found out? What if the minute Karen looked at her she could tell what had happened? Cara had never been good at keeping a secret. As she lay there, staring at the ceiling, she decided this was one secret she'd bury very deep. She'd have to if she wanted to remain friends with Karen and stay out of trouble. Her mother would be furious if she found out.

How would she stay away from Mr. Walker? Cara never wanted to see him again, but she had no way to avoid him. What if he wanted to do it again? What would she say? He was bigger than her, he was stronger, and he was their neighbor and her father's law partner.

Besides, he said he did it because he loved her. How could someone say they love you, and then do that to you?

When she heard the door creak open, Cara pretended to be asleep.

Her mother said, "Maybe she is sick."

Cara kept her back turned away and stared at the wall. She had to make sure she was never alone with Mr. Walker. That's what she had to do. She'd never go to Karen's house again if he was the only person home, never. She could manage that. He was hardly ever home anyway. She had to forget this. She had to forget this ever happened. Everything would go back to the way it was. She and Karen would still be best friends. Mr. Walker would still be her father's golfing buddy. The two families would still throw that big Christmas party together. It would be okay.

Cara reached up and touched her cheeks, surprised to find they were wet. She didn't even realize she'd been crying.

Chapter 2

The morning had grown hot and Cara lay on her bed, reading. She heard someone enter through screen door. Whoever it was tried to be quiet, but the screen door made a soft, metallic scraping sound whenever it was opened or closed. She bolted upright. She was supposed to be home alone.

After her parents left for Des Moines she'd locked the front door behind them, but the day was so warm she'd left the heavy back door wide open. The gates were closed and latched. She hadn't expected anyone to come through the backyard. It couldn't be Karen. She and her mother had left yesterday to visit relatives in Idaho. It couldn't be her parents either. They'd driven away only an hour ago, and besides, they would have come through the garage.

Cara's skin prickled. She was trapped in her bedroom. The only way out of the house was down the stairs, and he was there, Mr. Walker was there, she knew it. She tiptoed to the door of her room, listening. She didn't hear the sound of footsteps, but she was certain someone was walking around because every so often she'd hear a floorboard squeak. She wondered, for an instant, if it was all her imagination. Maybe she was just a "nervous Nellie", as her mom had been calling her for the past month.

Then she heard his voice. "Cara? Are you up there? Your mom and dad asked me to check on you while they're gone."

Cara's legs began to shake. For the most part, she had managed to avoid Mr. Walker since the thing that happened in his basement. Twice, he'd caught her alone in Karen's bedroom, once when Karen had been in the bathroom. That time he tried to kiss her, but when Karen flushed the toilet, he left in a hurry. The second time, he'd come home early while she and Karen were up in Karen's bedroom. He'd sent Karen downstairs to help her mother with supper. He said, "I'll walk Cara home."

Cara hadn't known what to do. She'd nodded her head and tried to push past him, hurrying after Karen, but he'd blocked the doorway. He'd grabbed for her, pressing his hips against hers, shoving his hands under her shirt. Cara had stood frozen in place, unable to utter a single word. She'd been terrified Karen might hear. Or worse, Mrs. Walker might hear. That time he had held her jaw with his hand so she couldn't turn her head away. He'd tasted like stale tobacco.

Just the memory made Cara gag.

Now he'd come into her own home when she was all alone. She had to figure out what to do before he came upstairs. The door to her bedroom was open. She didn't dare shut it now. He would know for sure she was home. With a quick motion, Cara smoothed the quilt on her bed. Her closet door sat ajar. Cara gauged the opening. She was just thin enough to slip through without touching anything. If she crawled on the floor she wouldn't disturb the hanging clothes.

Cara slipped past the door, going down onto her knees and then onto her belly, sliding carefully along the hardwood floor towards the back of the closet.

The closet was the reason Cara had chosen this bedroom when they'd moved in. The roof angled down at the far end. It was so low that anyone taller than four feet couldn't stand upright. Her father had installed shelving for her books and shoes and he'd left a space behind the shelves that was just large enough for one child to sit and play.

Trying hard to ignore the approaching footsteps, she climbed over the shelves. If she thought about Mr. Walker and what he might do, she'd make some kind of noise. Cara dare not give herself away. The closet was dark and she was hidden by hanging clothes, shoeboxes and books. There was enough room for her to lay down flat on her stomach below the sloping roof. If Mr. Walker wanted to find her, he'd have to crawl into her closet on his hands and knees, and then reach over the shelves and feel for her. As far as Cara could tell, if she stayed right where she was, she would be invisible.

Cara heard the door to her room creak open.

"Hey, anybody home?"

Cara pressed her chest against the floor, biting her lip to keep from making a sound.

"Cara?"

It seemed to Cara he was standing right in front of the closet. Feeling air move over her bare legs, Cara knew he'd opened the closet door. She squeezed her eyelids shut, terrified of what Mr. Walker would do if he found her.

"Cara?"

She was suddenly very grateful her father had never remembered to install a light in her closet. She breathed through her mouth, making an effort to keep each breath shallow and quiet, just like she did whenever her mother was in one of her moods.

She could hear him shuffling her hanging clothes around, but even if he took them all out, he wouldn't see her way in the back. Besides, she knew he wouldn't take her clothes out. If he did, her mom might ask her questions and Mr. Walker wanted to keep everything a secret. He wouldn't want her to have to answer questions. When the clothes stopped moving, Cara blew out a long, slow exhale.

She listened for a long time. She didn't hear anything, but that didn't mean Mr. Walker had left the house. For all she knew, he could be sitting on her bed. She wondered how longer it would be before her parents got home. They'd been gone more than an hour. She imagined they'd go to lunch before shopping, so the soonest she could expect them back would be suppertime. Unless Mr. Walker got tired of waiting and went home she'd be stuck on the floor in the back of her closet for a long time.

Cara's mind darted back and forth, her imagination working overtime. Was he sitting on her bed? Standing in the hallway? Waiting for her in the kitchen? Maybe he'd walked back across the yard, through his own gate and into his own home. Short of leaving the closet she had no way of knowing anything. How long could she stay there? Not moving? Barely breathing? She already needed to use the bathroom, and her muscles were beginning to cramp.

But Cara was scared. If she left the closet and he was waiting in her room, he'd be angry that she'd hidden from him, upset that she didn't trust him. He was her dad's law partner and close friend, their next door neighbor and Karen's father.

Cara wondered if all he really did want to do was check on her. Maybe she should trust him. He was an adult, and her mother had always told her she was supposed to trust adults to know what was best for her. Her mother told her to be respectful and do as she was told.

Cara decided she was being silly. She rose to a crouch, climbing back over the bookshelves. Mr. Walker had probably gone home. She peeked through the closet door. Her room was empty. Cara let out a sigh of relief and got to her feet. That's when she saw him, leaning against the wall. He came towards her, slamming her bedroom door behind him.

"Why were you hiding from me? What are you afraid of?"

"I-I wasn't hiding," Cara stuttered. "I was. . . I was cleaning my closet and I thought I heard a burglar so I-I kept quiet."

"You didn't hear my voice? I called for you."

"Um, no, I, uh, I heard something but I didn't know it was you. I'm fine, Mr. Walker. You can go home. I'm fine."

"You're afraid of me Cara. Why are you afraid?"

Cara tried to stop her legs from shaking. "I'm-I'm not afraid. I was just surprised someone was in the house."

"I told you I'd never hurt you, Cara. I told you I love you like my own daughter. I'd never, never hurt you."

Mr. Walker moved closer. He ran his hand along the side of her face.

"You are such a beautiful girl. I really want to kiss you. Will you let me kiss you? There's no reason to be afraid. I won't hurt you."

"No, Mr. Walker, I'd rather not. I don't want to kiss you." Cara backed away from him.

He grabbed for her wrist. Cara jerked her arm out of his reach. She shook her head.

"No, Mr. Walker, I'm not doing that again."

"C'mon, honey, I promise it won't hurt this time. Remember? I told you it wouldn't hurt the next time, that maybe you'd like it."

"No!" Cara surprised herself by shouting at him. "I'm not doing it again."

"Cara, honey, calm down. I'm not going to hurt you."

"Then get out of my room."

Mr. Walker sat on her bed. He patted the spot next to him. "Sit."

Cara shook her head. She backed toward the door.

"Do you want me to tell your mom and dad that you hid in your closet when I came to check on you today? Do you want them to ask you why? They might think it's a pretty disrespectful thing to do."

"You won't tell them," Cara said. "Because they might find out what you did to me. I don't think you were supposed to do that. My dad doesn't do that."

Mr. Walker laughed. "Sure he does, Cara. He does it all the time. Just not with you. He does it with his secretary, Elaine. She doesn't seem to mind."

"Uh-uh. He does not. I don't believe you." Cara felt a cold sensation spread through her chest. *Her father and Miss Madsen doing that?* It was unthinkable. She pushed the revolting picture out of her mind. Her father wouldn't do that. Not with Miss Madsen. She wasn't even very old, maybe twenty-one or twenty-two.

"Cara, be a big girl and come over here. I won't hurt you."

"No." She opened her bedroom door and made for the stairs.

Mr. Walker moved fast. He was on her in two seconds. He wrapped one hand around her waist, pressing the other over her mouth when Cara let out a shriek. He dragged her back into her room. He threw her down on the floor next to her bed and stood over her.

Her eyes wide, she watched him unbuckle his belt.

"I don't want to hurt you, unless you make me hurt you. If you fight me, I promise you it will hurt. If you go along with me, if you do what I tell you, I won't hurt you. I promise you that. I'm doing this because I love you, Cara. Don't make me hurt you because if I have to, I will."

Cara's heart pounded so hard she thought it might burst. She was terrified, too terrified to do anything. She'd never heard Mr. Walker sound like this, so mean, so cruel. She felt more afraid than she'd felt the first time, because now she knew what he intended to do.

"Take your clothes off. Now."

Too scared to cry, Cara did as she was told.

Chapter 3

Christmas 1967

The office Christmas party was held at the Walkers' home this year. Mr. and Mrs. Walker laid out cigarettes and ashtrays, silver bowls with mixed nuts, crackers with soft, smelly cheeses, but mostly they served drinks. Cara's dad hired a bartender for the occasion. Cara sat with Karen in the den, both dressed in uncomfortable frilly party dresses, following their mothers' admonitions that children should be seen and not heard. They watched and listened as the grownups told jokes and laughed out loud, their heads wreathed in smoke, hands holding tall, frosted glasses.

Cara's dad drank martinis. She didn't understand the appeal aside from the olive. He'd let her have a taste once; then chuckled when she grimaced and gagged. It tasted like poison. He said, "It's an acquired taste."

That's what Mr. Walker said about what they'd been doing together, that it was an acquired taste, and one day she'd like it. Cara hated it and she hated Mr. Walker for making her do it.

Since the day Mr. Walker found her in the bedroom, Cara had become a recluse. She'd made her father put a lock on her bedroom door, and she spent every afternoon and evening shut up there. She refused to stay home alone. If her parents were going out, she insisted they take her to her grandmother's house. If her mother disagreed, Cara threw a screaming fit until she gave in.

Cara's mother even dragged her to the doctor. He couldn't find a single thing wrong with her. He had no explanation for Cara's stomachaches, her lackluster appetite, her noticeable weight loss or her sudden temper tantrums. He said "Cara is just a nervous child, and there isn't much to do for her. She'll grow out of it. Some children hit a rough patch during adolescence."

Cara had no idea what adolescence was, nor did she care. The only thing that mattered to her was keeping out of Mr. Walker's reach. She'd managed to avoid him for weeks. Of course that was because it was the holiday season and now the Walkers had a houseful of company.

This was the first time she'd entered the Walkers' home in months. She and her mother had a big fight about the Christmas party. Cara had relented, agreeing to attend, but only because her father intervened.

She barely spoke to Karen anymore. In the mornings, Cara left early and walked to school, refusing a ride from Mrs. Walker, despite the fact that the junior high school was nearly three miles away. Everybody, including Karen, thought Cara was weird for walking. The only things that remained unchanged in her life were her grades. Cara was still a straight *A* student, the top student in her class. She could lose herself in school work. While reading or drawing, Cara could forget about Mr. Walker, even if only for a few hours.

Besides, Cara had noticed that the change in their friendship didn't seem to bother Karen much. With her dance and gymnastics background, Karen was the first girl picked for the cheerleading squad. She'd made new friends, fun friends, who giggled, wore lipstick and were popular. Because of Karen, Cara was tolerated by that crowd, but she was considered too serious and too shy to be included in anything really fun.

Now the two girls sat together, an uncomfortable space between them. They spoke only when spoken to, watching the adults.

Karen yawned. "You want to come up to my room?"

Cara took a surreptitious look around for Mr. Walker. She didn't want him following them upstairs. Since he didn't appear to be nearby, she agreed.

When they reached Karen's room, her friend flipped the door shut and flopped onto her bed.

"God, this is so boring. I don't know how they stand it."

"Yeah, it's pretty boring," agreed Cara. She perched on the edge of the other twin bed.

"What is up with you? You've changed so much. You're quiet. You got a secret boyfriend or something?"

Cara was taken aback. "No, of course I don't have a boyfriend. I don't want a boyfriend."

"Well I do." Karen sighed. "Mark Smith is dreamy. Haven't you noticed? He's a ninth grader, but boy, I don't care. He is so cute."

"Mark Smith?"

"You know, the tall guy, blond hair, captain of the basketball team? C'mon Cara, don't tell me you haven't noticed him. All the girls notice him."

Cara shook her head. "No, I guess I haven't noticed him. I've been pretty busy with school."

Karen looked at her, criticism in her eyes. "There's more to school than school work, Cara. You used to be fun. What happened to you? We used to have a good time together. We used to tell each other everything. Now you hardly say two words to me."

Cara just shrugged. She didn't have an answer for Karen, at least not one she was willing to voice out loud.

Karen rolled onto her back. She raised her hands toward the ceiling, staring at the pink polish on her nails.

"I'd let Mark get to second base with me." Her voice was so soft Cara almost missed the comment.

"Second base?" Cara was confused. "You don't play baseball."

Karen sat up and stared at her friend, a look of incredulity on her face. "Don't tell me you don't know what *going to second base* means?"

Cara nodded. "It means when you play ball and run to second base, like when we play softball."

Karen laughed out loud. "No you idiot! It means when you let a boy touch your boobs!"

Cara felt that awful pain in her stomach, the same pain she got whenever she saw Mr. Walker, whenever he touched her.

"Don't you know anything about this stuff? You know, like first base, second base, third base, going all the way?"

Cara shook her head. Her mouth felt dry as a desert. She was afraid to ask, but equally afraid not to.

"You know, sex," said Karen. "Don't you know anything about sex?"

Cara shook her head again.

"You are unbelievable! You mean your mother didn't tell you anything about it? Haven't you talked to any of the kids at school? Did you even start your period yet?"

"My period?"

"Oh my gosh." Karen laughed out loud. "When you bleed every month, your period. Women bleed every month, something about ovulation and all that." Karen flopped back down. "I use tampons. Rebecca explained how to use them in the girls' bathroom at school. I don't use those stupid pads my mom buys."

Cara didn't know what a tampon was, but from watching her mother she knew about the pads and the monthly bleeding. Suddenly something clicked. She wanted to know exactly what Karen was talking about. She was almost desperate to know. There was a link between what Karen was talking about and what Mr. Walker had been doing to her for months.

"Um, no, I don't know. My mom's never talked about any of this stuff. I don't, I mean, I haven't started my-my period yet. I don't know what a tampon is."

"These." Karen rolled over and opened her bottom drawer. She pulled out a box and with a careless motion, tossed it at Cara.

Cara held the box in her hand, cautious.

"What are you afraid of?" Karen laughed again. "It won't bite!"

As if she was entering the door to another realm, Cara pried open the cardboard lid. Pulling out a tampon, she turned it round and round in her hand. Unfolding the directions and illustrations, she gazed down at the line drawings and things began to click. She felt like Helen Keller, the day she remembered the word *water,* and everything Annie Sullivan had been trying to teach her suddenly made sense. It wasn't difficult for Cara to make the connection between where a tampon went and where Mr. Walker put *that* part of his body. Her stomach began to burn.

"Karen, what do you mean first base and second base and all that? What does *sex* mean?"

"You are such an innocent." Karen giggled. "I can't believe you don't know this stuff." She reached into the same drawer and pulled out a booklet. "Here, read this. My mom gave it to me last year."

Cara's hand shook as she took the booklet from Karen. She stole a glance at her friend's face. Fortunately Karen didn't seem to notice her discomfort.

"First base is kissing," Karen explained in a grown up voice. "Sometimes it's French kissing. That's when the boy sticks his tongue in your mouth. I don't know why it's called French kissing. Maybe they do it that way in France or something. Anyway that's first base. Second base is when you let a boy touch your boobs, like I said. Third base is, well, third base is when a boy sticks his hands down your pants. I'm not exactly sure what happens because, you know, I've never done it and I don't know anyone who has. Fourth base is when you go all the way."

"Go all the way?"

"Yeah, um. . ." Karen gave her a knowing smile. "When the boy sticks his thing into you. Married people do it. Well, usually it's married people who do it, but sometimes high school kids do it. They're not supposed to. Rebecca told me that some of the older kids have gone all the way. It's how you get pregnant."

Cara clutched the booklet to her chest. She felt short of breath and the room seemed to spin around her. This is what Mr. Walker had been doing to her, sticking his *thing* into her. If Karen's explanation was true, he wasn't supposed to do that. She wasn't supposed to let him do that. Even though she hadn't eaten anything all day, Cara felt like she was going to throw up. With a stiff motion, she rose from the bed and headed towards the adjoining bathroom.

"Are you okay?"

Cara sat down on the edge of the tub, trying to will the nausea away.

"Yeah, I haven't been feeling well lately."

Karen moved to stand in the doorway. She looked a little uncomfortable. "You do look pale, and you're really skinny. My mom said you'd been sick a lot. Is that why you haven't been over here much?"

"Um-hm. . . Yeah, I just haven't been feeling well enough to go out."

"Do you want me to get you anything? A pop or something?"

"No, no thanks. I just need to sit here for a few minutes. Usually it goes away after a while."

"Okay, well, I'm going to get something to eat. You sure you don't want anything?"

"I'm sure. Thanks anyway. I'll be right down."

Karen turned and vanished into the hallway. Cara listened until her footsteps faded away, then she got up and closed the door to the bathroom, locking it. Cara's gaze fell on the booklet still clutched in her hand. Her palms were sweating so much she left smudges on the cover. She closed the lid to the toilet, sat down, and opened up the booklet. She read it from cover to cover, understanding at last what she had done with Mr. Walker.

Cara sat in silence, appalled and humiliated. She had done something awful. She knew there was no one, absolutely no one, she could tell about this. Nobody would believe her and even if they did, they would despise her. The kids at school would never speak to her again. The teachers would treat her like she was trash. Karen would hate her. Mrs. Walker would hate her. Her own parents would never forgive her. The only thing she could do was make sure it never, ever happened again.

Cara put her ear against the door, listening for any noise in Karen's room. She didn't hear anything, but that didn't mean Mr. Walker wasn't out there, waiting. She lay on the floor, turning her head sideways so she could look under the door. As far as she could tell, the room was empty. Cara left the bathroom and stuffed the booklet in Karen's bottom drawer, along with the box of tampons. She glanced out into the hallway.

Downstairs people laughed and told jokes; enjoyed their cocktails. She could hear ice clink in the glasses. Smoke from their cigarettes wafted upwards, creating a gray-blue haze that swirled into spirals along the high ceiling.

The Christmas party meant nothing. It was mere noise. The people there meant nothing to her. She didn't even want to go home. She wanted to vanish completely. Disappear. Drift unnoticed like the smoke eddies above. Cara stood at the railing for a long time before she made a decision. Without catching anyone's eye, she walked down the stairs and straight out the front door, opening and closing it behind her without a sound. Her grandmother lived a few miles away. Cara decided she would walk to her house tonight. She didn't know what else to do.

Chapter 4

Christmas Day 1967

"How dare you!"

Cara staggered back a few steps from the force of her mother's slap.

"How dare you worry us like this? What's wrong with you, Cara? Can't you think of anyone besides yourself?"

Her mother was crying. First she had seemed to be crying tears of relief, but now she seemed furious.

"Louise. . ." Cara's father grabbed her hand. "I don't think it's necessary to get physical with her."

"What would you know?" Her mother turned on him. "You're not the one who's had to put up with her for the past six months. Put up with her pouting and her screaming. Change your busy schedule just to accommodate her. Run the selfish little brat to the doctor all the time for no good reason."

"Cara, come here." Her father beckoned to her. "Why did you run off last night? You had us scared to death."

Cheeks flaming, Cara approached. She cleared her throat, attempting to steady her voice despite the fact that she was about to burst into tears herself. "I-I didn't run off. I went to Grandma's. We tried to call you, we did. We called the Walkers' and later we called our house but no one answered. Grandma said she would talk to you first thing in the morning."

"But why would you do such a thing? Walk off into the snow without even a coat on Christmas Eve, without a word to anyone?"

Cara stared down at her shoes, ruined from walking in last night's snow and the salty slush in the street. She watched a tear dot the dirty black patent leather.

"She's a manipulative little witch," hissed her mother. "The sooner you realize it the better off we'll all be. This is her fault!" She stormed out of the room.

Cara's father leaned back on the sofa. He pulled a pack of cigarettes from his shirt pocket. He tipped one out of the package and lit it with his silver cigarette lighter. Cara stood before him, watching him inhale. He blew the smoke off to the side, away from her.

"We didn't answer the phone last night, Cara, because there was a problem."

Cara blinked at him.

"I'm going to ask you a question and I want an honest answer. Did Mr. Walker ever touch you?"

Cara's legs began to shake. She pressed her knees together to try to stop them, but that seemed to make the shaking worse. "What. . .? What do you mean?"

"Did Mr. Walker ever touch you in places he wasn't supposed to touch you? Parts of your body other people aren't supposed to see? This is important Cara. I need to know. I want the truth."

"Why?" Her voice was a whisper.

Her father inhaled again, a long slow inhale followed by an even longer exhale.

"Cara, do you know what rape is?"

Cara shook her head.

"It's when a man does something to a woman he's not supposed to do, something she doesn't want him to do. It's a very bad thing and it's against the law. Did Mr. Walker do that to you? Did he make you do things you didn't want to do?"

Cara wanted to slide under the rug, or melt into a pool of water like the Wicked Witch of the West in *The Wizard of Oz*.

"Just shake your head Cara. Shake your head yes or no."

Eyes locked on her shoes again, Cara nodded. *Yes.*

"How many times?" her father asked her, his voice hoarse now.

Cara looked up at him. She met his eyes then she looked away.

Her father rose from the couch. "That's all I need to know." He put a big hand on Cara's shoulder. "We won't ever talk about this again."

The Walkers moved out before New Year. Cara watched from her bedroom window as the three of them climbed into their car and drove off. The moving van had already gone ahead with their furniture. They were moving to Nevada. Mr. Walker had found a new job with another law firm. Between Christmas Eve and the day they moved, she only saw Karen once. Karen's eyes were red from crying. She deliberately looked at Cara and mouthed *I hate you* before she turned away and disappeared into her house.

It was weeks before Cara found out what had happened on Christmas Eve. Her parents hadn't discussed it, but her grandmother told her the story.

Mr. and Mrs. Engels, neighbors who lived two doors down, had left the party early because they were expecting a long-distance Christmas Eve phone call from relatives. Their fourteen-year-old daughter, Connie, had stayed at home to watch her baby brother. When they entered the house, they'd heard Connie screaming. They ran to her room and found her struggling with Mr. Walker. He'd ripped off most of her clothes and he was trying to rape her. Mr. Engels hauled Mr. Walker off his daughter, and he slugged him, knocking him unconscious. Mrs. Engels called the police.

A police officer had appeared at the Christmas party, asking for Cara's father. The officer escorted him to the Engels' house. Cara's dad had found Mr. Walker half-dressed, his *thing* hanging out of his pants. Connie was covered with bruises, and the police insisted she go to the emergency room.

Cara's grandmother said Connie wasn't badly hurt, just scared out of her wits. Cara learned she'd told her parents and the police officers that among other things, Mr. Walker yelled at her that *Cara never gave him so much trouble.*

"That was how your dad found out."

Cara's face turned beet red when she heard her grandmother utter those words.

"You came here because of him, didn't you?"

Cara could only nod.

"I don't blame you," said her grandmother. "He should be in jail."

"Why isn't he? If what he did is illegal why isn't he in jail?"

"Because your father is a big name in this town and it would be bad for business. Your mother doesn't want a scandal. She's afraid of losing her country club membership."

"But what about the Engels?"

"They agreed that if he'd leave town they wouldn't press charges." Cara's grandmother shrugged. "They didn't want Connie to go through a trial. They didn't want her to be forced to see him again. Your father felt the same way about you. He wants you to forget about it."

Cara saw sympathy in her grandmother's eyes. "What if I can't forget it?"

"I'm sorry for you," she said. "But you can't undo what he did. You'll have to find a way to live with it."

Cara tried and failed to stop her words. "Mom hates me for it. She thinks everything is my fault. She said the other day that I had ruined her life."

Cara's grandmother patted her shoulder. "I know it's hard, honey, but as time passes things will get better. You're a smart girl, smarter than your mother. She'll come around."

Chapter 5

April 1971

Cara's head lolled forward.

"Damn, that's good shit." She gazed around the cluttered Volkswagen van, trying not to slur her words. Randy and Jackie spooned on the ratty old mattress. Her friend John leaned against the wall, his eyes half-closed; bong resting in his lap. Cara couldn't remember how long she'd been there. Fifteen minutes? An hour? Two? That was the thing about dope, you lost track of time. She had a final in art class today.

Shit! She had a final in art class.

"John." Cara poked at him with her foot. "John, what time is it?"

John stirred and glanced at his wrist. "I don't know," he said with a grin. "It's upside down."

Cara slid over to the other side of the van and held up his arm. She tried to make sense of the hands on his watch.

"I gotta go. Art final. I'm late." Cara looked for her bag, the multi-colored paisley shoulder tote she'd sewn herself from remnants she found at the fabric store. She grabbed for it and slung it over her shoulder, pulling the dime bag out, tossing it in John's direction. "Keep it for me."

"Sure thing," he mumbled. He stuffed the baggie into his backpack. She could trust John with her dope. Randy and Jackie were a different story. They would smoke what they wanted then sell the rest.

Cara climbed out of the van, keeping an eye peeled for Mr. Ringer, the assistant principal, also known as the resident fascist. He was always on the lookout for students skipping class. Cara was on his hit list because she hung with the hippies and druggies and she'd been tear-gassed at an anti-war protest over the winter.

He hated the fact that she had a dispensation from her shrink to come and go as she pleased, yet she managed to maintain straight *A's* in every one of her honors classes. He spent an inordinate amount of time trying to catching her smoking pot or doing something untoward, something he could use to suspend her, but he couldn't pin a thing on her. Cara had him pegged. Whether he realized it or not, Mr. Ringer followed a pattern. Where he would be, when he would be there and what he would do, was all very predictable. Cara made a point of studying his pattern. Once she had it figured out, she pretty much ignored him. Still, one had to be on guard, she never knew when he might change his pattern, so she just to be on the safe side she checked the parking lot for his big protruding gut, his white shirt and his skinny black tie.

He'd tried to get her suspended for refusing to adhere to the strict dress code rules. Cara had walked away when he'd ordered her to get down on her knees in the hallway so he could measure her skirt. He had responded by phoning her parents and firing off a letter to the FBI, accusing her of being an anti-American subversive. The call to her parents got her grounded for a month. The letter to the FBI had made her the talk of the high school. Well that, and her relationship with notorious bad boy Rick Shea. That relationship had been over for a while and Rick had graduated last May, but it had lasted nearly a year and it seemed like everybody at all three high schools in town knew about their relationship, following its progress from the day it began to the day it ended.

Yeah, everyone knew about the nightmare ending.

Cara reached the door to the art room without any interference from the assistant principal. She'd have to stay late if she wanted to complete her painting. Her teacher wouldn't care. She loved to have students spend time with her after school and in any case, she had a soft spot for Cara. Thanks to her art teacher, Cara had been admitted to a senior art class at the beginning of her sophomore year. The principal couldn't very well say no, since a watercolor Cara painted had been chosen to hang in the Capitol Rotunda in Washington D.C. by none other than the President of the United States himself. It was the painting that had brought her into contact with Rick Shea.

One Saturday morning Cara received a call informing her that one of her paintings had been entered into a national competition by her art teacher. What Cara found most astonishing was not that her work had been chosen by the President, but that it had been selected in the first place from among the hundreds of works submitted to the governor of the State of Iowa by every public high school.

To Cara it was just another abstract painting, no better and no worse than anything she'd done before. Cara hadn't given much thought to the results at the time. What she recalled was that while she painted it she'd been completely oblivious to the world around her. Sometimes that happened when she painted or worked on a sketch, she could shut off her brain and let her hand move of its own accord. Cara had known her teacher liked it, but she never expected the work to end up anywhere besides the classroom wall. She was surprised and a little uncomfortable at the unfamiliar surge of pride she felt upon hearing the news. Cara spent most of her time flying under the radar. She worried that any mention of her name would remind everyone of David Walker.

When she'd called, the teacher had asked Cara to come to the school so they could take a picture for the yearbook. She'd also said she was making arrangements for Cara to meet with the mayor and a reporter from the local newspaper.

Cara's mother agreed without hesitation. She loved that kind of publicity.

Aware that she hadn't done much her mother could be proud of, instead of wearing her usual baggy jeans and letting her thick hair dry into the natural waves her mom hated, Cara styled her hair, blowing it straight and tucking the ends under. She donned a cute blue seersucker miniskirt with a baby-blue sleeveless top and matching seersucker jacket. She declined her mother's offer of pantyhose, but she wore a pair of wedges that lengthened her long legs even more.

To Cara's astonishment, she was joined at the photo shoot by Rick Shea. Apparently his sculpture had been the other work of art chosen.

She knew who Rick Shea was, despite the fact that he was a senior while she was a freshman. His reputation definitely preceded him. He was the boy every girl in town wanted to get with. Cara had heard a lot about him. Who hadn't? He was the epitome of cool.

He was tall, broad shouldered and well-built. His hair was almost jet black, a gift from his Cherokee grandmother, along with his high cheek bones, an angular nose and a chiseled jaw, but his eyes were a cool ice-blue, inherited from his Irish father. He had strong hands. His father was a cabinetmaker and Rick was his apprentice.

Although she'd occasionally seen him at the soda fountain after school, usually with one girl or another, Cara never considered approaching him. The guy was way out of her league. Besides, she'd kept her distance from boys. Teenage boys touched teenage girls and they expected to be touched back. Cara figured she understood the concept better than anyone.

Rick made small talk all during the photo shoot and the interview. Cara found him pleasant enough. He was polite and kept a respectful distance making Cara wonder if his reputation was exaggerated. The interview finished, Cara sat in a chair, watching her mother through lowered lids as she chatted away with the mayor and the reporter, expounding upon Cara's wonderful qualities as a daughter. Cara wanted to laugh. She knew what her mother really thought of her.

"You want to go outside for a smoke?"

Cara hadn't even heard Rick come up behind her.

"Sure."

They exited the newspaper offices through the side door, walking around to the back of the building so her mother wouldn't see. Rick stuck a Camel unfiltered in his mouth, struck a match, lit it and handed it to Cara. Then he lit one for himself. Cara felt an unexpected thrill go through her as she took the lit cigarette from his hand. His gesture unnerved her. It slid like silk through the barriers she'd erected over the past few years. She had never smoked an unfiltered cigarette before. It seemed quite daring. She put the cigarette to her lips, feeling the dampness from his mouth, inhaling deeply. She did her best to look dainty as she picked a piece of tobacco off her tongue before she exhaled. Rick leaned against the old red bricks, blowing smoke rings into the chill spring air.

"I've seen you around."

Cara didn't respond to his comment, she just looked at him, keeping her expression carefully neutral.

"I've seen you at the soda fountain after school. You play basketball in the gym at night. I've watched you play. You're pretty good, you know, for a girl."

"Thanks." It was all Cara could think of to say. Rick Shea had noticed her?

"I saw your painting before your teacher sent it off," he said. "It was on display in my art class for a couple weeks. It was well done. Nice choice of colors."

Cara was surprised by her own reply. "Tell me about your sculpture."

"Not much to tell," he said, taking a drag from his Camel. "I sculpted a woman out of clay. Abstract of course. I think it was the combination of glazes I used that got their attention. The judges, I mean. Or whoever chose the two works from Iowa."

"Weird coincidence that the two final selections are from Iowa, from the same town," said Cara.

"Yeah," Rick said. "It is interesting."

Cara heard her mother calling for her. She dropped her cigarette on the sidewalk, crushing the lighted tip.

"Thanks for the smoke," she said. "I gotta go."

"Yeah, see you around." Rick leaned back against the building.

Cara had the distinct feeling that he watched her walk away, watched her until she rounded the corner. She was too shy to turn around and wave.

As Cara read in her room that night, she heard the phone ring. Her mother answered. Cara's eyes lifted from the page at the sound of her mother's voice. It almost sounded as if her mother was flirting. Cara shook her head in disbelief. It was difficult to imagine her uptight mother flirting with anyone.

"Cara," she called out. "Cara, telephone."

That was surprising. Cara didn't get phone calls.

Cara's mother met her at the bottom of the stairs. "It's that nice Rick Shea," she whispered in Cara's ear. "Be polite."

Cara shot her mother a glance before heading into the kitchen to get the phone. Apparently even her proper mother was not immune to Rick's charms. Why on earth was he calling?

"Hello?"

"Hi, Cara, this is Rick. I just wanted to let you know how much I enjoyed meeting you today. You're quite an artist."

Cara knew perfectly well he had an angle. But her wayward heart beat fast nonetheless. Rick Shea was calling her.

"Thank you." She made an effort to keep her voice neutral. "How did you get my number?"

"Easy. Everybody in town knows your dad. Besides, my brother's girlfriend works as a file clerk in the courthouse."

Cara could almost hear the grin in his voice. Her father had been appointed to the Superior Court last year. Their phone number was unlisted as a result. Rick had obviously gone to some effort. She felt her heart speed up even more and she willed it to slow back down. Rick saved her the trouble of thinking up a response.

"Listen Cara, I'm wondering if we could meet tomorrow after school, at Evan's ice cream parlor."

"Um, I guess," she said, surprising herself by accepting. "What time will you be there?"

"Around three-thirty. I'll hold a booth for us. Look for me in the back corner."

"All right."

"Hey, I can't wait to see you again. 'Night, Cara."

"Bye, Rick."

Cara set the receiver back in its cradle. She stood still for a moment wondering what on earth she'd just done. What could Rick Shea possibly want with her? She wasn't one of the cool girls. She kept to herself and the other kids at school thought she was weird. Besides, a lot of people knew what had happened. Not everybody, but enough. Cara felt like some of the kids pitied her, but others looked at her like she'd asked for it, as if she'd gone along with Mr. Walker willingly. Everyone who knew anything about that Christmas Eve was protective of Connie Engels, protective of her reputation. Unlike Cara, Connie had fought back. Her parents made it clear to everybody who expressed concern that what had happened was not Connie's fault.

In contrast, Cara's parents never said a word about Mr. Walker. They told Cara she was not to discuss it. Although Cara wasn't certain how her dad felt about what she'd done, her mother called her a disgrace. She said, "It's a miracle that we can even hold up our heads in this town." Cara felt like a leper.

"What did he say?"

Cara nearly jumped out of her skin, whirling around. "Jeez, Mom, what are you doing standing there? You scared me to death."

Her mother ignored her. "Why did he call? He's such a polite young man. You barely said two words to him."

"He just wants me to meet him at Evan's after school, to get some ice cream or something. It's no big deal."

"No big deal? A boy like that calls you and you think it's no big deal? You're lucky any boy is calling you at all after what happened."

Cara's eyes grew wide and she felt the blood drain from her face. She stared at her mother.

"Well, what do you expect? You're no raving beauty and everybody knows. . ."

"Everybody knows what, Mom?"

"That you, well. . . I don't have to spell it out for you."

Cara's voice rose. "Spell what out, Mom? Maybe you should spell it out. I'd like to know what everybody. . ." She stopped when her father entered the room.

"Why are you yelling, Cara? Don't speak to your mother in that tone. Apologize to her immediately."

Cara stared at the floor.

"Cara," her father said in what she'd come to think of as his *judge* voice.

Cara spoke through gritted teeth, "Sorry, Mom."

From over her father's shoulder she watched her mother shape her lips into a smirk. She said, "You should be a little more respectful to your parents, young lady."

Blinking back tears, Cara asked, "May I please be excused? I have homework."

Her father nodded. As she headed up the stairs, Cara could hear them discussing her behavior. She heard her father's deep bass notes, but she couldn't make out his words. However her mother's shrill voice came through loud and clear.

"That girl gets more disrespectful by the day. Do you know that she didn't even stay to talk to the mayor today? She snuck out after the photographer was finished. It took me twenty minutes to find her. She was off somewhere in the back of the building doing who knows what. She smelled like cigarettes when she got in the car."

Her father's voice rumbled.

"That may be," replied her mother. "But I think she behaves like a common. . ."

Cara reached her room and closed her door, shutting out the remainder of the conversation. She was sure her mother's last word would be *slut.* Possibly *tramp.* Her mother was right. Why would Rick Shea, the most popular boy in three high schools, want anything to do with her?

Despite Cara's doubts, Rick was waiting for her the next day, exactly as he'd promised, in the back booth at Evans soda fountain. He rose from his seat when she approached, greeting her politely, and then helped her with her backpack, sliding next to her as she slipped onto the vinyl bench.

"I'm really glad you came," he said. "I was afraid you'd change your mind."

"I-I almost did," Cara stuttered, surprised to hear the truth spill from her lips.

"Why would you change your mind? I won't bite. Well, not yet."

Cara laughed. "I don't go out much. To be honest, I don't go out with guys at all."

"Yeah, I heard. I don't really understand why. You're the most beautiful girl I've ever seen. I should have to beat the other guys off with a stick."

Cara felt her heart jump. If this was a line, it was the best line she'd ever imagined.

Cara shrugged. "Most guys think I'm weird."

"Their loss," he said. "I already ordered for you. I hope you don't mind. One scoop of French vanilla with hot fudge, no nuts, no cherry, no whipped cream."

"How did you know?" Cara was stunned.

"I told you yesterday. I've noticed you. I pay attention."

The time flew by. Cara hadn't opened herself up to another person in ages. When there was a break in the conversation and she finally noticed the time, it was nearly five thirty. She was late.

"I was supposed to be home at five," she said. "My mom is going to have a fit."

"I'll give you a ride." Rick was nonchalant. "My bike's out back."

"Your motorcycle? I've. . .I've never ridden a motorcycle before."

"There's a first time for everything." Rick grabbed her backpack and slung it over his shoulder. "C'mon."

His bike was beautiful, a royal blue Harley Davidson. Rick mounted the seat, flipping down the footrests behind him. Cara stood frozen in place for a moment, unable to quite believe this unexpected chain of events. He started the bike with a roar.

"Hop on."

She didn't hesitate. He handed her the backpack, and she secured it over her shoulders before climbing onto the seat behind him. She slid down the slick leather until she was pressed against his body. Cara didn't know exactly what to do with her arms. Rick solved the problem for her by reaching back to pull her arms forward. He tucked them snugly around his waist. That brought Cara's cheek in contact with his hard, muscled back. She inhaled. He smelled spicy, musky, like Pub aftershave. She caught a bit of the sweet fragrance of wood and saw-dust that clung to his soft sweater.

Rick pulled the bike out into the back alley and after looking both ways, took off. The ride home was the most exhilarating experience of Cara's life. She threw her head back and laughed. Beneath her hands and her chest she could feel Rick join her, his laugh deep and throaty. Just like that, Cara was caught.

Chapter 6

"Why?" Cara asked, as she lay on her side, Rick's slow and steady hand sliding along her naked hip. "Why did you notice me?"

"Are you kidding?" Rick looked incredulous. "Have you seen your reflection in a mirror recently? Do you even have a clue what you look like?"

"What do I look like?"

"Like a goddess," he replied. "When I told you at Evan's that you were the most beautiful girl I'd ever seen, that wasn't a line of bull. I told you the truth. From the moment I laid eyes on you months ago, I decided you, and only you, would be my girlfriend."

"But you can have any girl you want."

"I don't want any girl. I want you."

"I still don't understand."

"You don't have to understand. Relax. Be my girlfriend. Enjoy what we have."

Cara and Rick had been together a month. Step by slow step, he'd convinced her that it was all right to let him near her, to be with him. She'd listened to his kind words, but more than that, Cara blossomed beneath his gentle touch. She'd dropped her guard and opened her heart, willingly following Rick into his bed. He taught Cara she didn't have to fear him, treating her with respect. Rick showed her how it felt to be loved and cherished.

Today his mom was in the kitchen, making lunch for them. There was a world of difference his household and hers. Rick, his older brother Jessie, and his younger brother Mark had a relaxed relationship with their mother and an indifferent relationship with their hard-drinking father.

The boys brought home whomever they chose, whenever they chose and neither parent ever said a word. At first Cara was terribly embarrassed by the situation, but when Rick teased her about her flaming cheeks in the same smoky voice that got him whatever he wanted, Cara forgot her discomfort. She found she couldn't withhold any part of herself from him.

The first time Rick had tried to kiss her like Mr. Walker had kissed her, Cara ran from him, flying down the stairs, racing blindly into the woods behind his house. Rick chased her down, took her into his arms and held her until she stopped shaking. He led her back to his room where he sat her down on the bed, admitting to her that he'd heard a version of the story. Cara stumbled to his bathroom and threw up. When she lifted her head, she found him waiting for her, a cold can of pop in his hand.

"We're going to take this slow," he said. "I won't do anything you don't want me to do, but you need to get over him."

"I-I can't," Cara replied, her voice shaking. "Whenever anyone touches me, it's his touch I feel and I get sick."

"That's because he wasn't supposed to do that to you. I mean, maybe old guys think about it doing it with young girls but they're not supposed to do it."

Cara blurted out the whole story. Rick listened to her in silence.

"I didn't want him to. I tried to stop him. I tried to get him to leave me alone, but he wouldn't. I know everyone thinks I just let him, that I let him do whatever he wanted, especially after what happened to Connie. But it wasn't my choice. I didn't have a choice. Even my parents think I let him. Rick, I didn't even know what he was doing to me."

"I'm not him," Rick said. "It's okay when you do it with me. Really Cara, it's okay with me. I'll explain everything to you. Anything you want to know, anything you don't understand, I'll explain, and if you'll let me, I'll show you. Really, honey, you are the sexiest thing I've ever seen, and I can fix this for you. It will feel good with me. I swear to you, it will feel good with me."

Cara didn't know whether to believe him or not, but when he spoke to her in that soft, smoky voice and he used words like "sexiest thing I've ever seen", Cara felt an odd clench in her stomach and she found herself wanting to trust him, wanting to do exactly what he wanted her to do.

Rick was right. It did feel good with him. Rick's touch was nothing whatsoever like Mr. Walker's.

When he was at her home, Rick behaved like the perfect gentleman. He watched the network news with her father, joined them for supper, showed off his impeccable table manners, and always remembered to bring flowers for her mother.

As the months passed, Cara came to realize Rick was a real pro when it came to reading people. He took great care, spinning charming webs of nearly invisible silk, catching whatever he wanted with a minimum of trouble. Despite knowing that, she was stuck fast. He had set the perfect trap. Rick Shea wanted her and he got her. He touched her, she quivered. He kissed her, she burned. Their relationship was the talk of the school. Everyone who had ignored Cara for two years treated her with a newfound respect, even awe. After all, she was Rick Shea's girlfriend.

When Rick told her he'd planned something special for her birthday, she knew it would be spectacular. He instructed her to make up some reason to stay out all night. She just had to let him know where to pick her up.

After convincing one of Karen's former cheerleader friends to cover for her, Cara told her parents she'd been invited to a slumber party. Her mother was excited about the invitation, even offering to bring by a midnight pizza. Cara declined, saying that everything had already been arranged.

She packed up her pajamas and toothbrush, and grabbed a sleeping bag. Her dad volunteered to drive her to the party.

"You don't have to pick me up. I'll walk home in the morning," Cara said.

"Call in the morning and we can decide," said her dad.

"Okay. See you tomorrow."

"Have fun." Her father drove off.

She waved until he'd vanished around the corner. A few minutes later Rick showed up on his Harley. He kissed her. Cara could feel his eagerness in his kiss. He tossed her things into the woods across the street. "We'll get them in the morning," he said.

Cara climbed onto the back of his Harley and they headed out of town.

The sun was low in the sky by the time they reached their destination, a pond in the middle of nowhere. Rick had already set up a large tent stuffed with blankets and fluffy pillows. A fire burned in a fire pit and he'd stuck a bottle of champagne on ice. Cara had never tasted champagne.

A cooler sat nearby. It held two rib eye steaks, cooked green beans, enough salad for two and gooey chocolate brownies, Cara's favorite. Cara blinked back tears. No one had ever before gone to so much trouble for her. For the first time in her life, she felt beloved.

Rick covered a space for them on the grass with a blanket, inviting her to sit, while he took charge of preparing her birthday dinner. The champagne bottle opened with a pop and he poured her a glass. Cara held it, admiring the bubbles. He'd even brought glass champagne flutes.

"Take a sip."

It was cold and crisp, fruity and slightly bittersweet on her tongue. It tasted nothing like her dad's martinis. She sipped, cautious, watching Rick grill the steaks. She'd heard that if a person drank too much, she got sick. The last thing she wanted to be tonight was sick.

Rick knelt before her, offering her a plate. Together they reclined on the blanket, feeding each other morsels of food. Cara couldn't imagine a more romantic evening.

After dinner, the two sat arm in arm, watching the vibrant pink light of the setting sun fade from the sky. When darkness had fallen and the crickets began to chirp, Rick led her to the tent. They had the entire night together. For the first time since they'd been together, Rick spoke the words she'd been waiting to hear. "I love you, Cara."

Cara shattered. She clung to him, tears of joy streaming down her cheeks. "I love you too. An entire night spent in Rick's arms was heaven.

The next day was something more akin to hell.

Chapter 7

Cara snuggled against Rick on the Harley, brushing her lips over his back as they rode into town. She felt like she was a part of him, something she'd never felt with another human being. He turned to wink at her, tucking her arms even tighter around his waist. Cara turned to press her cheek against his sun-warmed leather jacket, comforted by his gesture. There was no need for words. His actions said it all.

They rounded the corner near Amy's house. Rick planned to drop her off so she could gather her things and walk home. They rode directly into two police cars and her parents. Cara felt Rick's muscles tense. She sensed he was about to turn the bike around and flee.

"Don't," she whispered. A move like that could get them both in a lot more trouble than they were in right now. Cara knew Rick's parents wouldn't be angry with him, but her parents could ruin his life.

"Stop," she said. "Stop here and let me off. Don't say a word. Let me handle it. Please."

Cara didn't know what her parents had in store for Rick, but he didn't deserve to be punished. Her father was powerful enough to run his family out of town on a rail. She couldn't let that happen. Rick sat frozen while she unwrapped herself from his body and slid off the bike. As Cara approached the two police officers and her parents, she decided that the best defense was a good offense. Her mother stood half hidden behind her father's bulk, arms crossed over her chest, a smirk on her face.

"What the hell do you think you're doing?" Cara stared at her mother, mustering all her strength.

Her father's voice rumbled, ominously low. "Shut your mouth and get over here young lady."

"No," shouted Cara. "I won't go home with you. I hate you! I hate you both!"

Her mother stepped around her father. She slapped Cara, knocking her back a step. "Why you filthy little liar. . .How dare you?"

Cara's face flamed. Refusing to look back at Rick, she sprinted down the sidewalk, hoping for nothing more than to get away from her parents. Within seconds she heard pounding feet behind her and she was tackled, knocked to the ground. Cara threw her arms in front of her face to shield her head, but her right arm hit the pavement at an odd angle. She felt the bone snap with a cracking sound.

Cara tried to roll from out from beneath the policeman, but she was caught in his grip, in pain and struggling for breath. He hauled her to her feet. He wasn't gentle about it.

He dragged her back to her parents. "Take your medicine like a good girl."

Holding her limp right arm with her left hand, Cara felt the blood drain from her face. She stole a brief glance at Rick, catching the horror and the humiliation in his eyes. He was as white as a sheet. He climbed off his bike, shaking, and he took a step in her direction.

Cara's father said, "If I were you, young man, I'd climb back on that machine and get the hell out of here. I never want to see your face or hear a word about you. If you call my home, if you ever try to see my daughter again, I will have you thrown in jail."

Rick stood where he was, indecisive. She looked into his eyes. "I'll be all right," she said, her voice trembling. She knew he was lost to her forever. "Go."

Cara climbed into the back seat of her parents' car and they drove her to the hospital. She shed silent tears, all the while her mother screamed at her. Cara tuned out the words. There was no reason to listen. She'd just said goodbye to the only good thing in her life.

Dr. Emmett, their new neighbor, met them in the emergency room. Cara assumed her parents called him, asking him for a favor because they didn't want to be embarrassed. He set her arm without saying a word, refusing to provide her with any medication for the pain. When he finished he escorted her from the curtained cubicle. Cara looked around for her parents, assuming she'd go home and face their wrath. To her great surprise, they were nowhere to be seen. Dr. Emmett walked on ahead.

"Where are my parents?"

"Just follow me. There's something else we need to do."

He and Cara entered an elevator, riding it to the fourth floor. When the elevator doors opened, two burly male hospital attendants stepped inside. Cara's heart began to pound and she backed against the elevator wall. She clutched Dr. Emmett's jacket with her free hand.

"What are you doing? What's going on?"

He didn't reply. The men flanked her, one on either side.

"Watch the arm," Dr. Emmett said.

"No." Cara let out a scream. "No!"

Desperate, she fought the two men as they dragged her from the elevator, knowing it was futile. Each man weighed a good two hundred pounds or more and both were solid muscle. But a cornered animal will fight back, and Cara was a cornered animal. The two men dragged her, kicking and screaming, down the hallway to a set of locked metal doors. One of the men held her in some kind of stranglehold while the other pulled out a collection of keys. He unlocked the door and pushed it open, holding it while Cara was hauled inside. The sight that greeted her was terrifying. When she heard the door clang shut behind her, she fought even harder, knowing it was futile.

Her parents had sent her to a locked mental ward. The residents shuffled around in filthy, ragged pajamas, their hair hanging in greasy strings around gray, vacant faces. Many had feces or vomit smeared on their clothing, their hands, and their bare feet. When they heard Cara's screams, many became agitated and began to yell right along with her.

"Shut her up," ordered a nurse, and one of the men obediently put a heavy hand over Cara's mouth.

Cara gagged. The stench of the place was enough to make her vomit. She felt relief when the two men half-carried her to a small room adjacent to the main room, but that sense of relief vanished when the men shut the door behind her. Under the direction of the same nurse, they began to tug at her clothing.

"No!" Cara fought with all her strength, but she was no match for the two men as they removed her clothing.

She tried to cover her nakedness, but it was impossible with her right arm in a cast and one of the men holding her left arm. She was reduced to begging and pleading with the nurse who supervised, stone-faced, immobile.

The two men lifted Cara, stretching her out on a bare mattress. As one man held her down, lying on top of her, forcing the breath from her lungs, the other pulled up metal rails, one on each side of the bed. Cara felt them tug on her legs and her left arm. Her legs were spread and a leather restraint closed upon each ankle. She felt the straps tighten as her legs were tied to the bed. The same thing was done with her left wrist. The nurse wrapped the restraint around her right upper arm and made sure the binding was short enough that Cara could not reach across her body.

She asked the men to hold Cara's left leg. Cara tried to jerk it out of their grasp, but she could barely move. She felt a needle pierce the big muscle in her thigh. Then the three of them moved away from her and left the room, shutting the door and locking it behind them.

Cara gazed around in a state of utter despair. The walls were white, padded. The padded door was topped with a tiny barred window. To Cara's right, beside the bed, was another barred window. The glass was opaque and was filthy. A muted sun was the only light source. There was nothing in the room aside from the bed with its bare mattress and Cara.

At that moment, she prayed for death. She prayed for someone, anyone to take her out of her body: an angel, God, or even the devil himself. She was not crazy, but she knew if they left her like this for long she would be.

Cara turned her head and stared out the small window beside the bed. She pretended she could see a hint of blue sky. She focused all her attention on that, digging deep, calling upon every single ounce of strength, every tiny bit of reserve she had, in an attempt to shut the room and her helpless condition out of her conscious mind.

She pictured Rick and thought about their night together. She relived it over and over again until at last, she was able to block out every single thing that had happened since. Cara closed her eyes. She decided if necessary she would keep them closed forever.

Chapter 8

The next morning a nurse entered the room and released Cara from the restraints. To her shame, Cara had already wet the bed twice during the night. She'd had no choice. She'd held it as long as she could. With the nurse's assistance, Cara slid to the edge of the mattress. When she tried to stand, every muscle in her body cramped and she collapsed onto the floor. The nurse helped Cara to her feet, and helped her to dress, taking care not to hurt her aching arm.

This nurse was young and pretty. She seemed perturbed, apologizing over and over again about the fact that she couldn't offer her a bath or a shower. She helped Cara to the sitting room, the room that had terrified her the day before. She unlocked the door to the Nurse's Station and said, "Stand right here." She returned shortly with a folding metal chair. She set it next to the door and urged Cara to sit. She said, "Don't worry; I'll keep an eye on you."

One after another, the residents approached Cara, exploring her with their dirty hands, touching her hair, her face, the cast on her arm. It was as if she was a visitor from another planet. Cara cringed, but she didn't have the strength to fend them off. The previous day and night had literally and figuratively stripped her bare.

She was terrified of what lay in store. The pain of her broken arm was negligible in comparison to that fear. Layered over all was the deep, visceral knowledge of what she'd lost. It wasn't only Rick she'd lost. How could she return to her home? Parents didn't do this to their children.

The door opened once more, and the nurse asked, "Do you want some breakfast?"

Cara shook her head. She couldn't remember the last time she ate or drank, not that it mattered to her. Her stomach was tied in knots, her throat constricted and aching from her struggle the previous day and the tears she'd shed all night long.

The nurse returned to her station.

Without a wall clock or any exterior windows to gauge the time of day, Cara had no way to determine the passage of time. She didn't know if she waited in the chair for twenty minutes or several hours. At last the nurse reappeared.

"Someone will be coming to take you to your room," she said.

Cara lacked the strength to ask *what room*, so she merely nodded, indicating she understood the words if not the meaning behind them.

A young man entered the unit. He looked Cara up and down before disappearing into the nurses' station. When he emerged, he carried a manila folder in his hand.

"Follow me."

Cara rose from the chair, her movements slow, awkward.

The young man ignored her. He headed to the door hand in his pocket, searching for the key. The young nurse stepped out of the nurse's station. She lay a soft hand on Cara's arm, stopping her. Leaning her head close to Cara, she pressed her mouth against her ear.

"You'll be okay," she whispered. "Don't make waves and you'll get out of here sooner rather than later. When they give you pills, put them under the back of your tongue and hide them until after they check your mouth. Spit the pills into your milk carton." The nurse took a breath. "Be careful what you say to Dr. Kent."

When the nurse let her go, Cara almost fell on her face. The young man glanced back, impatient now. The nurse steadied Cara and gave her a little shove in his direction.

"She hasn't had a thing to eat or drink in nearly two days," she said. "And make sure she gets help with a shower. Female help," she added. "I'll be down to check on her later."

Cara stumbled after the young man. He led her to a bank of elevators, pressing the button for the farthest one. He and Cara stepped inside and she noted the elevator only went to two floors, two and four. They descended to two. The elevator doors opened onto a short, well-lit hallway. The gray linoleum floors were scrubbed clean. Doors opened off the hallway into bedrooms. The rooms resembled dorm rooms but they each contained only one bed and a dresser. There were no knobs on the doors, no locks, simply a handle on the outside.

They passed what appeared to be an arts and crafts room. Patients worked on various crafts. One man used a potter's wheel. Several women were painting. A few people knitted, some made those simple, childish potholders Cara had made back when she was a Brownie.

She continued to follow her guide down the hall toward another locked Nurse's Station. The farther she walked, the more lightheaded Cara grew. She forced herself to remain upright. The last thing she wanted to do was faint and be at *their* mercy, whoever *they* might be. The young man unlocked the door and left her standing in the empty hallway. Cara watched him hand the manila folder to a woman in a white uniform. She heard him repeat the other nurse's parting instructions.

"Cara Franklin?"

Cara nodded.

"Let me show you to your room and I'll see what I can do about getting an aide to help you with a shower. I believe there are some clean clothes waiting for you. Lunch will be served in an hour. After lunch, I'll let you know what's expected of you. Looks like you've already had your meds this morning so we can skip those today. Oh, it appears you have an appointment with Dr. Kent at two."

Cara was relieved at the professional tone in the nurse's voice. She would rather kill herself than have a repeat of last night. Unfortunately, most of what the woman said went in one ear and out the other. Cara struggled to focus. She didn't want to mess up. *She'd already had her meds this morning?* Cara was quite certain the nurse upstairs hadn't given her any medication. She sent up a silent prayer of thanks to the universe in general and to that nurse in particular for her help.

Dazed, Cara followed the woman down the hall to her room. The nurse tried to be informative, but Cara was incapable of absorbing much. Finally the nurse gave up her futile attempts to illicit a response. She made a comment about needing some time to adjust to the new medications.

Cara was content to let the woman think whatever she wanted to think. She had gone into physical and emotional overload and her cognitive systems were shutting down. She waited passively on her assigned bed for an aide to come to her room and take her to the shower.

The aide, a good-natured middle-aged woman, wrapped Cara's cast in a plastic bag and escorted her to the shower room. Weak as a kitten, Cara had to lean on the aide's arm for support. She stood, helpless, beneath the stream of hot water, unable to shampoo her hair or even hold a bar of soap.

The woman lowered Cara to the wet floor and left, returning with a plastic chair and the nurse in charge. Cara sat, staring at the blank white wall, while the aide shampooed and showered her with the nurse's assistance. The aide dried her and helped Cara into clean clothes. With a vague sense of unease, Cara noticed that the clothes were her own. She helped Cara to her room where she combed out Cara's thick, tangled hair and braided it neatly. When she finished, Cara slumped across the bed and promptly fell asleep.

"Cara, wake up," a voice intruded on her dream. "Cara, wake up and drink this."

"Leave me alone," Cara replied. It hurt to talk "Don't touch me." She tried to move away from the voice, but her body refused to obey.

"Cara wake up and drink this or we're going to start an IV."

Cara struggled to open her eyes. They felt gritty, like she'd rubbed sand into them. Her mouth was dry as burned toast and her throat felt raw. Every joint, every muscle in her body ached.

"C'mon sweetie, sit up. Dr. Mack, could you please come over here and help me get her up?"

Cara felt herself pulled gently into a sitting position. Someone slid behind her. Limp as a dishrag, she leaned against the person. Cara pried her eyes open.

"That's better," the woman said. "Do you know where you are? Do you remember me?"

Cara blinked and looked up. The woman's face seemed out of focus, but she wore a white uniform. Suddenly Cara remembered. "Oh God," she cried out. "Don't hurt me again."

The woman muttered something under her breath. "No one is going to hurt you. I'm sorry. I'm so sorry. It's not going to happen again. Now drink this. Please. Drink this so we don't have to start an IV. You're very dehydrated. You've slept for over twenty-four hours since we brought you down yesterday. Do you understand what I'm saying?"

Cara nodded and reached for the glass the woman held out in her direction. She stopped and looked at her right arm, confused by the sight of a cast. Then she remembered how that happened too.

The woman helped her to drink the entire glass of juice and poured her another one, making her drink that too.

"All right, that's better. You stay here with Dr. Mack while I get you something to eat. You're going to eat all of it and then I'll help you get cleaned up and we'll talk. My name is Debbie, by the way. I'm your nurse today."

Cara watched the woman leave the room. With a sigh she leaned back, but then what the nurse said registered and she remembered there was still a body behind her. Cara jerked herself forward.

"Get away from me."

Dr. Mack, as the nurse referred to him, disengaged himself from her and stood up. He walked around the bed until Cara could see him.

"I'm James Mackie," he said. "I'm a medical student."

Cara looked at him through narrowed eyes. "I thought I was supposed to see another doctor," she said, rubbing her sore throat with her left hand.

"Dr. Kent," he replied. "He's not here right now."

Cara couldn't think of anything to say. She was too tired for questions. Besides, she wasn't certain she wanted to hear any of the answers. Cara collapsed back onto the pillow and shut her eyes. It seemed as if only a few seconds had elapsed before Debbie was shaking her again.

"Cara, wake up. You've been asleep for nearly an hour. C'mon, sit up. I brought you toast and a couple of boiled eggs and some fruit. You need to eat right now."

Debbie helped Cara to sit at the edge of the bed, pulling a bedside table over. A tray of food sat on it. An involuntary groan escaped Cara's lips as she moved into a sitting position.

"Does your arm hurt?"

"Everything hurts."

"I know," Debbie said. "We'll try to make it better after you eat. I have a pain pill for you, but I want you to have something in your stomach first."

Using her left hand, Cara reached for a piece of toast. She nibbled at it while Debbie peeled the boiled eggs for her. "Um, it's just a pain pill, right?"

"Yes," said Debbie. "It's just a pain pill."

"I remember what you said the other morning. I remember about the pills. Why did you do that? Why did you help me?"

Debbie remained silent for a few moments, as if considering how much to tell her. Finally she said, "I don't normally work on that ward. And we don't, we're not. . ." Debbie stopped speaking for a moment. "What happened to you upstairs was wrong. I don't know how it happened."

Cara stared down at the tray of food. "Do my. . .? Do my parents know? Did they tell the nurse to do it?"

Debbie cleared her throat. "I don't know how to answer that. Maybe you'll have an opportunity to ask them."

Cara stopped nibbling on the toast. "I can't."

"I believe your father will be here later today," Debbie said.

"What if I don't want to see him? Do I have to see him?"

"No, you don't have to see him."

Cara refused to meet with her father, preferring to remain closeted in her room. While he spoke with the doctor, she huddled on her bed, left arm hugging her knees tight to her chest. He didn't meet with Dr. Kent.

Debbie said, "You've been assigned another doctor, Dr. Bowman. Do you have any questions?"

Cara shook her head. There were so many questions running through her mind that even if she'd wanted to ask something, she didn't know where to begin.

She'd been locked in a mental hospital. A cast covered her right arm from a close encounter with a concrete sidewalk and she was covered with bruises, courtesy of the two men who had dragged her into the locked ward and stripped her clothes from her. Her ankles and her left wrist were raw from pulling against the restraints, and she had a huge purple welt above the cast where the nurse had restrained her right arm.

Try as she might, Cara couldn't wrap her brain around the events of the past three days. Yes, she'd lied, but there had to be some other way for her parents to punish her. She reminded herself, her parents weren't some other parents. They were *her* parents. Her father was a judge. He sentenced people to prison. He believed people should behave in a certain way. In his world things were black and white. You were wrong or you were right. He didn't allow for shades of gray.

Despite that, Cara knew he loved her. She wasn't quite sure how she knew, she just did. What she couldn't understand was why he let something like this to happen to her. Why did he give his permission for this? How could her own father let them hurt her like this?

Her mother was another story. She could barely stand to be in the same house with Cara. Sometimes it seemed it seemed to Cara like her mother had to force herself to breathe the same air. She had never forgiven Cara for the situation with Mr. Walker. For that matter, her mother had never forgiven Cara for anything. Not for being tall. Not for being a tomboy, wearing jeans and tie-dyed tee shirts instead of pretty dresses. Not for having red hair. Her mother compared it to horse hair.

Cara wasn't pretty or blonde, petite or graceful. She didn't enjoy shopping, she didn't wear makeup. Most unforgivable of all, Cara wasn't part of the 'in-crowd'. She might be considered a *brainiac* by the other students, but her mother didn't value grades, and she had little interest in Cara's artwork. Cara was being punished for all those sins, she was certain of it. The fact that she'd lied and stayed out all night with Rick was nothing more than an excuse.

Cara closed her eyes. It was better not to think about it. It was better to sleep and dream about waking in the warm circle of Rick's arms.

Or better yet, what if she fell asleep and woke up a thousand miles away, in another body, living the life of an entirely different person? That would be perfect. Cara figured she'd spent more than enough time being Cara.

James Mackie tapped nervous fingers on the arms of the chair. This was the second time he'd been asked to recount the events of yesterday. The second time he'd been required to describe the condition of the patient when she'd been brought down from the fourth floor. The second time he had to repeat the conversation he'd heard in the stairwell.

He wasn't even supposed to have been in the psych ward. He was finishing up his second year in medical school and he was only here to do an emergency room rotation. It just so happened that a patient on the psych ward had fallen and needed to have a scalp laceration stitched up.

Dr. Mack, as he was known to the nursing staff, had been suturing lacerations and setting broken bones successfully for a couple of months. The supervising physician had been busy with a motor vehicle accident so he'd trusted James to handle the laceration on his own. James had no idea when he walked onto the ward that he'd get involved in something like this, that he'd be filing a formal complaint against the chief of staff of psychiatry.

He'd happened to be standing at the nurse's station when the charge nurse had called for him. She'd just admitted a young woman who had been upstairs in the locked ward overnight. The charge nurse was concerned because the girl was unresponsive and nobody could reach Dr. Kent.

James had no idea what to do. This wasn't his area. He suggested they call his attending to take a look at her. Unfortunately when they'd called down to the ER, the attending said it would be a good hour before he could swing by. He'd instructed them to put in a call to Dr. Bowman, the psychiatrist available for emergencies, and he'd asked James to stay with the patient until Dr. Bowman arrived.

James stood in the room while the nurses catalogued the girl's injuries. He was appalled by what he saw. The girl was bruised from head to toe, her ankles and her left wrist scraped raw from tight leather restraints. Her right arm had obviously been broken and a new plaster cast applied, but just above the cast, the skin on her arm was red and bleeding from another restraint that had been applied improperly.

While he waited, another nurse joined them, Debbie. James made note of every word of the conversation.

Shaken, Debbie said, "I arrived on shift and found the patient naked and restrained, lying on a bare mattress. She'd been left there, uncovered and unattended, with nothing to eat or drink, for nearly twenty-four hours. The night staff on the locked ward claimed they'd been following Dr. Kent's orders. According to his notes, the patient had stayed out all night with her boyfriend. Her parents were concerned about promiscuity, and they wanted to scare some sense into her. Dr. Kent claims this is a technique he's used before with teenagers to produce dramatic changes in behavior, to induce compliance. He claims it's as effective as electroshock therapy."

From what James gathered, Debbie knew the family. She said, "The patient's father is a judge, her mother a snooty pain-in-the-ass. The girl is a straight A student, she's never been in any serious trouble, but it's pretty common knowledge that several years ago she was sexually abused by her father's former law partner. He preyed on young girls."

James didn't think stripping a patient naked and tying her to a bed for twenty-four hours made for effective therapy, especially after hearing of her history. It was barbaric. The young woman didn't even stir when they'd undressed her, turned her over to check her back, and changed her into a hospital gown. The bruises covering the patient's body sickened him.

Doctors took an oath to do no harm. In this case, James believed a great deal of harm had been done. He knew that despite the fact he was only a second year medical student, he had no choice. He had to report this abuse. He suggested to the charge nurse that she call the girl's parents and let them see the results of Dr. Kent's plan of treatment.

As James followed the two nurses down the hallway, Dr. Bowman entered the unit. James was familiar with him. The emergency room staff called on him when they needed an initial psychiatric intervention or evaluation. The man was pleasant enough. Dr. Bowman hurried past them, disappearing into the girl's room. The nurses hastened to join him. When he reappeared, his round, usually jovial face was beet red. He seemed quite flustered. Grabbing the girl's chart, he disappeared into Dr. Kent's office.

James returned to the emergency room and explained the situation to his supervisor, informing him he planned to make a formal complaint against Dr. Kent. His supervisor pointed out the obvious, that it was risky for a second year medical student to open his mouth about anything, especially since James wasn't even on a psychiatric rotation.

Then he said, "Dr. Kent's a major asshole. Go for it."

After his shift, James headed to the stairwell, planning to go to the medical library, hoping for a quiet place to write down his observations and review his notes. He heard male voices a floor up. At first he ignored them, but then he'd heard one of the men speak the patient's name. Despite any discomfort James felt about eavesdropping, he listened. It didn't take a genius to figure out that he was listening to the two orderlies who had dragged Cara to the locked ward.

His fury growing by the minute, he listened to them rib each other about getting the biggest hard-on of their lives when they'd stripped her and tied her to the bed. One of them mentioned that he'd tried and failed to lift the keys to the girl's room so he could use that hard-on. That was as much as James could stand. Tempted to beat both men senseless, he stormed to the office of the hospital administrator and demanded to speak with him.

Now here he was, a day later, waiting to see if the girl's father had any additional questions for him. Apparently Dr. Bowman wasn't quite as passive as James thought. After James left the psych ward, Dr. Bowman had called Judge Franklin and insisted he come to the hospital. Judge Franklin may have wanted some sense knocked into his daughter, but he didn't want her manhandled and mistreated until she was black and blue. He never expected she'd be tied to a bed, helpless and humiliated. How could he know she'd be vulnerable to an attack from those two cretin orderlies, and dehydrated almost to the point of shock?

James was glad to learn the judge had raised holy hell.

This morning when James checked in with Debbie, she was within seconds of starting an IV. If the girl hadn't come around when she did, he would have started it himself to get some fluids into her. They were all lucky she hadn't gone into renal failure.

In a low voice, Debbie said, "Dr. Kent's hospital privileges have been suspended, two orderlies were fired, and the nurse has been placed on leave of absence. The entire psychiatric department is under investigation by the hospital board."

James was relieved his complaint hadn't been the only one filed. Both the charge nurse and Debbie backed him up with statements of their own, as did the nurse's aide who'd helped the patient when she'd collapsed in the shower.

James looked up as the door to the administrator's office opened and Judge Franklin stepped out. His movements heavy, ponderous, the man dropped into the chair next to James. For a few moments he said nothing. At last he cleared his throat.

"I'd like to thank you. I imagine as a medical student it must have been difficult for you to come forward. You might have endangered your career by speaking up."

James looked Judge Franklin in the eye. "What happened to your daughter was wrong. It shouldn't have happened. I would have endangered my career if I didn't speak up. I don't think I would make a very good doctor if I looked the other way."

James wanted to ask the judge what he would do now, what would happen to his daughter, but he knew it really wasn't any of his business.

The judge said, "Cara's refusing to see me."

"Is that so surprising?"

Judge Franklin raised his eyebrows. "She's my daughter."

"Well, that's the point. She's your daughter, yet you and your wife brought her here and gave her over into the care of Dr. Kent."

"How were we supposed to know this would happen?"

"You didn't know what would happen and you left her anyway."

Judge Franklin leaned on the arm of the chair and rubbed his forehead. "When I think of what those men did, what they could have done, it's worse than. . ."

"Worse than when she was raped by your law partner?"

Judge Franklin's head flew up. "How do you know about that? For Cara's sake I went out of my way to keep it quiet."

James shrugged. "Things have a way of getting out. It's a small town."

"I didn't know what to do," the judge said. "Maybe I was wrong to keep it quiet. Maybe I should have gotten Cara some help then. Tried to find out exactly what happened. But I didn't want to know. I honestly didn't want to know what he'd done to my daughter. I thought maybe, maybe we could all put it behind us. That it would be better for her if we never talked about it."

James wondered why the judge was telling him this. Perhaps the man found it easier to unburden himself to a stranger, a stranger who would be gone in another few months.

"I'm at my wit's end," the judge said. "My wife won't shut up about Cara, constantly going on about her, claiming she lies and manipulates everyone, yet I've never see any sign of it. At least I hadn't until the other night. Cara's always behaved respectfully towards me, but she's quiet. She doesn't talk much. She doesn't confide in me, or in anyone for that matter. I have no idea what's going on in that head of hers." He paused for a moment. "She's talented you know. The top student in her class, and she's a wonderful artist. Last year a painting of hers was chosen to hang in the Capitol Rotunda in Washington D.C."

"Have you ever seen the painting?"

Judge Franklin seemed to hesitate. "No," he said, "I guess not. I've never seen it."

The older man and the younger man sat side by side in silence. James didn't know what else to say. He wondered if the young woman would recover from this. To her, this must seem like one punishment added on top of the other. He imagined she felt completely alone, abandoned by the two people who were supposed to protect her—her mother and her father. What a lousy deal. He felt bad for her. From what her father just admitted, she had a lot going for her. She was intelligent, talented. Certainly she was one of the prettiest young women he'd ever seen, even in her weakened state, despite the bruises.

"Will you leave her here?" James asked.

"Dr. Bowman seems to feel she may need some time to recover and he thinks this might be the safest place for her." Judge Franklin looked into his eyes as if asking for confirmation.

James wasn't her doctor. He wasn't a doctor at all, yet the man sitting next to him seemed to expect an answer. Whether he liked it or not, James was involved. He had involved himself by filing a formal complaint against Dr. Kent.

"I agree with Dr. Bowman. She's probably still in shock. Who knows how she'll feel or what she'll do over the next few weeks? She'll be safer here."

The judge turned towards him and James could see that his eyes were filled with remorse. "Have I destroyed my daughter?"

James wanted to yell at the man, *most likely, you fucking jackass*, but he knew how much the judge was hurting.

"Give her some time," James said. "She's young. Maybe she's stronger than you think. Just give her some time."

Chapter 9

Three long days passed before Cara left her room. Just dragging herself out of bed to take a shower or use the bathroom was exhausting. It seemed like Miss Mandy had to help her with everything and not just because of the cast. Cara had a tough time finding the energy to do much more than turn over in bed. Debbie finally pulled some clothes out of the closet, ordering her to get dressed and meet her for lunch in the dining room.

"I don't remember where the dining room is," said Cara.

"You're a smart girl. You're perfectly capable of finding it," Debbie replied.

Movements slow, Cara pulled on a pair of baggy jeans and a loose tee shirt. She wandered down the corridor, searching for the dining room. She joined Debbie at a table, the other residents shooting her curious looks. This was Cara's introduction to the world of psychiatric medicine.

The life Cara led in the inpatient ward was very circumscribed. She met with Dr. Bowman every day of the week except Sunday. She spoke with the nurses. Debbie was her favorite and she looked forward to the days she worked. Miss Mandy was usually available if she needed help, although Cara became quite adept at using her left hand to hold utensils, dress herself and even paint. Writing gave her problems but she rarely had to write.

During one group therapy session, Dr. Bowman encouraged Cara to write a letter to her parents. She refused.

She said, "I can't write with my left hand." She continued to decline visits, despite the fact that her father dropped by or called at least once a day.

Two months passed and Cara barely noticed. It didn't even register with her that school had ended for the summer. She passed through every day in a semi-stupor, as if she only marginally inhabited her own body. The medical student, James Mackie, came by one day to remove her cast. In silence, Cara watched him pry the plaster away from her pale, wasted arm.

"I'm ordering a little physical therapy for you, so you can regain the strength and mobility in this arm."

Cara nodded, but she didn't really care what he ordered.

She appeared for meals, sitting at the table with the younger patients, but she ate very little. She attended group therapy three times a week and kept all her appointments with Dr. Bowman. She responded politely when she was spoken to. She learned to play poker and a mean game of billiards. In the arts and crafts room, she used the potter's wheel to create beautiful pots, plates and vases, which were very popular with the other patients and the staff. Cara gave them away without a second thought.

A week before school was scheduled to begin Dr. Bowman called Cara into his office. Her father stood there. Cara took one look at him and turned away without a word.

"Cara," her father called out. "Wait. Please. Wait."

Cara stopped walking, but she didn't turn around.

"It's time for you to come home."

Her father's words didn't quite register. "Home?"

"Yes, it's time for you to come home. Dr. Bowman is releasing you."

"Why?"

"What do you mean why?"

"Why would I go home? Why now?"

Her father walked up to her. He seemed cautious, like he was approaching a wild animal.

"School starts next week. You need to go back to school. You need to come home. Your mom and I want you to come home, Cara."

"I think you're ready to be discharged," said Dr. Bowman. "You're feeling better, aren't you, Cara?"

Better than what? Better than the night I was dragged in here? She turned to her father. She looked into his face for the first time in nearly three months. He looked older, weary. "I don't want to come home," she said at last. "I want to go to boarding school."

"But why. . .?" Her father seemed genuinely confused.

"Because everybody knows, everybody at my school knows what happened. I'll have to see it in their eyes every single day."

"It won't be that bad. I'm sure you'll still have your friends. This is nothing a girl like you can't handle."

Cara stared at him. *Friends? What friends? A girl like me? Do you know anything about me at all?*

She was careful to keep her face expressionless. It was a lesson that first night in the inpatient unit had taught her. *Don't let anyone know what I really feel. Don't let him know how much he's hurt me. How much he can hurt me. If I let someone in, if I allow myself to love someone, if I allow myself to care, I will have to pay a heavy price.*

"I don't want to come home," Cara repeated.

"Honey, please, I'm begging you, please come home with me. I've missed you. I've missed you something awful."

This was the first time her father had ever called her 'honey'. Cara felt her façade crack. The crack was infinitesimally small, but it was just large enough to admit his words. With trepidation, she agreed. He had no idea how hard it would be for her to face the kids at school. They would all know what had happened with Rick. They would know she'd been in a mental hospital. She'd be dubbed the crazy girl.

Cara turned to Dr. Bowman. "I'll go home on one condition. I want a note from you, or I want you to call the school. Tell them I have permission leave class whenever I want. I won't leave school and I'll keep up my grades up. I'll go to the library or something, but give me permission to leave class if I need to, if it's too much for me. If you do that, I'll go home."

Dr. Bowman agreed to do as she asked, so Cara said goodbye to Debbie and Miss Mandy. She tossed her few possessions into a paper bag and left the ward. On her way out the door, she and her father ran into James Mackie. Her father stopped to chat with the young doctor.

James said, "I'm leaving too, heading back to medical school at the University of Iowa. Good luck, Cara."

She said, "Thank you." She accompanied her father to the parking lot without a backward glance.

Cara returned to school. She picked up right where she'd left off. She attended to her work and received excellent grades, but her classmates went out of their way to avoid her. John was her only friend. His family had moved to the Midwest from California and he sought out Cara, claiming she was the only person at this provincial high school who was weird enough for him.

Feeling something akin to desperation, Cara hung out with him. He was eager to introduce her to marijuana, LSD and psilocybin mushrooms. Cara wasn't much into hallucinogens, but the marijuana numbed her, making it easier to function at home. She managed to be courteous to her mother and reasonably friendly to her father.

John also introduced her to Randy and his girlfriend, Jackie, both drug dealers. Cara was quick to see the advantages of hanging with them. Randy had a roving eye and he gave her a lot of freebies because he thought she was cute, but Cara knew better than to trust him. Randy could come on pretty strong at times so she made sure she was never alone with him. John accompanied her when she bought her drugs. One thing Cara wanted to avoid was a physical relationship with anybody, especially someone like Randy.

Her father was satisfied with her grades, but once again, to her mother's never ending aggravation, she didn't date. Cara skipped every single high school dance.

Desperate to get away, Cara accelerated her high school work and graduated a year early. She'd been looking at colleges since the previous fall and she'd applied to a number of small, elite colleges out east, hoping to get as far from home as possible. More than anything Cara wanted a fresh start in a new place among new people who didn't know anything about her, her family, or her past.

Her father encouraged her. He talked at length about the opportunities that would be available to her when she graduated. He and Cara were thrilled when she was accepted to each of her top three schools. The two of them sat up half the night talking about her options. She hadn't felt this close to her dad in years. Before she went off to bed, he even hugged her, telling her how proud he was. Cara felt like she'd finally given him a reason to feel that way.

"You know, you could get a summer internship with a congressman or a senator," he said. "Maybe go to law school, get involved in politics. You've already thrown your hat into the ring." He teased her about her foray into the anti-war movement.

"I don't know about politics." Cara flashed him a smile. "I'm more into art and literature. I'm thinking maybe a degree in art or perhaps a double major in art and art history."

Her father leaned back in his chair and lit a cigarette. "I've never told you how much I enjoy looking at your painting." He'd hung the painting from Washington D.C. in his chambers when it had been returned last year. "People ask about it all the time."

"Really?"

"Yes, lawyers, judges, law clerks. The District Attorney has told me many times how much he loves it. He's even offered to buy it."

Cara laughed.

Her father smiled. "It's good to hear you laugh, honey. I don't remember the last time I heard you laugh."

The next morning Cara ran to answer the phone. It was her father's secretary, but the woman was incoherent. She finally managed to say, "Your father suffered a heart attack in his chambers. He's dead. His body has been taken to the hospital."

Cara dropped the phone and ran. The doctors had already drawn a sheet over her father, but she threw it to the floor, covering his cooking body with her own, completely unaware of her mother's arrival.

The emergency room staff decided to call Dr. Bowman. He arrived with Debbie, and together they managed to pull Cara off her father's corpse and sedate her. It was Cara's grandmother who took responsibility for getting both Cara and her mother home so the body could be moved to the hospital morgue to await an autopsy.

The following day Cara found her mother in bed, unable to function. She left Cara and her grandmother to deal with the coroner and the local press, and to make the funeral arrangements. Forced to set aside her own sorrow, Cara took over the household responsibilities and went about the business of death.

It seemed as if the entire town planned to attend Judge Franklin's funeral. Cara roused her mother and helped her to bathe. Cara did her hair for her and applied her makeup, making sure to put some blush on her pale cheeks. With her grandmother's assistance, she helped the silent woman to dress, propping her in a chair in the living room while she made herself ready.

Because of the number of people she expected, Cara opted for a graveside service. Despite her mother's faint protests, the casket would be closed. Cara couldn't bear the thought of anyone seeing her father's dead body. She'd picked out his favorite suit for him to wear and his secretary had given the mortuary his judicial robes. He was to be buried in them, along with his gavel.

The night before the funeral Cara went to her father's office and pulled her painting from the wall. She removed the painting from its frame and rolled it into a cylinder, tying it with a red ribbon. She asked to mortician to place it beside her father in the casket. When she buried her father, she would bury the best piece of herself.

Cara's sole consolation was her memory of their final conversation. Her father had made her laugh.

Any differences of opinion, any lingering animosity were forgotten for the time being as Cara and her mother stood hand in hand during the service. Cara felt her mother's knees buckle when the casket was lowered into the ground. One of her father's friends retrieved a lawn chair.

She was grateful for the distraction. Cara knew that if her mother hadn't collapsed, she might have. Watching her father's casket slide into a dark hole was the worst moment of her entire life.

After the service Cara drove herself and her mother and grandmother back to the house. The three women rode in silence. By the time they arrived home, the street was already filled with cars. The staff from her father's office had come by to drop off flower arrangements and the front door to their home sat open. As Cara escorted her mother up the front walk, she could see that the house was full of people. Her father would have loved it. He liked nothing better than a good party.

Cara turned her mother over to the women from her Bridge Club. She retired to her room for a few moments of solitude. She pulled a small plastic bag of marijuana out of her bottom drawer, rolled a joint and lit it.

Cara sat on the floor, leaning back against her bed and inhaled deep and slow, waiting to feel the buzz. She closed her eyes.

Dear god, she wanted to get so high she'd forget that her father was dead.

Cara finished that joint and rolled another one. Finally, after the third joint, she decided she was wasted enough to go downstairs and face her guests. Trading the black dress that smelled of pot smoke for a dark brown skirt and white blouse, she kicked off her shoes off and left them off. Cara glanced in her mirror. Her eyes were red-rimmed, but it didn't matter. Everyone would assume she'd been crying.

Cara was surprised to find Debbie among the guests, along with James Mackie. From the way Debbie kept her arm through his, Cara assumed they were dating. Debbie seemed happy, though she tried hard not to seem too happy in front of Cara.

Cara said, "I didn't thank you for rescuing me at the hospital."

"There's no need to thank me. I'm glad I could be there."

Always polite, Cara turned to James. "What year are you in now in medical school?"

"I just completed my final year. I'll be starting a residency in Internal Medicine in Iowa City this fall."

Cara swallowed over the hard lump in her throat. "My dad died of a heart attack, you know."

"Yes," he replied. "I know. Debbie told me. I'm very sorry."

"He didn't have any warning. He just, he just died. The autopsy showed that he had some atherosclerosis, but not much. The pathologist termed it *sudden cardiac death*."

"It happens sometimes. I've seen it happen to patients in the hospital."

Cara absorbed his words in silence. She looked down when James put his warm hand on her arm.

"My father died when I was just a boy," he said. "I know how you feel."

James felt like he should explain to Cara what the words *sudden cardiac death* meant, but at the same time he got a gut feeling she really didn't want to know. At least not right now. She appeared to be running on fumes.

"It happens," he repeated, wishing he could offer Cara some comfort. She seemed so very alone, exactly as she had when he'd met her two years ago. Even the air around her felt absolutely still, almost painfully so. It was as if noise of the everyday, the commonplace, of home and family, laughter and love didn't or couldn't reach her.

Her loss touched him more than he expected. Cara seemed so solemn, so adult. He wondered if she'd ever experienced a single carefree moment in her short life. At least she could function. He'd attempted to engage her mother, but the woman couldn't even muster an answer to his greeting. He realized Cara must have made the funeral arrangements.

Two years ago it had always been Cara's father, not her mother, who came to the hospital. Even though Cara had refused to see him, her father had usually made a point of swinging by the emergency room to have a word with him.

Aside from filing the formal complaint against Dr. Kent and removing the cast from Cara's broken arm, James had no official involvement with the case. He hadn't had access to Cara's psychiatric chart and he'd never spoken with Dr. Bowman about her. Yet James always sensed that Judge Franklin somehow felt connected to his daughter through him, as if he'd thought of James as a conduit to Cara.

Watching Cara float through the room, James believed with his whole heart that the loss of her father had been a tremendous blow. Cara had very little to fall back upon. She couldn't count on her mother and her grandmother appeared to be quite elderly.

Although the girl wasn't as thin as the last time he'd seen her, she still seemed frail, and just as she had when she'd been hospitalized, she kept her eyes veiled, her face blank and smooth, making it difficult for him to read her.

Two years ago he couldn't help being concerned for her. Even after he'd returned to medical school, he'd caught himself wondering from time to time how she was doing. Now he felt that concern resurface. James shrugged. Maybe it was force of habit. He'd just spent four years training to be concerned about nearly everything.

He and Debbie stayed for another hour before tracking Cara down to say their goodbyes. James was struck by an odd sensation as they walked down the porch steps, he felt almost as if he was throwing Cara to the wolves. In truth, there was nothing he could do for her. He reminded himself that he wasn't a part of her life. What she made of herself, what she did from this point on, what happened to her, was none of his business.

So James wondered why it was that his chest ached as Debbie's car pulled away from the curb. And why his eyes traveled back to Cara standing alone on the porch, her slim profile turned away from them, her shadow stretched long across the grass.

Chapter 10

January 1974

In hindsight, Cara often referred to the twelve months following her father's death as her "Black Hole of Calcutta" year. She felt like she'd been shoved into a suffocating little box from which there was no escape. College was out of the question, at least for the time being. Her mother was too depressed to climb out of bed, let alone deal with insurance adjusters, fill out the forms required to receive her father's social security payments, or make any arrangements for the transfer of her father's pension funds.

Fortunately their house was paid for, but Cara wasn't a signee on her parents' accounts and despite her grandmother's help, there was no family member other than Cara to pay bills or even buy groceries. Taking the initiative, Cara contacted one of her father's former law partners, Phil Jackson. He agreed to help Cara with the paperwork, and her mother was relieved to hand over control of all their assets.

While her father's insurance payout was helpful, it wasn't enough to live on for a prolonged period of time. Neither was his pension. He hadn't been a judge long enough to accrue much retirement. Within weeks, Cara found two jobs. Despite her mother's feeble protests that the job was beneath her, she worked as a waitress during the lunch hour in the grill at her mother's country club. Evenings and weekends, Cara worked at a women's clothing store in the mall. In addition, she registered for a full load of classes at the local junior college, arranging her class schedule around her work schedule. She shopped, did laundry, cleaned the house and prepared meals for herself and her mother. Her grandmother made herself available, but as the months passed,

Cara could see that her grandmother's health was failing and it was just a matter of time before she too would need assistance.

Cara managed to scratch and crawl her way through every day for nearly eight months, until the night her grandmother suffered a stroke.

Her grandmother lay in a bed in Intensive Care, minimally responsive, for three days. When she woke from the coma her cognitive functioning remained intact, but she was paralyzed on her right side.

Sitting at the bedside, holding her grandmother's hand, Cara listened, shocked, as the older woman apologize to her.

She spoke slowly, trying to enunciate clearly, despite the paralysis on the right side of her mouth. "I feel so sorry for you, my dear. You have so much on your shoulders."

Cara blinked back tears. "Don't apologize, Grandma. It's not your fault. We'll work it out. I promise you, we'll work something out."

The neurologists told Cara her grandmother's prognosis was guarded. With physical therapy, she might regain some function and perhaps partial independence, but they didn't hold out much hope for a full recovery. Once her grandmother was stable, she would be transferred to a rehabilitation unit and then, depending upon her progress, she'd either transfer into a nursing home or Cara would have to hire help to care for her.

An anxious Cara left the hospital that evening, intending to go straight home. She needed to check on her mother and give her an update. In recent weeks, her mother had begun to show some interest in helping out around the house, she even answered the phone on occasion.

As she pulled out of the visitors' parking lot, Cara worried what she'd find when she got home. When her grandmother had the stroke, her mother suffered a huge setback. The news about her grandmother's prognosis could make things much worse.

Halfway home, Cara felt dizzy. It was almost as if her grip on reality began to slip. She swore she was leaving her body and standing outside, a stranger, watching.

Panic stricken, short of breath, heart thudding in her chest, Cara struggled to maintain control of the car. She had so little feeling in her body that the hands steering the car might as well have been made of ice. With an abrupt jerk, Cara turned the car down a side street, banging the front wheel against the curb. Throwing the car into park, she ripped the key from the ignition and jumped out, shaking like a leaf.

Cara clutched at her chest and leaned back against the car door, struggling to get enough oxygen.

Cara was nearly overcome by the urge to run away, but she didn't know where in the world she would run to and she had no idea what she'd be running from. Whatever this was, she knew it wasn't anything she could see, it was inside, pounding at her along with the pounding of her heart. She might run forever and she'd just bring it along with her.

Randy, he was the solution. She had to find Randy tonight. Cara hadn't gotten high in months, but she was desperate to get wasted now before she did something stupid, like drive into a ditch or over a bridge or hit another car head on.

She'd always stayed away from Randy unless her friend John went with her, but John and his family had moved back to California. She'd have to handle this on her own. At that moment, Cara didn't care. She was too terrified to worry about what Randy might say or do. The need to control her fear far outweighed her fear of Randy.

Cara started the engine. Terrified she'd screw up, Cara stayed under the speed limit all the way to Randy's neighborhood. She left her car parked down the street and walked up the hill. As she expected the main house was dark, but the van sat in its usual spot. She tapped lightly on the van's back door. It swung open and Randy peered out, his head wreathed in pot smoke. He looked her up and down.

"Long time no see."

"I've been busy," Cara said, struggling to keep her voice even.

"Yeah, I heard," said Randy. "Your old man kicked. Too bad."

Cara didn't know how to respond and an uncomfortable silence settled between them.

"So, you want to get stoned or what?"

"Yeah, yeah I do."

"Got any money?"

Cara already knew she didn't have money with her, but she checked her pockets anyway, just for show. "Uh, no, sorry, I didn't bring anything with me. It was kind of last minute. . ." Her voice trailed off. Cara cleared her throat. "Can you comp me some pot, just a couple joints? I can pay you tomorrow."

Randy blinked at her. "Maybe," he said. "I've got some new stuff. You can try it first, be my guinea pig. It's my treat."

"Yeah, that sounds good." Cara agreed, before Randy could change his mind.

"Climb in." He turned his back to her, disappearing toward the front.

Cara crawled onto the dirty mattress, closing the door behind her.

Randy pulled out a hash pipe. Cara didn't normally smoke hashish, but at this point, she would have smoked, ingested or even injected anything to slow the pounding of her heart.

She watched Randy remove the foil wrapping from a small chunk of dark, slightly oily hash. He stuffed it into the bowl of the pipe. He handed the pipe to Cara, holding a cigarette lighter to the bowl as she inhaled deeply. Cara smoked three bowls, so intent upon distancing herself from her own fear the fact that Randy didn't participate escaped her notice.

A welcome silence descended. From a great distance, she saw the hash pipe drop from her open hand. She felt her head fall forward onto her chest, and then, nothing.

When she opened her eyes, Randy's face loomed above hers. She didn't understand why his features appeared so distorted and she couldn't remember why he was there. Why on earth was Randy Johnson in her bedroom? At that moment, she felt a hand between her legs. Was Mr. Walker lying on top of her, in her bed? Who was it, Randy or Mr. Walker?

It looked like Randy, but Randy would never be in her bedroom. Mr. Walker knew how to get into her room.

"No," she muttered, fumbling with the groping hands.

Cara made a weak attempt to shove him off, but he was heavier than she was, stronger than she was and for some reason, she didn't seem to have control of her extremities.

"C'mon, Cara, c'mon. . ."

She shook her head, thrashing from side to side now. She somehow managed to clench her legs together. Judging by the sound of his voice, Mr. Walker was angry. He would to hurt her, she knew it. He was going to hurt her and then he would rape her. She felt him pull at her clothing. Her shirt ripped.

"Stop," she cried out, the word thick and oddly slurred. "Stop it. Get off me."

"Shut up! Shut the fuck up, bitch!" His fist connected with the side of her face and Cara flipped onto her side, stunned.

She tried to gather her wits, but doing anything, even thinking in a complete sentence, was like slogging through quicksand. She didn't want to be raped again. Oh God, she didn't want to go through it again.

Someone grabbed her shoulders, jerked her head forward. Cara remembered where she was. It was Randy on top of her, not Mr. Walker. He flipped her onto her back and tore at the waistband of her jeans. Cara felt them unsnap. One of his hands held the waistband, the other tugged at the zipper.

"No!" she screamed, clawing at Randy's eyes, raking her nails over his cheek and jaw.

Randy yelped and let go for an instant, long enough for Cara to kick free of him and lunge for the door to the van. He grabbed her by the hair, dragging her backward. He straddled her, sitting on her chest, slapping her over and over until she felt like she would either throw up or pass out. Finally he sat back, panting.

"You stupid fucking bitch." He pressed a hand against his bleeding cheek. "You think you're too good for me? I know what you are. Everybody knows what you are, a fucking slut. You're a fucking slut." He slid off her and kicked her in the ribs.

"Get out!" Randy yelled. "Get the fuck out of here and don't ever come back."

Gasping for breath, Cara crawled to the door. She managed to open it and drag herself out, falling headfirst into the dead grass beside the van. She didn't know if she could stand, but she had no choice. She needed to get as far away from Randy as possible. Cara lurched to her feet and stumbled down the drive. The direction of home was vague, but her body turned left, running on autopilot.

Maybe she'd get hit by a car, she thought. Maybe she would be very lucky and get hit by a car.

"Damn I need this."

James left the med center in Iowa City as soon as he'd finished afternoon rounds. The week had been intense, but fortunately the drive was easy and it gave him time to unwind. The weather held up too. Iowa was between winter storms. A couple days with Debbie would do him some good. He felt like he deserved a little rest and relaxation. Debbie was very adept at providing it.

The two had an easy, uncomplicated relationship. They had fun together. No demands. No distractions. James couldn't afford any distractions right now, not in his first year of residency. Debbie didn't even know he was coming. He'd decided at the last minute and he figured she'd be at work. Since she'd given him a key to her place James assumed she wouldn't mind. If she was busy, he'd kick around for a day or two, maybe do some cooking, watch a little basketball. Spend some quality time in bed with her when she got home.

It was late by the time James hit the city limits. He sped down the main street, hoping the cops were busy elsewhere and made a sharp right turn, heading onto the winding road that led to Debbie's place. His sports car chewed up the pavement. He was no more than a couple blocks from Debbie's house when, from out of nowhere, a ghostly figure darted in front of his car.

"Jesus Christ!" He slammed on his brakes, swerving to avoid it. *What the hell?*

James pulled his car to the side of the road. The adrenalin rush had his heart pounding. He was pretty sure a woman had just flung herself in his path. He ran back to where he'd seen her, hoping to God he hadn't hit her.

At first he was in such a panic he couldn't focus on anything. Then he saw her stumbling along the side of the road. Before he could reach her, she fell to the pavement. James ran to her side.

"Damn."

The young woman was half-naked. James ripped off his jacket and dropped to his knees beside her, wrapping it around her bare torso. Her skin felt ice cold beneath his hands.

"Did I hurt you? Are you hurt? Did I hit you?"

The girl looked up at him. He sucked in a sharp breath. The woman was Cara Franklin. Shit. She stared at him, eyes blank, face stark beneath the pale winter moon.

"Cara, it's me, James. James Mackie. It's me."

Cara closed her eyes and slumped against him. Without another word, James wrapped his arms around her and lifted her, holding her close to his chest as he ran with her to his car. There wasn't time to call an ambulance and he doubted anyone would open their door to him this time of night. He reached down and flipped open the back door, positioning Cara on the bench seat. Before he let her go, he laid his cheek over her mouth to see if she was still breathing. He could feel some air movement, but her respirations were shallow. He had to get her to the hospital. He was pretty certain he hadn't hit her, but it was clear she was suffering from hypothermia and under the dim glow of the car's interior light, he could see she'd been beaten. Her face and chest were bruised, and she had an especially nasty purple welt on the left side of her jaw. She was dressed in only a pair of faded denim jeans. The zipper had been ripped apart, exposing pink silk panties beneath. She was barefoot and her feet were dead white.

Dear God, James didn't even want to think about what had happened to her. He just wanted to get her somewhere safe, somewhere she could receive the care she needed.

Tires screeching, James turned his car around and raced to the hospital. He pulled up directly in front of the emergency room entrance. He reached into the backseat for Cara, where she lay still as stone. He pulled her limp body towards him. James ran for all he was worth straight into the ER.

With a yell for help, James flew through the double doors, the girl flopping in his arms like a rag doll. Cara's lips and extremities had turned blue and her skin was as white as alabaster. Her pulse was weak, her respirations shallow. James knew she was heading for a cardiac arrest from hypothermia. They couldn't even get a blood pressure on her. It took fifteen excruciating minutes for her body to warm up enough to get an IV started.

James breathed a sigh of relief when Cara's vital signs began to improve, but she didn't arouse like he would expect. She remained lethargic, her speech rambling and incoherent. James overheard the ER doc put in a call to a neurologist and he listened to him order a chest x-ray, a skull series and some stat labs and a toxicology screen.

A nurse put a hand on James' arm. "You'll need to step outside, Dr. Mack."

James nodded. He assumed they intended to see if Cara had been raped, she just didn't want to say that out loud.

"The police are waiting to talk to you," she said. "But you'd better move your car first because we have an ambulance on the way."

James rose from his chair, running a tired hand through his hair. He'd never felt so helpless in his life. He didn't have privileges at this hospital anymore. All he could do was answer questions and wait like everyone who brought a loved one into the ER had to wait. It was agony. He felt out of control, and that was a damned uncomfortable feeling.

In a fog, James made his way back out the double doors. He moved his car, parking it in the patient lot and then returned to the desk. The ward clerk pointed out an empty exam room where two police officers waited. James didn't know what he could tell them. He had a lot more questions than he had answers.

The officers took down all his personal information and then they asked him to tell them his version of events. He complied, giving them the approximate location of the spot where Cara had run in front of his car.

"How do you know Cara Franklin?"

"I've known the family for several years," he replied.

"What brings you to town so late at night, Dr. Mackie?"

James bristled at the suggestion that he might have something to do with Cara's condition. "I have a few days off and I planned to surprise my girlfriend. If you want to check with her, she's probably working upstairs in the psych ward right now. She's a nurse." James crossed his arms. "Someone needs to call Cara's mother. I would have done that myself, but I don't have her phone number."

One of the officers indicated he would go by her house to check in with her mother and break the news.

"I plan to stick around here until a family member arrives," James said.

Leaving the officers, he headed toward Cara's cubicle. The police officers trailed after him. He knew they wanted to talk to the ER doc, to see what he'd learned. For some reason that thought pissed James off no end. Cara shouldn't have to go through something like this again. He didn't want her problems to become police business, but he reminded himself where that sentiment had gotten her in the past.

"Hey," James called into the curtained cubicle. "Can I come back in?"

One of the nurses stuck her head out. "Yes, we're done."

James didn't want to ask the question, but he did anyway. "Was she. . ."

James breathed a sigh of relief when the nurse shook her head.

He pushed the curtain aside, pulled up a chair and sat near the head of the gurney. Cara's eyes were still closed, but he could follow the regular rise and fall of her chest. IV fluids were flowing in and he was relieved to see that color had returned to her cheeks.

He asked the ER doctor, "Has she been able to answer questions?"

"Not really. She mumbled a name I think, but I couldn't catch it."

"You think she has a concussion?"

"Either that or she's overdosed on something. I didn't see any needle marks. We'll know more when the toxicology screen comes back, but as you know, it'll take a couple days."

"Are you going to admit her?"

"Yes, I think I'll admit her overnight for observation. I want to make sure she wakes up." The doctor waved an arm in Cara's direction. "Nothing like frying your brain on a Saturday night."

"I don't think that's what happened." James tried hard to keep the anger out of his voice. "Look at the bruises on her face, on her chest. Consider her state of undress. Everything indicates she was attacked."

"Probably." The man shrugged. "But how do we know? Chances are she was at a party, got stoned and hooked up with the wrong person. Maybe things just went a little too far."

"Are you implying this is her fault?" James asked.

"No, I'm just saying it happens." The ER doctor glanced at James. "Look Mack, I'm not saying it's right, I'm just saying it happens." He left the cubicle to speak with the police officers.

"Fucking asshole," James muttered under his breath and he felt better.

Abruptly Cara stirred to life, thrashing about on the gurney. She threw her hands in front of her face as if fending off an attacker.

"Cara, Cara," James repeated in a low voice, leaning close to her ear. "Cara, it's me, it's James Mackie. I'm right here. Right here beside you."

Cara moaned in response.

"Open your eyes. Open your eyes and look at me."

She complied with difficulty. Her eyes were swollen and red, the blood vessels burst. He was convinced now that he was right. She'd been attacked.

"Where am I?"

"You're in the emergency room."

"Why. . .? Why am I in the emergency room?"

"Do you remember, Cara? Do you remember how I found you? Can you remember anything?"

Bleary-eyed, Cara looked around the small cubicle. She tried to focus on James' face. James had found her? Where had he found her? Where had she been?

Out of the blue, Cara remembered his face, his eyes staring into hers.

She'd been cold, so cold. He'd wrapped her in something and picked her up. Why? Why did James wrap her up. . .?

Oh god, Randy. He'd attacked her. What had he given her? He must have put something in the hash. Cara tried to remember what he'd said to her. He's said something about some new stuff and wanting her to be his guinea pig. What an idiot. She was a stupid idiot. Yeah, she was Randy's guinea pig, all right. Cara closed her eyes, feeling hot tears squeeze slide down her temples and into her hair.

"Go away, James. Go away."

"I'm not leaving, Cara. Not until you tell me what happened."

Tears still flowing, Cara opened her eyes and stared at the ceiling. "I'm stupid," she said. "That's what happened. I'm stupid. Haven't you figured that out by now? I'm a complete and utter fool. Go away James. Leave me alone."

"Look, the police are already here. They know you were beaten up and the doctor did a rape exam. Now either I go get them and you tell them the truth or you tell me and I take care of it for you. Those are your choices."

Cara looked at him, not quite believing his words.

"I'm serious, Cara. I understand why you'd hesitate to talk to the police, but goddamn it, tell me. I'll deal with it. I'll take care of it. I'll keep my mouth shut unless you say otherwise."

"But it was my fault, James, it was my fault. I shouldn't have even been there in the first place. I knew better. I knew what he was capable of."

Abruptly, her stomach lurched and she bolted upright. James grabbed for an emesis basin, supporting her as she retched violently despite the fact that her stomach was empty. A nurse poked her head through the curtains.

"Everything all right in here?"

"Might need a little anti-emetic," James said.

"No," Cara waved her off. "Nothing, please, no more drugs."

"Are you sure? Let me go get the doctor."

"No," said Cara, "Not yet. Give me a minute. Just give me a minute. Please."

The nurse grimaced. "I should get the doctor."

"No, I'm okay," Cara replied. "Just give me a minute or two and then you can go get him."

"Two minutes," the nurse said. "That's all you get."

Cara needed James' help to lie back down. She was drenched with sweat, feeling as sick as she'd ever felt in her entire life. She knew she had to tell James. If she didn't, Randy would do this to someone else, some young high school girl.

"He gave me something, some kind of drug. I don't know what it was. I thought I was smoking some hash. That's all, just some hash. But I passed out and when I woke up he was on top of me."

James listened in silence, his fury mounting, as Cara's story spilled out. He was anxious to know who this 'he' was she talked about, but he needed to let her tell the story at her own pace.

"I tried to fight him off, I tried, but he was too strong for me. I remember that I couldn't seem to move. He hit me, here." Her finger grazed the purple bruise on her jaw. "Then I scratched him across the face and he sat, oh god, he sat on my chest and started slapping me. I think after that he threw me out of the van. I don't remember anything else until I saw your face."

James looked at her, a question in his eyes.

"No." She shook her head. "He tried but he didn't. I swear he didn't."

"Who did this, Cara? Who is he?"

Cara began to sob. "He's a drug dealer. His name is Randy. Randy Johnson."

"Where does he live?"

"He lives on Valley Lane, at the very end of the street. He lives in his old Volkswagen van. It's parked on the side of the house, under the apple tree. James, promise me you won't tell anyone."

James hesitated a moment before agreeing. "I promise, Cara, but I want to know why. Why can't I tell the police?"

"Because it's my fault this happened. I shouldn't have been there in the first place. It's my fault. I knew better. I knew better than to go to him alone."

With a sigh, James sat back in his chair. He would deal with this Randy Johnson character later. Right now, he needed to deal with Cara.

"It's not your fault. It's never been your fault. Men aren't supposed to do that to women. Men aren't supposed to frighten you or beat you or rape you. Men are not supposed to force you to have sex with them. Nobody is supposed to do that to you. Do you hear me? Nobody has the right to do that to you."

Eyes wide, cheeks streaked with tears, Cara just stared at him.

"I'm not bullshitting you Cara. Nobody has the right to do that to you."

"Then why do they keep doing it?"

James clenched his fists to keep from hauling her off the gurney and burying her against his chest. He spoke through gritted teeth. "I can't answer that. Honest to God, I can't answer that. I only know it's not your fault, Cara. It's not your fault."

She closed her eyes and James thought she'd drifted off to sleep. He began to rise, but stopped when he heard her murmur his name.

"James, I think I need to see a real psychiatrist, not Dr. Bowman."

"Why? Why now? Is it because of what I just told you?"

"No, because of what happened, what happened before I went to Randy's place."

"What happened, honey?"

For some reason, his concern seemed to make Cara uncomfortable. She cleared her throat and turned her gaze to the far wall.

"I was driving home from here, from the hospital. My grandmother had a stroke and she's in Intensive Care. I had just met with the doctors and they'd given me her prognosis. I needed to go home and tell my mom about it. As I was driving, it was like. . .I don't know how to explain. It was like I couldn't see anymore, as if I was going blind or something. My heart pounded so hard I thought it might jump right out of my chest, and I felt like I couldn't breathe. James, I thought I was going to die. I was so scared. I didn't know what to do. The only thing I could think of was to get stoned. I know it was stupid of me. I didn't know what else to do. I wanted the feeling to go away. I just wanted it to go away."

"Do you get stoned often?"

"No. Well, I did for a while," she said. "But not much since my dad died. The last time I smoked a joint was a few weeks after the funeral. I mean until last night. I've never been to Randy's alone before, never."

"Well, I guess now you know your instincts were right about him. You could have died, Cara. If I hadn't driven by, if you hadn't darted in front of my car. . .Do you understand? Jesus. I don't even want to think about it." James rubbed his forehead, distracted by his thoughts of what might have happened.

"Can you ask Debbie to find me a doctor, a good one?"

Shit, Debbie. He'd forgotten all about Debbie.

"Yeah, I can. Cara, what you had is something called an anxiety attack. It happens to people when they're under a great deal of stress. It's okay. It can be fixed."

The doctor entered the cubicle, accompanied by the one of the officers. They asked James to step outside. He took Cara's hand and gave it a reassuring squeeze. She squeezed back. As he turned to leave she said, "James, can you check on my mom? Please? Someone needs to check on my mom."

Before James could answer, the police officer said, "My partner's leaving for your house in a few minutes, Miss Franklin. He'll let your mother know what's going on and he can give her a ride over here."

The look of horror on Cara's face told James that might not be a good idea.

"Cara, how is your mom doing? How's she been since your father's death?"

"She's not well," Cara said, and James heard the panic in her voice. "Please, she's not well."

"I'll go." James volunteered. "I'll make sure Mrs. Franklin gets here tonight. "Please," Cara said. "Please let Dr. Mackie go in your place."

"All right," he said. "Let me talk to my partner. I'll be right back."

"Thank you," Cara whispered to James. "Thank you for everything."

Chapter 11

James didn't drive straight to Cara's home. He headed up Valley Drive, past the place he found Cara, clear to the end. He found the old van parked underneath the apple tree, exactly as Cara had described. James left the motor running in his car, then climbed out and strode to the rear of the van. He pounded on the metal door. For a few seconds he heard nothing.

At last a voice called out, "Fuck off, Cara! You ain't getting no more shit from me!"

"I'm not Cara."

The back door of the van opened. James stared at a half-dressed, scruffy looking man in his early twenties. He had several deep red slashes along one cheek.

"Who the fuck are you?"

"Your worst nightmare." James hauled him out the back of the van and slammed him against the apple tree. "You beat up a girl tonight. She's a good friend of mine. You tried to rape her, didn't you? Didn't you?"

"Nah, man, I didn't try to rape her! Get your fucking hands off me! I didn't try to rape her! You got it wrong. She asked me for it. She was begging me for it. She's a fucking cunt. . ."

James fist connected with Randy's face, knocking the back of his head against the thick tree trunk. "What did you say? I don't think I heard you right. You said she asked for it?"

"Yeah, man." Randy spat, holding a hand to his bleeding mouth. "She offered it up in trade man. You know, I give her dope, she gives me. . ."

James' knee jerked up into Randy's groin.

"Jesus Christ man!" Randy squealed like a piglet. He would have doubled over but James kept him pinned to the tree.

"I'm sorry," said James, his voice sweet, "But I didn't hear that last thing you said. She offered what?"

Randy tried to catch his breath. "Nothin', man, nothin'. She didn't offer me nothin'. She just. . ." He grunted, unable to speak for a moment. "I just misunderstood, that's all. I must have misunderstood what she wanted. There's no problem, man. No problem. Let me go. I won't touch her again."

James held onto him with both hands, jerking him around until they stood behind the van. Randy's legs shook.

"You're damn right you won't touch her again. You speak to her, you touch her, you even think about her, you have one teeny-tiny wet dream about her and I'll fucking kill you. You got it?"

"Yeah man, I got it," wheezed Randy, his face white, his eyes bulging from his head.

James abruptly let go and Randy dropped to the ground like he'd been shot. James stalked to his car and peeled away from the curb, making a U-turn. He pointed his car down Valley Lane and headed to Cara's house. *That felt good*, James thought. *That felt very, very good.*

James stood on Cara's front porch. He rang the bell for several minutes. When there was no response, he pounded on the front door. Eventually he went around to the back where he could see Cara's mother through the picture window, huddled on the couch, wrapped in a thick blanket.

James called her name in a loud voice, but she gave no indication that she heard him. *So this was what Cara has been dealing with since her father's death.* Exasperated, he pounded on the glass window, hoping to startle her into reacting. He didn't care if she called the police. At least she would be doing something besides staring off into space. The woman appeared to rouse herself. Standing with the blanket clutched tight to her chest, she peered through the glass into the dark backyard.

"Cara?" she called out. "There's somebody in the backyard. Cara? Where are you?"

"Mrs. Franklin," James yelled. "I'm Dr. Mackie. James Mackie. Cara was in an accident tonight. She's in the hospital. She sent me to get you."

Mrs. Franklin stared at him.

"Mrs. Franklin, did you hear what I said? Cara's in the hospital. Open the door and talk to me. If you're afraid to talk to me then for god's sake call the police and talk to them."

He wished he could shake the woman out of her stupor. Damn, if he was in Cara's position he'd probably use drugs too. He watched as Mrs. Franklin walked in slow motion to the back door, dragging the blanket behind her like a little kid. She flipped on the floodlights, illuminating the entire backyard. James followed her to the door, standing a few feet away, hands in front of him, giving the woman lots of space. He didn't want to spook her any worse than he had already.

Louise Franklin opened the door. "What's she done now?"

"Cara hasn't done anything Mrs. Franklin. She's been hurt and she's at the hospital. The police want you to come down."

"I don't like to leave the house. Cara knows that."

"She said you weren't feeling well," he said, forcing himself to use his best bedside manner. "She asked me to check on you."

"Oh. When is she coming home?"

"She has to stay overnight. It would be nice if you could come to the hospital with me. I'm sure Cara would appreciate it. She's all alone there."

"But I told you, I don't like to leave the house."

James patience came to an end. If anyone was in need of her mother, it was Cara. He couldn't disguise the contempt he felt. "Look Mrs. Franklin, maybe Cara will put up with your whining, but I won't. Your daughter needs you. She's been hurt and she's scared. For once in your life act like a goddamned parent. Get your shoes on, get a jacket and I'll drive you to the hospital. It's either me or the police. You decide."

At first, Mrs. Franklin seemed to withdraw from him even further. Then anger crept over her features. James decided anger was much better than complete apathy. She dropped the blanket and stomped upstairs like a petulant child, reappearing a few minutes later with a pair of boots and a suede jacket.

Poor Cara. James knew exactly who was the adult in this household.

As they walked to the car, James said, "I expect you to behave yourself when we get to the hospital. Cara didn't do anything wrong."

"Who do you think you are that you can. . .?" She bristled, but James cut her off.

"I'm a friend. I'm a friend of Cara's and I was acquainted with your husband. I'm aware of the way you've treated your daughter and I'm telling you right now I won't put up with it. If you can't be kind, you can at least be respectful.

"You have no idea what I've had to deal with all these years."

James frowned. "I think it's more accurate to say you have no idea what your daughter has had to deal with all these years. Now get in the car."

She pointed a long finger at him. "You are a very disrespectful young man."

"Yeah, well, I'm not as nice as your daughter. I don't have a lot of patience for people who abuse their children."

Mrs. Franklin slapped his face. James didn't make a sound. He just looked at the woman. At least he'd gotten a rise out of her. Indignation was an improvement over the lethargy he'd witnessed. The epitome of politeness, James held the car door open for her and watched her climb in. The woman sat, stone-faced, on the drive to the hospital. James didn't try to engage her in conversation. He didn't see the point. His only concern was how she'd respond to Cara. If she uttered one word of criticism, one single word, he'd turn her right around, march her outside, drive her back home and leave her there alone to stew in her own juices. Maybe it would do her good. Cara should go off to college and leave her mother's issues behind. It might be the best thing for everyone.

James escorted Mrs. Franklin into the emergency room. The ward clerk informed them that Cara had been transferred to a bed in the Medical unit. He got the room number and walked with Mrs. Franklin to the elevator.

"You don't have to come with me," she said.

"Yes actually, I do."

She turned up her nose, but remained silent.

As they walked side by side down the hallway toward Cara's room.

"Look Mrs. Franklin, your daughter's been beaten, and whoever did it tried to rape her. She was able to fight him off, but she was out in the cold for god only knows how long. I'm the one who found her nearly dead from hypothermia. I should warn you, Cara looks pretty bad." James put a hand on the woman's shoulder, forcing her to come to a halt. "Do you think you can at least pretend to be sympathetic? If you plan to be a bitch about it, I'd just as soon take you home right now."

Louise Franklin took a deep breath. In a voice reeking of sarcasm, she asked, "Why are you making this your business? What does my daughter mean to you anyway?"

"You may not realize this, Mrs. Franklin, but your husband and I spent a great deal of time together during Cara's previous hospitalization. He cared what happened to his daughter. He's gone now. Somebody needs to care about her. It might as well be me."

Louise Franklin stared at him. Her voice softened just a bit. "Regardless of what you may think of me, Dr. Mackie, Cara is my daughter. I care about her." She paused. "I'll do my best to be sympathetic."

"I'm glad to hear that."

They continued down the hallway in silence.

Cara was asleep. Mrs. Franklin sucked in a breath at the sight of Cara's battered face, the bruises visible beneath the dim light. Hands over her mouth, she began to back out of the room, but she backed right into James where he stood blocking the doorway.

"I can't," she muttered. "I can't look at her."

She tried to get by James, but he held her arm. "She needs you. She needs her mother. Stay."

James felt a tremor go through the woman. He studied her face, wondering if she felt faint, if he should sit her down. An odd, fractured look came over her, as if her facade had cracked. The tears began to flow and Mrs. Franklin crumbled against him. Her shoulders shook for a long time. All at once, she quieted and pushed herself away.

James gazed into the woman's eyes. She seemed worn out, far older than her forty years, but now he saw some strength in the set of her jaw, some spark of life in her features. He pulled a chair from the corner of the room and set it next to the head of the bed. Mrs. Franklin sat down, laying her hand lightly on the bed covers. It was something. Cara stirred, but she didn't wake.

With weary steps, James made his way down the hall. He walked straight to his car, drove on autopilot to Debbie's house. Her car was parked in the drive and her house lights were on. He decided to knock rather than let himself in with his key. Debbie opened the door to greet him, but James didn't feel much like talking. He threw his bag in her room, showered and went to bed. That night he tossed and turned, his dreams filled with disturbing visions of a pale bruised face surrounded by waves of auburn hair. He knew he'd disappointed Debbie, but James wasn't in the mood to stay. He left for Iowa City after breakfast.

Over the following six months, Cara tried hard to hold herself together. She continued to struggle with anxiety attacks, but James had kept his word. Debbie gave her a list of psychiatrists who specialized in stress-management.

Cara and her new psychiatrist, Dr. Kenny, met together twice a week. When he suggested they try some new techniques, Cara agreed without hesitation. She absolutely dreaded the heart-pounding terror she felt during an attack.

One weekly session involved hypnotherapy. In the beginning, Cara's anxiety increased and the attacks became more frequent. As part of his treatment, Dr. Kenny instructed her to come up with a trigger word, something that had positive connotations for her. He put her under hypnosis and asked Cara to relive the circumstances that triggered the first attack. He then guided her through the relaxation techniques he'd taught her. He used her trigger word to invoke feelings of security, safety and warmth. The trigger word Cara decided upon was *James*. Only she and Dr. Kenny knew the reason for that particular word.

Cara continued to attend her classes and work both jobs. In incremental steps, her mother resumed her management of the household, doing the cooking, the cleaning, the grocery shopping, and to Cara's great relief, paying their bills. She and Cara shared the task of driving Cara's grandmother to physical therapy sessions, and she helped Cara contract with a private home care agency. Mrs. Franklin also rejoined her bridge group at the country club and to all appearances, managed to have a sense of humor about the fact that her daughter regularly served the group lunch.

Cara was shocked to overhear her mother say, "There's a lot to admire about Cara's work ethic."

At last Cara felt confident enough to make a late application to the University of Iowa. She received her Letter of Acceptance, and with her mother's blessing, packed her things and moved to Iowa City as soon as her junior college semester ended. With the help of the Housing Office, she rented a furnished studio apartment in the attic of an old Victorian a block from campus.

Cara loved her compact apartment, especially the dormer window in her bedroom. It overlooked a green common area, so she positioned her bed in the alcove where she could watch students jog, play Frisbee and touch football, meet for outdoor study groups, sunbathe and simply kick back. The mere existence of the window and the energetic scene below made her feel happier than she'd felt in ages.

Her bathroom was tiny and lacked a shower, but the short, deep, antique white porcelain claw-foot bathtub made up for that. She couldn't wait to run the water for a long hot soak.

The kitchen consisted of a café table and a couple of chairs, a sink, a row of shelving and a two-burner stove. There was no oven, but Cara didn't mind a bit. The place was all hers and she reveled in her freedom. And it was freedom, pure and simple, despite her appointment at the Office of Financial Aid in the morning to find out about work-study options. While Cara had saved enough money to pay for her own housing, tuition and books would be paid for by a combination of grants and work-study. Rent came to eighty-five dollars a month so it would be necessary to work only one part-time job. She'd have all the time she needed to study.

Cara twirled around her bedroom, scarcely feeling the wood floor beneath her bare feet. For the first time in years her heart felt light, as if the breeze blowing in through the open windows drifted clear through her chest, caressing her inside and out. She had already registered for classes, which left her nearly a week to unpack and organize her apartment to her satisfaction, arrange her work schedule, buy her books and learn her way around Iowa City. Never in a million years had she expected to feel this kind of excitement. Cara was starting fresh as she'd longed to do. It felt like heaven.

Chapter 12

May 1976

"How do you do it?"

"Do what?"

"Make every single man in this office stop whatever they're doing and stare. Their tongues hang out when you pass by. Sheesh, they practically slobber all over their statistics."

Cara laughed out loud. Jeanie, the administrative assistant and her boss, was quite a tease. "I don't think it's me." She couldn't resist a snort. "I think it's the calfskin briefcase you loaned me." Cara slapped it on her desk to emphasize the point.

Jeanie shook her head. "No, honey, it's you. Believe me, it's you." She sifted through the paperwork on her desk. "How's the schedule coming? Have you been able to set up the number of cholesterol screenings we need for this month?"

"Things are looking good," said Cara. "I've got the VFW Hall lined up in Pella, the Lion's Club in Newton, I'm waiting to hear back from our contact in Anita and I'm still working on Dubuque."

"Who have you called in Dubuque?"

"The Chamber. Someone's supposed to get back to me today about possible locations. Katie and I went out last week and contacted the local doctors. We've got our flyers all over Pella and Newton. We should be good for this Saturday and next."

"Do we have nurses and the phlebotomists lined up?"

"Yes. Plus Dr. Marsh said he was going to send some of the residents along for the ride. He mentioned something about a field trip."

"More like punishment," Jeanie said.

"For whom?"

"You. You'll have to hold their hands. Residents never leave the Med Center."

"Yeah, well, I can send them out for coffee and doughnuts."

Jeanie laughed. "How long has it been Cara? Two years?"

"Since I started?" Cara thought for a moment. "Almost two years. I think it will be two years on June first."

"I remember when you first showed up here in your jeans and your little pink tee shirt. You were so skinny and so shy I thought you were one of the doctors' kids."

Cara blushed.

"Look at you. You still blush at the drop of a hat." Jeanie walked over to Cara's desk and dropped a pile of files onto it. "The results from last week. No one has had time to sort through them yet. Do you mind?"

"Not in the slightest." Cara pulled the pile towards her.

"I don't know how you do it," Jeanie repeated.

"What now?" asked Cara, opening the top folder.

"Work so efficiently. Ever since you started here you've taken a full load of classes. You're busy painting, doing research. And you still find time to do this. You were originally supposed to be half-time, you know."

Cara glanced up at the older woman. "I like it." She shrugged. "I'm accustomed to being busy. Besides, the money's good. And I enjoy working with you and Dr. Marsh."

"Dr. Marsh and I are old enough to be your parents. Well, I'm old enough to be your parent. Dr. Marsh could be your grandfather." Jeanie laughed. "Don't you want to hang out with young people?"

Cara smiled at her. "How do you know I don't?"

Jeanie rolled her eyes. "In all the time you've worked here, you've never talked about a single *kegger*. You haven't mentioned a single date. You've never come in hung over. You don't call in sick. You've never once received a personal phone call. You bring an apple for lunch and you sit in the courtyard and read. I've worked with student assistants for a long time, my dear, and you are not the typical student assistant."

"I don't know whether to be flattered or insulted."

"Neither," said Jeanie. "You're an enigma."

Cara just smiled in answer and sifted through her files. She needed to double-check the results before she called the test subjects.

Those subjects whose cholesterol level fell within normal limits or was just slightly elevated would receive a form letter explaining their results and informing them that they did not qualify for the project. Those whose cholesterol was significantly elevated would receive a phone call inviting them to enroll in the program and if they were willing, Cara would make an appointment for them with the intake staff. She'd always follow up the phone call with a packet of information explaining the program in detail, along with a form for their personal physician to fill out regarding their health history.

The job had nothing whatsoever to do with art or art history. That was one of the things she enjoyed about it. Another was the fact that the staff was like one large extended family and she'd grown comfortable with them over the past couple years. Cara felt comfortable with very few people. So what if she didn't have a social life? She was better off.

The past two years had been the most uneventful of Cara's entire life. She performed well in her classes, receiving praise from her professors for her work. She'd already presented a series of watercolors in two exhibits. Even though Jeanie didn't think school work could be considered *fun* by any stretch of the imagination, Cara had taken electives like ballet and ballroom dancing, fencing, canoeing and riflery. She had her favorite running routes along the Iowa River and every Friday night she allowed herself some time off to hit the basketball court in the gym for a pick-up game with some of the guys.

Sure, she got asked out but she preferred to study, paint and read in her apartment or in the sunny park beneath her bedroom window, alone. The anxiety attacks were under control for the most part. If they did occur, it seemed to be when she went home or when she was thinking about going home, so she limited her visits to the holidays. She'd lived two summers now in Iowa City and this coming summer would be her third. She and her mother had a much easier time keeping their relationship cordial if they didn't live together.

Cara would actually graduate in January with a double major in Art and Art History, but she hoped to continue working with the project while she attended grad school. She shared a nice clean office in the Med Center with professionals who behaved like professionals despite Jeanie's claims to the contrary. And as Cara said, the money was good. It helped pay her expenses and she'd managed to put some aside for grad school. Asking her mother was for financial assistance was out of the question. Her mother still struggled at times with depression and Cara felt guilty enough as it was about leaving her alone to care for her grandmother. She didn't want money to become an issue too.

Cara smiled as she thought about Jeanie's comment. She had worn jeans and a pink tee shirt the first day on the job.

Jeanie had sized up Cara's deficiencies and taken her under her wing. She taught her how to dress like a professional. Even though Cara was merely a student assistant, a large portion of her job involved meeting with city officials to arrange for cholesterol screenings and with physicians to try to recruit their high-risk patients. The shops in Iowa City didn't have much in terms of business attire, so Jeanie had taken Cara up the road to Cedar Rapids. They even made an occasional weekend foray into Des Moines just for fun.

Jeanie showed her how and where to look for bargains, how to mix and match her clothes so she appeared to have far more outfits than she actually did, and she taught Cara about the judicious use of makeup. She also helped her find the right styling products to control her unruly hair. Cara learned how to straighten her curls and for work she kept it pulled back in a neat French twist.

The one area Cara refused to compromise was comfort—she would not under any circumstances wear pantyhose. Cara detested the suffocating feel of them against her skin.

Jeanie had winked at her and said, "Well, your legs are long enough and pretty enough and tan enough that I'm guessing no one will care."

Cara had been grateful to Jeanie for taking an interest in her. She imagined this was the kind of thing normal mothers and daughters did together. They shopped, they went to lunch, they gossiped. Cara couldn't place all the blame on her own mother. Maybe if she had been a normal daughter, the kind of child her mother had hoped for, the two of them could have had some fun together.

"Cara," Jeanie's voice interrupted her musings. "Cara, Dr. Marsh is in the conference room with our new volunteers. Do you want to go fill them in on the screening?"

"The doctors are here already? Sure."

Cara rose from her desk, automatically smoothing down her form-fitting knee-length gray skirt and straightening her crisp white blouse. Her heels clicked against the tiled floor as she proceeded down the long corridor to the conference room. Volunteers came and went.

Usually they were medical students. Residents rarely volunteered, they were too busy. Because of that, she was certain the group would be small. It shouldn't take long to give them the details. All they had to do was show up for the van on time, stethoscope in hand and have a decent bedside manner.

The worst thing they might have to deal with would be a patient with a fear of needles or blood. Cara had seen an occasional subject faint when the tech stuck him. Once in a great while a medical student might be asked to do a tough stick, but most of the time the techs and the nurses could handle it. It was a plus though, if they could field some questions about cholesterol testing and heart disease. Cara had observed that middle-aged men seemed to trust any information they received from a physician far more so than they did the same information received from a nurse.

Cara walked through the doorway. The director of the program, Dr. Marsh, rose from his seat. He stepped forward to take her arm and introduce her. There were three other men in the room. Cara glanced at the two standing next to the coffee-maker, cups cradled in their hands. One wore standard issue green scrubs, the other dark trousers and a blue button-down shirt covered with a white lab coat. Then Cara turned her gaze to the third man where he leaned against the edge of a table, dressed in faded jeans and a dark brown long-sleeved Henley. She looked up from the leather sandals on his bare feet, took in his lean, muscular legs, his narrow hips and waist, his broad chest and the arms crossed in front of it. She met his eyes. He was staring at her, faint amusement evident in his half smile. Cara blinked in surprise. It was James Mackie.

"Gentlemen, thank you for coming," said Dr. Marsh. "This is Cara Franklin, one of our assistants. She works directly with the program coordinator and she schedules all our test sites, our community outreach and our patient intake. She'll explain what you can expect on Saturday. Cara, they're all yours."

Still staring at James, Cara cleared her throat and dragged her eyes away from his face. "Good morning, gentleman. As Dr. Marsh said, I'm Cara and I am one of the student assistants. I work with Jeanie Anderson, our program director." She turned towards the two men near the coffee pot. "You are?"

"William Donovan," said the doctor in the scrubs, extending a friendly hand in her direction. Cara shook it firmly, back in control.

"Dr. Ezra Payne," said the second man. The hand he extended was limp, his handshake less than enthusiastic. He set his coffee cup down and crossed the room on long, thin legs. "Dr. Marsh, may I speak with you for a moment?"

"Is there a problem, Dr. Payne?"

Dr. Payne didn't mince words. His voice was harsh. "I had no idea when I volunteered for this project that I would be reporting to a student assistant, let alone a woman. I thought you were in charge of this project."

Dr. Marsh's face flamed with anger, while Cara's turned just as red, but with embarrassment. She noticed Dr. Donovan trying hard not to laugh.

"Could we step outside for a moment please, Dr. Payne? Excuse us, Cara, gentlemen." Dr. Marsh left the room, Dr. Payne close on his heels. The door shut behind them.

"Yeah, he's a pain all right," William Donovan said. "Don't take it personally. He treats everyone like that. Dr. Marsh will chew out his ass and he'll do his job. He won't be happy about it, but he'll do it."

"Thank you for saying that," said Cara, grateful for his good humor.

"Cara." The voice belonged to James.

She turned abruptly. It had been two and a half years. As she watched, he lazily pushed himself away from the table and approached her. He took both of her hands in his and held them. If it had been any other man, Cara would have pulled away, but she couldn't pull away from James. She stared into his eyes. She saw the same amusement she'd seen when she entered the room, but there was more, *male admiration, male interest.* Not something she had ever expected to see in his eyes or had even allowed herself to imagine. If James was smart, he'd leave her alone. If she was smart, she'd let him.

"You two know each other?" William's voice came from behind her.

"Yeah," answered James, still holding her hands. "Yeah, we do. We're old friends."

"How-how are you?"

"I'm fine. How are you?"

"I'm fine."

"You look. . .fine," he replied grinning at her. "You look very... fine."

"Hey," said William. "Knock it off, Mack. I was hoping for a chance."

"Not on your life," said James, his eyes focused directly on Cara's face. "She doesn't date residents."

William guffawed. "And that makes you?"

"A volunteer, pure and simple."

Dr. Marsh and Dr. Payne reentered the room. Pulling her hands free, Cara whirled around, her cheeks still hot. Cara hoped Dr. Marsh would assume she was flushed because of Dr. Payne's comments, rather than from the overwhelming, heart-pounding excitement she'd felt when James had taken her hands and looked into her eyes.

Cara had buried any feelings, any desire to have a relationship with a man long ago. She'd shut down that part of herself the day she'd been dragged to the mental hospital. Since that day, since Rick, the only man she'd let come physically close to her was James and even then, the contact had been brief and necessary. She trusted him, but she didn't know if she could trust herself not to do something stupid. Stupid was her pattern.

"I think we've settled everything, Cara," said Dr. Marsh. "Why don't you go ahead and explain what happens at the testing site, how we screen our subjects, the instructions we leave with them and what might be expected of the doctors. I'll be in my office." He shot Dr. Payne a last look of warning before he disappeared down the hall.

Cara began by thanking the three doctors for their willingness to volunteer for the project. She explained the screening process and discussed the typical questions patients might ask. She ended with instructions about where and when to meet the vans on Saturday morning—the vans that would take them to the VFW Hall in Pella—and she handed them printed information about the drug. When Cara finished, Dr. Payne stalked off without a word. Cara couldn't help but glance at James. Despite her embarrassment, her mouth turned up when she saw that his broad shoulders were shaking with suppressed laughter. William Donovan, just behind him, was actually laughing out loud.

"Don't feel singled out for special treatment, Cara," William said. "You should have seen the look on his face when one of the nurses asked him to get a rectal temp. I thought his brains would blow out his ears. The nursing staff knows how he is and they love to get a rise out of him."

Cara smiled at him over James' shoulder.

He shot a quick sideways glance at James. "So, this thing about not dating residents, is that true or is Mack here just acting like your big brother?"

"I don't date," Cara answered, looking at James. "If you'll excuse me, I need to get back to work. It's nice to meet you, Dr. Donovan. Goodbye, James. I'll see you both on Saturday."

Cara turned on her heels and strode out of the room with what she hoped passed for confidence. Inside she trembled. She could still feel the warm pressure of James' hands around hers.

"Damn." William whistled long and low after Cara had gone. "She is something."

"She's not for you," said James.

"Why the hell not?" William's tone was flippant.

"Because to you she'd just be a fling. Cara's not that kind of girl."

William seemed to consider James' words. "She may not be *that* kind of girl but she's certainly *my* kind of girl, unless you have a prior claim on her, of course. And since you're a year ahead of me. . ." William gave him a big grin. "I'd certainly defer to you."

James didn't answer.

"Do you, Mack? Do you have a claim on her?"

"Maybe," said James. "Maybe I do."

Chapter 13

James had the afternoon free. After the unexpected encounter with Cara, he found himself in need of distraction. He crossed the river and walked up the hill to Prairie Lights Bookstore.

He couldn't get her out of his mind. He wondered if he had the right to say anything more to Cara, to do anything more, the right to touch her again.

How he wanted to touch her again.

He perused the shelves, not really seeing the books. My god, Cara was striking, but then he'd been aware of that from the first. Years ago he'd felt the urge to protect her, to rescue her. He still had that same feeling, the sense that he should protect her, but she wasn't a girl anymore. That fact had smacked him in the face the minute she stepped through the door to the conference room in her tight gray skirt and her tailored white blouse and those high heels.

Cara claimed she didn't date. No surprise there. If he were in her shoes he would be cautious around men too. She'd known more than her share of misogynist jerks. But he wasn't like that. He adored women. He didn't like the thought that a woman like Cara might spend her life alone. It wasn't right and it wasn't fair. She should be loved.

How old is she now, he wondered, *twenty-one?* With her hair up she looked older and it was hard to tell. He tried to remember how old she'd been the last time he'd seen her. *Seventeen, or was it eighteen?* He guessed she was around twenty-one while he was almost twenty-eight. When Cara had been seventeen, the age difference had been a chasm. Now seven years seemed insignificant. She had appeared mature this morning and so confident that in fact it seemed as if there wasn't much of an age difference between them at all.

James wondered if she was as confident as she looked or if she was putting on a show. He remembered Cara had always been good at hiding her true feelings. But the color he'd seen in her cheeks when she'd looked into his eyes wasn't a show. That was the real deal. She'd blushed when he took her hands and she hadn't pulled away. That alone spoke volumes.

What happened to Randy? James had no idea whether or not Cara ever told the police who had attacked her. He hadn't gone back to find out, and he hadn't seen Debbie again. He'd called her, ending their relationship over the phone and he'd mailed back her key. It wasn't the most courageous thing he'd ever done, and he wasn't particularly proud of himself. He cringed when he thought of the hurt he'd caused her, but something had shifted in that relationship and he wasn't interested in seeing her.

Debbie had probably provided Cara with a list of psychiatrists regardless of what she thought of him, because that's the kind of person Debbie was.

Cara hadn't seemed plagued by anxiety this morning. Payne had thrown her a curve, but she'd carried on like a professional. James wondered what her major was. He doubted very much she was pre-med. She'd always been interested in art. Well, he'd do his best to find out on Saturday. He was glad there would be other people around. Their presence would keep him from coming on too strong. That was last thing he wanted to do with Cara. He remembered very clearly how fragile she'd been the night he'd left her in the hospital two and a half years before.

James turned over one book after another without focusing on a single cover. His lack of concentration frustrated him, but he knew the source. The instant he'd seen Cara this morning he felt a stirring in the very marrow of his bones.

So what if he wanted her? James had absolutely no idea how to go about getting her or even if he should. He could seduce a woman with the best of them. He'd spent years perfecting his techniques, sensing when he should hold back and when he should make a move. Understanding exactly how much to put into a kiss and how and when to leave a woman wanting more. He knew instinctively when a slow and sweet approach was called for, or if a woman just plain wanted him—now.

Every woman he'd been with had meant something to him. They just didn't mean something to him for long. Cara was a different animal altogether. He couldn't do that to her. Seduce her, enjoy her and move on. Like he'd warned William, she wasn't that kind of girl. Her presence was a complication he hadn't planned on. He was leaving for Durham, North Carolina, at the end of August to begin a Cardiology Fellowship at Duke.

Damn, he should leave well enough alone.

James returned the book to the shelf and headed towards the door. That's when he saw it taped to the window, the poster advertising a student art show. *The Body Beautiful, Watercolors by Cara Franklin.* Today was the last day of the exhibit. James stared for a moment; then he abruptly tore the poster from the window and left Prairie Lights. He strode back toward the river and the bridge that led to the art building.

Cara finished up with her phone calls and left the office early. She had a full afternoon of classes and she wanted some studio time. There was a face she needed to paint. The image of a man's face was stuck in her head, James' face. She hadn't been able to get the sight of him leaning against the table out of her mind. She hoped if she put him on paper she could gain some perspective, put some distance between James and the direction of her thoughts. Maybe she could view him with the same clinical detachment she viewed all her subjects.

There was no disguising, even to herself, the immediate attraction she'd felt. She'd seen the same interest in his eyes. She also recognized the danger. What if she acted on her attraction? What if she opened herself up and he crushed her? What if he saw what she tried so hard to hide? That she was tainted. Dirty. What if she dropped her defenses, exposed her inner self, warts and all, and he rejected her? Cara didn't know if she could survive that. Not with James.

What had happened with Randy was awful, but she'd moved beyond that low point in her life, at least to the extent that she could. Randy's behavior was what she'd come to expect from men—no more, no less. Fortunately after that night, Randy had kept his distance. Besides, she'd completely stopped using drugs and last she heard, he'd moved to Omaha. The police never learned the truth and she kept her mother in the dark. Life was easier that way.

James was not just any man. He was another animal altogether. Cara cared what James thought of her to the very depths of her soul. He was a good man. He was intelligent, articulate, courageous and determined. He was beautiful in an intimidating masculine way, but she also had vivid memories of his kindness and the gentle way he'd treated her. James respected women and he deserved her trust.

On the other hand, Cara wasn't certain she deserved a man's kindness or respect.

Feeling her heart pound in her chest as she ran up the stairs to her apartment, Cara hoped to God she wasn't about to have an anxiety attack. She called up her trigger word and a semi-hysterical laugh escaped her. It was *James* in the flesh.

She checked the clock. Damn, she needed to get a move on. Cara kicked off her shoes, tossed her skirt and blouse on the bed, and she pulled on her favorite old faded jeans with the holes in the knees and the rip in the back pocket.

When she slipped the paint splattered white tee shirt over her head her hair fell out of the twist, so she shook out the remaining pins and left it down. She grabbed her flip-flops and her backpack. Cara ran across the green grass barefoot, appreciating the feel of spring warmth between her toes. She slid into her flip-flops when she hit Market Street, trotting down the hill toward the bridge that led to the art building. She didn't want to be late for her art history class. Cara had a brief presentation to make today.

Head down, rushing across campus, Cara tuned out her surroundings as she mentally reviewed her material. In the middle of the pedestrian bridge she banged into a hard body. Cara landed on her backside with a *whomp*, her pack tumbling off her shoulders.

"Sorry." She groped for her pack. "I wasn't watching where I was going."

"No problem."

Cara knew that voice. Her head spun around and she stared up into James' face. He grinned from ear to ear. She got to her feet in a hurry.

"I like your hair down." He tucked a long auburn curl behind her ear. "It makes you look like you."

Remember to breathe. Cara could feel herself blushing again. Just that slight brush of his fingers made the side of her face tingle.

"What are you doing on this side of campus?"

"Well, nice to see you too," James replied with a laugh. "I was checking out the student art exhibit."

"No. You weren't. You didn't."

"Yeah, I did. Why? Is there something wrong with that?"

"No. It's just that. . ." Cara stopped speaking and stared at him.

"It's just what? That it's your work? Is that what you're trying to say?" He laughed again. "You weren't so tongue-tied this morning. Is it me?" James looked directly into her eyes. "You're staring at me. Do I have dirt on my face or something?"

That her smile.

"No, it's just that I'm, well, I'm sort of shy about my work. It's pretty personal stuff."

"You could say that I guess," replied James, a thoughtful expression on his face. "You could also say it's pretty damn beautiful stuff. I was blown away."

Cara was pleased. "You saw the entire exhibit?"

"Yeah, I did. And I kept this." He pulled the folded poster out of his back pocket and showed her.

It was Cara's turn to laugh. "Thank you," she said.

James heard the warmth in her voice. It felt like a caress. *Careful*, he told himself. He could get caught up in the sound of her very fast. They stood there in silence for a moment, just looking at each other.

"I have to get to class," Cara said at last.

James leaned over and brushed his lips against her cheek. She gave a little gasp. God, she smelled heavenly, like fresh air and sunshine. "It's good to see you again, Cara," he whispered, his lips moving over her ear.

"You too," she said. She sounded a bit breathless, standing there on the pedestrian bridge a moment longer than necessary. Suddenly she pulled away, slinging her pack over her shoulder. Cara jogged toward the art building.

James leaned against the rail, looking after her. Just before she entered the building she turned. She seemed surprised that he was still there, but she waved and then disappeared inside.

She had him. He was caught, thrashing helplessly like a fish on a hook. All Cara had to do was reel him in and she didn't even know it.

He'd looked at her paintings and it was as if he'd seen her soul on display. Everything her eyes shielded from the public was as clear as day in her work. She spilled her secret heart onto canvas, or whatever it was one called watercolor paper. Her feelings of lingering despair and loneliness were evident, but at the same time the paintings made him aware of her strong sensual nature, her natural vivacity and the powerful energy she buried deep inside. Cara's interior world was filled with pain, true, but in contrast to the obvious pain, her paintings teemed with color and light and hope. The dichotomy was fascinating. It's probably why she'd merited her own exhibit.

James had never been more physically and mentally aware of a woman in his entire life. He prayed there was a chance Cara might reciprocate. He dismissed the doubting voice in his head, the voice insisting this could end badly. He would do his best to see that it didn't. James wasn't completely clear about what he wanted, but there was no question that it was more than a one-night stand. He most definitely wanted more than a one-night stand with Cara.

Once her classes were done for the day, Cara painted. She chose acrylics because she wanted more vibrant colors and if she messed up her work she could always fix it. She became so caught up in portraying the light she'd seen in James' eyes that she couldn't leave the studio until she'd managed to capture it to her satisfaction.

She loved his golden brown eyes. She loved the way the pupils enlarged, nearly covering that golden brown expanse when he saw something he liked, or when he was aroused or angry about something. She'd seen him upset and angry before—the night he'd brought her to the hospital. She'd seen his eyes today, twice.

The crinkles that appeared in the corners of his eyes when his mouth turned up in that devilish grin of his fascinated her. She smiled to herself as she painted, remembering the deep, warm, round tones of his laughter. Cara wasn't much into life drawing although she'd included some charcoal sketches in her exhibit. She preferred abstract. This painting of James would be an abstract, aside from the eyes.

By the time Cara cleaned up her brushes and her work area, it was quite late. She wasn't afraid to walk home in the dark. The campus was busy with students finishing projects, papers, taking tests. Someone was always around. Cara preferred the dark. She needed to examine her feelings about James and she didn't want a single thought exposed on her face.

Cara remembered back to that winter night two and a half years ago, the night James had rescued her. He not only saved her life, he seemed to care about what had happened to her. She remembered his words to her. *It's never been your fault. Men aren't supposed to do that to women. Men aren't supposed to frighten you or beat you or rape you. Men are not supposed to force you to have sex with them. Nobody is supposed to do that to you. Do you hear me? Nobody has the right to do that to you.*

Something changed between them that night. Cara wasn't quite sure what it was at the time, but James had become very important to her and not just as her trigger word. He was her ideal. If she ever decided to be with a man again, she'd want the man to be like James. In all honesty, she was forced to admit to herself that she'd want the man to be James. The problem was a man like James could have anyone, any woman he wanted. Why on earth would he want her? Yet she couldn't deny the overt interest she'd seen in his eyes. No, Cara couldn't deny the truth of that.

She'd learned the signs long ago. She knew when men were interested and she'd steered clear of that interest for over two years. She guessed she was pretty enough, at least Jeanie said she was, but being pretty was beside the point. The point was trust. Cara was terrified she'd do something she would regret, as she'd always done in the past.

Cara didn't regret the time she spent with Rick, but she had never fully recovered from its aftermath. That episode was an indelible part of her now and it colored every decision she made. Just like David Walker was a part of her. Though the man had moved away long ago, she still carried him deep inside.

What if James touched her and she ran from him? What would he think of her then? That she was crazy?

Cara realized she'd already felt his touch a number of times and his touch hadn't hurt. His hands had soothed and comforted her two and a half years ago, just as they had today. James' touch made her want things she had no right to want.

Cara reached the door to her house. She climbed the stairs and switched on the light in her apartment. She'd forgotten to eat all day so she heated up some leftover tomato soup and threw a handful of grated cheddar cheese into it. She dropped a slice of whole wheat bread into the toaster, then walked the few steps into her bedroom and opened all the windows while she waited for the toast to pop up. The day had been warm and humid, but the night felt cool. Cara loved to leave her windows open, let the breeze drift over her at night. The toaster made a clicking sound and Cara returned to the kitchen. She sat at the small wooden table to eat her supper, preoccupied with thoughts of James. She brushed her teeth and took a quick bath.

Cara climbed into her bed and lay down below the windows. The night was dark, the breeze pleasant, yet sleep wouldn't come. Restless, that's how Cara felt. Restless, wired, aroused. Her stomach churned with anticipation, as if it knew something she didn't. Cara tossed the sheet away and stood beside the bed. Other than the chirping of crickets the night was quiet. From an open window somewhere nearby, Cara heard a brief burst of female laughter. She listened to see if it would be repeated, but there was only silence.

Cara slipped out of her room and padded down the stairs. She opened the front door, propped it open with a rock, then hopped off the front porch and ran into the park beyond. The tender grass felt cool and springy against her bare feet. Filled with a sudden burst of energy, she skipped from one corner of the park to another until she collapsed onto her back into the soft grass, laughing. Something was coming. She could sense it. She could smell it in the soft night breeze as it drifted past. Something was definitely coming.

Chapter 14

The screening on Saturday went well. Better than Cara expected. The three doctors arrived early. The drive was uneventful. Dr. Payne didn't speak to Cara any more than was absolutely necessary, although William Donovan flirted shamelessly. James, on the other hand, sat in silence, gazing out the window.

Halfway to Pella they came to a stop at a railroad crossing and he caught her eye. He smiled and her heart skipped a beat. Then he turned his face back to the window. Cara did the same, but a corner of her mouth twitched and she nearly laughed as she'd done the night before in the park. The same anticipation she'd felt then was coiled in the pit of her stomach like a snake waiting for the right moment to strike.

As she always did at screenings, Cara set up a table near the entrance stocked with pens, screening forms and permission slips. She greeted participants with a reassuring smile. She helped them complete the forms, channeling them on to the nurses for vital signs. From there they moved to the phlebotomist for the blood draw and finally on to the three doctors so they could ask their questions and receive information about the cholesterol lowering project. Although James kept his voice quiet, as she worked Cara listened for it above the hum of all the other voices in the room. He sounded confident, smooth, soothing, reassuring. Cara could tell James was already a very good doctor. At least he had the bedside manner down pat.

The participants had been asked to fast before the blood draw. Cara and the other student assistant, Katie, made sure to provide orange juice, coffee and fruit afterward. The student assistant who'd held the position before Cara had always brought doughnuts. When

Cara took over she told Jeanie that she considered doughnuts in the same room with information about a cholesterol lowering medication a bit of an oxymoron. Jeanie had just laughed and told her to bring whatever she thought was appropriate, so Cara had run with that and for two years they'd provided fresh fruit.

When the screening ended and the last patient had gone, James and William helped pack up. Dr. Payne grabbed the medical literature they'd brought and took it with him to one of the vans. Cara noticed him fidgeting in the back seat while the rest of them finished their tasks. The phlebotomists and the nurses made certain the blood samples were safely stored on ice for the ride home. Cara and Katie folded the chairs, while James and William carried the tables back to the closet in the VFW hall. Finally the vans were packed up. Cara decided to ride in the van Dr. Payne was *not* in and James followed her. William trailed after James, grimacing when he realized there was no room for him.

"Shit," he muttered under his breath, shuffling towards the other van.

James snorted and looked after William's retreating back. He turned to Cara. "Good," he said, "I was hoping to have you to myself."

"We're not exactly alone," she said. "There are six other people in the van."

"Yeah, but Will isn't one of them."

Cara laughed. "I'm ignoring him."

"As if that's going to stop him, it never has in the past," said James. "Do you want to go get something to eat? When we get back, I mean?"

Despite the wonder she felt at her newfound confidence, Cara didn't hesitate to accept his offer. "I would love to," she replied.

"Pizza and beer?"

"I don't drink beer, but pizza sounds good."

"Pagliai's?"

"Absolutely."

They climbed into the van, both squeezing into the rear bench seat. Within twenty minutes Cara's eyes grew heavy. She hadn't slept much the night before, and she'd been awake at four fifteen and at the Med Center loading the van at five a.m. Her head bobbed forward and she drifted off to sleep.

When Cara opened her eyes at last, she found her cheek pressed against James' shirt. She was nestled into his shoulder, where she'd been sleeping soundly. His arm was around her, holding her in place. His head leaned against hers and she could feel the regular rise and fall of his chest against her cheek. Her face flushed with sudden warmth and Cara was afraid to move, reluctant to disturb James in any way, but the door to the van flew open and the other passengers began their noisy exit. James lifted his head from hers. He looked down at her and grinned. He stretched, his chest expanding for a moment against the back of her arm.

"C'mon," he said, taking her hand and tugging her towards the door.

"I have to unpack everything." Cara paused for an instant, just long enough to lose her balance and trip on the lip of the open door. James moved quickly to stabilize her, dropping her hand and grabbing her hips. Cara's heart raced at his touch.

"Sorry," he said, setting her upright. "I didn't mean to pull you so hard."

"You didn't. It's just me tripping over my own big feet."

"I don't think so." James shook his head. "You're very graceful, you know."

"You've got to be kidding." She laughed. "I am far from graceful."

"No," he said. "You couldn't be more wrong. You're what I would call lithe."

"Lithe?" Cara rolled her eyes.

"Yes, lithe."

They helped the group unload the vans, James waiting patiently while Cara filed the intake forms, made sure everything was tidy before she locked the office. They headed toward the river and Pagliai's. As they climbed the hill, James placed a warm guiding hand on the small of Cara's back. She felt a thrill go through her, a tingle of electricity shot up her spine.

"You don't have to help me up the hill," she said, hoping he'd ignore her words and keep his hand exactly where it was.

"I'm aware of that," James answered, his eyes crinkling. "I just like touching you."

Cara kept her eyes focused on some nebulous point at the top of the hill.

Pagliai's famous pizza looked and smelled as appetizing as ever, but Cara was on edge, and she didn't know if she'd be able to taste anything. James ordered a cold beer, Cara a soda. She felt awkward, shy under these unfamiliar circumstances, but it wasn't long before James' soothing, confident manner and his offbeat sense of humor put her fears to rest. She relaxed and attended to what he was saying in his smooth, deep voice. They discussed art, medicine, her plans after graduation, his current rotation in Infectious Disease, and the Cardiology Fellowship he'd been accepted to at Duke. He intended to leave Iowa City at the end of August, in a little over three months.

Before Cara knew it, they had long since finished the pizza and James was paying the bill.

The sun had set by the time the two left Pagliai's.

"Thank you, James. That was fun."

He stood still, looking at her for a moment before he spoke. "I hope you don't mind but I'd like to walk you home."

"It's not necessary," Cara said. "I'm not afraid of the dark."

"Let me put it another way. I'm walking you home."

"What about your car? You left it at the Med Center."

James shrugged. "I can get it tomorrow."

Cara backed away a half step. The implication of his words was not lost on her. Thoughts raced through her head, reasons why he shouldn't. . .why she shouldn't. . .and then she shut them all up. Cara felt her lips form his name and she reached for his hand. Without hesitation, his fingers curled around hers, big and warm, safe and eager.

Cara wanted James with every fiber of her being, with every single cell. She wanted him with a ferocity that was both terrifying and exhilarating. If she could let this decent man into her life, if she could expose herself to him in every way, drop her guard and let him enter, she would discover if she had healed—if time had healed her—or if she had really, truly given up all hope of ever loving, of ever connecting intimately with another human being.

James' hand in hers, Cara led the way to her apartment. Neither spoke on the walk back. It wasn't until they reached the house that James stopped to draw her into his arms.

"Are you certain about this? Because once we begin, there's no going back."

Cara buried her face against his chest. She inhaled, smiling at the scent of tomato sauce and garlic bread that clung to his shirt. Cara looked up into his warm, brown eyes.

"Yes, James," she said. "I want you to come upstairs with me." Cara unlocked the front door. James closed it behind them.

The morning breeze ruffled the curtains. It was dawn, and Cara had finally drifted off to sleep. James cradled her warm body, pressing her close, stroking her side with tender fingers. Her hip felt soft as satin beneath his calloused hand.

He scanned Cara's delicate features. She looked like a painting, like an angel in repose. Her shining hair lay scattered across the pillow. Her cheeks were flushed pink and he could detect very faint bluish circles under her eyes, beneath the thick auburn lashes. That was his fault. He'd kept her up all night.

Damn, she was the loveliest woman he'd ever seen. And making love to her came as close to heaven as he could imagine.

What he had done? What the fuck had he gone and done? He'd fallen in love, that's what he'd done. James Mackie had fucking fallen in love.

James had never, ever been with a woman who'd responded with such intensity to his touch. He had been concerned that after everything she'd been through in the past, Cara would be stiff and wooden, or icy and withdrawn, or hesitant, or fearful, or worse. But no, if anything, she'd been the opposite. She had welcomed him. She'd given herself to him without reservation, held nothing back. She'd trusted him to explore every silky inch of her, and she'd done the same to him, with eagerness and a hunger that had thrilled him.

God, he had never been so hard, so frequently, in the space of so few hours. Even now, even when it should be impossible, he felt himself stir as he pictured what they'd done just before she'd fallen asleep. He'd like to do it all over again so he could watch her face in ecstasy as she rode him like a wild thing. Listen to her moan with pleasure, feel her nipples peak into perfect rosebuds beneath his palms as she climaxed. Sense her body quiver around him while he drove deep inside her, pulsing with his own powerful, nearly simultaneous orgasm.

It bewildered him, the intensity with which he wanted her. James would be leaving Iowa City in three months and he wouldn't be returning. The Fellowship at Duke would last two years and then who knew? He might go into research, he might start a private practice, he could end up in Alaska or Chicago or Hawaii or New York City. He had no idea where he'd end up. He hadn't thought that far ahead. But he was clear on one thing, he would be with Cara. Somehow, somewhere, she had to fit into his future. She was the one he wanted.

James didn't make decisions lightly. The decision to apply to medical school was long-planned. The Cardiology Fellowship had been in his head for years. James had always prided himself on his serial monogamy. He'd never cheated on any woman he'd dated, but he'd never even once considered committing himself to a woman for longer than a few months, certainly not for a lifetime. This one night with Cara had been an epiphany. She was young and James wanted her to graduate from college and start work on her Master's, but he would marry her. Maybe not tomorrow, maybe not this year, but when she was ready.

James could be quite determined, even ruthless, when he set his mind to something. He did not intend to let Cara slip away, especially not now. He tightened his arm around her, possessive. Cara didn't wake, but she murmured in her sleep, throwing a long leg over his thigh. James smiled. He didn't have to be back to the hospital until Monday morning. They had the entire day and night ahead of them and he intended to make the most of it. Done thinking, decision made, he closed his eyes and promptly fell asleep.

Cara didn't know whether to dance, laugh, sing or simply yell at the top of her lungs, "James Mackie just fucked my brains out!"

She did none of those things. Instead, she turned towards him. He lay on his back, his breathing quiet, even, peaceful. Unable to resist, Cara put her lips on him. She started at his forehead, kissing her way down his face, over his closed eyes, kissing the tip of his nose, paying special attention to his soft and sensual lips, trailing light butterfly kisses along the firm line of his jaw, rubbing her lips over his delightfully rough day-old beard.

Cara could tell he was awake now because the corners of his mouth turned up. He managed to keep his eyes closed as she continued her ministrations, nibbling lightly on the tendons of his neck and the muscles of his shoulder. She knew he had come fully awake when the sheet began to tent above his groin, as she nibbled and licked her way down to his small, hard bud of a nipple and pressed her warm mouth against it, tugging on it with her teeth and rolling it with her tongue, while her fingers explored other regions. James had a body to die for. And he knew exactly how to use it.

When they'd walked back to her apartment, Cara had no idea she would respond to him the way she had. She'd surprised herself. Somehow, without even realizing it, over the past two years it seemed she'd healed. She'd just needed the right person to bring it to her attention, a person like James, but only James.

She found herself flipped on her back, his grinning face above her. Cara laughed.

"Are you too sore? Because I want to fuck you right now. But we can wait a while. There are other ways." He slid his erection along the inside of her thigh, spreading her legs.

Cara opened her legs wider and wrapped her calves around his, inviting him in. "I'm sore," she said. "But in a good way."

James could feel her welcoming warmth. "Then you don't mind?"

"Um-um." She slipped soft hands over the curve of his back, cupping his buttocks.

He entered her with care, as if a single thrust might break her. He heard her sharp intake of breath and he stopped for a moment, searching her face, afraid he had hurt her.

"No." She shook her head. "I'm not sore. It's not that. It's the feeling I get when you first. . ." she paused, "with that first thrust. I can't explain it. It feels so powerful, so natural, so. . .It makes me want to come the instant you get inside." She finished her sentence in a rush.

James took her face in his hands and kissed her lips. "Good," he said. "That's the way it should be when two people love each other." He moved within her again.

Cara tossed her head back, gasping. "Do we, James? Do we love each other?"

"Yes, Cara," he said. "Yes, I believe we do." He thrust again, deeper this time. Her hips arched toward him in response.

"Oh God!"

James was careful, he was gentle, and above all, he was thorough with his lovemaking. He saw the tears on Cara's cheeks when at last he reached his own climax. He held himself as still as he could for fear of hurting her. Shudders racked his body and a deep groan escaped his lips. He leaned over her, panting, unwilling to rest his entire weight on her. Cara's slender arms reached out for him and she pulled him down onto her chest with surprising strength.

"I love the weight of you," she whispered. "Don't hold back. Don't ever hold back. You won't hurt me."

James lifted himself up on his elbows and smoothed the hair away from her face. His thumbs followed the tracks of her tears.

"Why are you crying, Cara?"

"Because of you, because of what you've done for me."

"What have I done?"

"Made love to me, you've made love to me. And I've realized. . ." She stopped in mid-sentence.

"Yes?"

"I've realized that it's safe to make love you."

James understood what she meant. "It's more than safe," he said. "It's the right thing to do. It's perfect. We're a perfect fit."

James slid out of her and rolled onto his back, taking her with him, enfolding her in his arms. Cara sobbed while he held her, soothed her. He understood the tears she shed as no one else in the entire world ever would. It was time she let them go.

"So do you have eggs?" asked James as he rose from the bed and pulled on his trousers. "And bread and cheese and butter and syrup?"

"You're making breakfast?" Cara giggled.

"Absolutely," he said. "Breakfast is my specialty."

"A man who cook? Let's see. You can cure infectious disease, make love all night long like a superhero and you're good in the kitchen. What more could a woman ask?"

James chuckled. "Don't jump to conclusions. Infectious Disease is my least favorite rotation, so I put it off 'til the end. My culinary expertise consists primarily of stovetop macaroni and cheese, Rice-a-Roni, and hotdogs stuck on a fork and cooked over my gas burner. And. . ." James cleared his throat and winked at her. "The past twelve hours were an aberration. I may not be able to get it up again for a year."

Cara gave him a big smile. She wrapped the sheet around her and turned onto her stomach, propping herself up on her elbows to watch him dress. "That would be a shame," she said. "A damn shame. I was sort of thinking we could maybe. . .Well, I have a really nice claw-foot tub in my little bathroom."

"I noticed that," he said. "The thought did cross my mind. But I need to eat and so do you. So, do you?"

"Do I what?"

"Have eggs, cheese, butter, bread and syrup?"

"Yes, sir, I do. I have eggs, cheddar cheese, whole wheat bread, butter and maple syrup. That's all you need?"

"A frying pan and a couple bowls."

"Of course." Cara started to climb out of bed, intending to help him.

"Uh-uh." He wagged his finger. "You stay right there. Naked."

Cara raised her eyebrows.

"Naked."

"What are you making?"

"Cheese Frenchies."

"With maple syrup?"

"Trust me, you'll love it." James disappeared into the tiny kitchen.

Cara lay back on the bed. She covered her mouth with both hands, holding back a shout of joy. She kicked her legs against the sheet in exuberance.

"Hey, what's going on in there?"

"Nothing," she called, trying hard not to laugh. "Just caught in the sheet."

"Need any help?"

"Nope, I'm good. *I'm very, very good.*

Chapter 15

James' fellow residents and his family were stunned by the swiftness with which he committed to Cara. His friend, William Donovan, was the first to be won over to their cause, although he immediately took Cara aside to complain. "You never gave me a chance."

James' mother and his sisters were next. As soon as he had another free weekend, James drove a very nervous Cara up to Minneapolis to meet his family. James' mother and his two sisters were affectionate with each other and with James. Watching their interaction made it easy for Cara to see where James had learned how to treat a woman.

Cara's mother was another story altogether. She was vehement about her opposition to their relationship, yet she refused to give Cara any explanation as to why. James' mother insisted upon speaking with Louise Franklin personally, to discuss the situation and ask her to give James and Cara a chance.

After the phone call, Cara's mother admitted she felt a kinship with his mother, learning she too had lost her husband. Louise talked to Cara about how much the two of them had common, both widows and single mothers raising teenagers. The irony wasn't lost on Cara, but at least her mother stopped criticizing James.

The summer months passed in a flash. James rotation in Infectious Disease wound down, and he began packing in mid-August. He waited until Cara's semester finished so she could fly to North Carolina with him to help choose an apartment since she would be sharing it after she graduated in December. He'd be there for two years and neither wanted to be apart any longer than necessary.

Cara's plans for Grad school had now changed because of her involvement with James, and Cara hadn't yet decided where she would apply. Once James left for Durham, she figured she'd have plenty of time to consider her options. Between the nights she spent with him, the research on her senior thesis for Art History and her hours in the studio, Cara didn't have much time left to think about it. Besides, she and James were focused on other things. Like each other.

As a third year resident, James had more freedom than he'd had for the previous six years. He had Boards to consider, but he figured if he didn't know his stuff by now he never would so he didn't bother reviewing. He'd already arranged to take his Boards out in North Carolina where he wouldn't be so distracted by Cara. He found it hard to concentrate when he could smell the sunshine on her velvety skin, when she tasted like nectar and she fitted him like a kid glove.

Cara and James spent three days in Durham, renting an apartment near the med center that satisfied them both. It had a large kitchen for James and a lot of natural light for Cara.

The hardest part was returning to Iowa City to help James pack his things and load up his car. They wouldn't see each other again until Thanksgiving, when they planned to meet in Minneapolis.

James stuffed his sports car to the roof with his clothes, kitchen equipment, music albums and books. Cara loaded a box of glasses into the back seat, her eyes filled with tears. Since their first night together she and James had been in either her bed or his. He'd become an integral part of her life, flowing through her bloodstream with every single beat of her heart. She didn't want him to leave. Cara reminded herself that she'd see him in three months.

James came up behind her. His arms slid around her waist and he pulled her against him.

"It'll go by fast," he said, his voice low in her ear.

Cara leaned her head on his shoulder and closed her eyes. For a few moments she didn't trust herself to speak. She didn't want to make this parting any harder for him than it already was. James put his hands on her shoulders and turned her around to face him. She burst into tears.

"Honey, it's okay." One of his big hands moved beneath her hair to cradle the back of her head.

"It feels like. . .It feels like my heart is being ripped out of my chest." Cara sobbed. As James began to say something she put a hand over his mouth. "I know it's only for a few months. I know, but it seems as if I've just barely found you and I'm already losing you."

James laughed. "Losing me?" He tilted her chin up. "Baby, you couldn't lose me if you flew to the moon. Don't you get it? I'm yours. I am hopelessly in love with you. Let me repeat that. I am hopelessly in love with you."

James pressed his lips against hers, hard, claiming her. Cara twined her arms around his neck and returned his kiss with equal fervor.

God almighty, he takes my breath away.

"I have something for you," James said, breaking off the kiss.

"Hmm?"

He reached around her into a box he'd set on the roof of the car. He pulled out a stack of cassette tapes.

"I made these for you. My favorite music. I hope when you listen to the tapes you'll remember me." James flashed the grin that obliterated every one of Cara's defenses.

She held out her hands for the tapes. As into details as James was, he'd labeled each tape with the artist, the songs and the date of release. She smiled despite her tears. As if she'd forget the songs they'd made love to.

"Thank you."

"That's all you have to say? Thank you? Not thank you, James, I love you too? Thank you, James, I'm yours forever? Thank you James, I'll wait for you until the end of the world?"

Cara laughed. "All of the above. I love you too. I'm yours forever. I'll wait for you until the end of the world. Remember that. I will love you no matter what."

"Promise?"

"Promise."

"All right, sweetheart, I have to get going. You'll be okay."

"Yes, I'll be fine." Cara pretended a confidence she didn't feel. "Drive safe and call me as soon as you arrive."

James pulled her close for another kiss, and another.

"I will," he said.

James tossed the last box onto the floor of his car and climbed into the driver's seat. Rolling down the window, he grabbed Cara's tee shirt, drawing her towards him for a final kiss. Cara's lips tingled when they separated. She watched in silence as he pulled away from the curb.

James stuck his arm out the window and waved. She waved back, standing at the curb until the car vanished from sight.

Cara sighed and headed down the hill towards the river. The air seemed heavy as she walked back to her apartment. Despite the fact that the morning was already oppressively hot, Cara felt chilled. Thunderheads built in the western sky. She wondered if a thunderstorm was just what she needed. It would match her dark mood. Despite James' reassurance that all was well, she couldn't shake the feeling that something was off. Perhaps after the rain had passed her anxiety would pass with it. She decided to spend some time in the studio. She still needed to finish the portrait of James. When she was with him, she hadn't felt any urgency to get it done. Now she did. Yes, an afternoon in the studio would do her good. Concentrating on a painting would rid her of this growing sense of unease. *It's only because you've grown so accustomed to his presence. James is right, everything will be fine.*

Chapter 16

Thanksgiving 1976

Of course it rained on Thanksgiving. As anxious as she was to see James, she had her mother and her grandmother in the car, so she was forced to take her time. Her mother seemed more relaxed than she'd ever been. Cara suspected it had a lot to do with Phil Jackson, her father's old law partner. He'd lost his wife to cancer the year before and he and her mom were *seeing* each other. Her mother actually smiled often during the trip. She refrained from criticizing Cara's driving and she was quite attentive towards Cara's grandmother.

Well, if Phil had something to do with these improvements then Cara had to hand it to him. It was nice to see her mom happy for a change. Come to think of it, Cara wasn't certain she'd seen her mother happy. This was a revelation. The changes in her grandmother were another. Although her grandmother's mind was as sharp as ever, her physical condition had deteriorated. She now needed a wheelchair and she'd been forced to move out of her own home and into a nursing facility. Maybe the changes were more apparent because Cara didn't see her very often. She decided to make a point of visiting back home before she moved to North Carolina. Her grandmother might not have much time left.

Cara blinked away tears. It was hard enough to see the road with the rain coming down.

Unless there was a delay in Chicago, James' plane should have landed by now. He was due in at one thirty and it was almost three. Cara's stomach was busy turning cartwheels and her heart sped up whenever she thought of him. So did the car. Cara wished she could go a tiny bit faster, but James would be waiting for her whether it took her forty-five minutes or another two hours.

Regardless of how busy he was, James took the time to write to her. Cara read his letters over and over. James didn't waste words, he told her exactly what he was doing, what his plans were and how much he loved her. Cara cherished his letters. She stored them in a shoebox along with a few items he'd given her over the summer. . .Wildflowers that she'd dried and preserved between two sheets of waxed paper, along with a pencil sketch he did of her lying on his bed. The drawing was so awful it made her laugh, but every time she pulled it out of the box she remembered how he'd looked at her when he drew it. She would never forget the expression on his face or the way he made love to her afterward.

Cara negotiated the Minneapolis holiday traffic and pulled up in front of the house, rain still pouring down. James stood in the front yard, soaked to the skin, his shirt clinging to his broad chest. Shoving the car into park, heedless of the downpour, she raced towards him. With a big grin, James opened his arms. Running all out, Cara jumped into them, clutching his neck, kissing every part of him within reach. James laughed so hard he stumbled backward and sprawled onto the wet grass, Cara cradled in his arms.

James flipped her over and covered her with his hard body. For an instant Cara was aware of lying in an icy puddle, but she forgot the cold the instant James' eyes locked on her face. His pupils dilated, changing from golden brown to black, exactly the way she remembered.

James lowered his mouth to her, kissing her like he was a starving man. Cara's fingers slid up over his shoulders, threading their way into his wet hair in a desperate attempt to pull him closer. He pressed against her, both of them heedless of the rain and the eyes that stared at them from the car windows.

"Hey! Hey! Take it inside! What the hell is the matter with you two?"

James growled against her mouth, expressing his unhappiness at the interruption. Cara pulled away and tilted her head back. She stared upside down into William Donovan's grinning face. Cara laughed at the sight.

"What are you doing here?"

"What do you think? Hanging out with my best bud and his girl. There wasn't time to fly back to New York, so here I am." He pointed toward Cara's car, squinting. "I think you need to get your grandmother inside."

"Oh shit!" Cara placed her palms against James' chest, trying in vain to shove him off.

"Uh-uh, not yet," he said. "I like you all wet beneath me." He lowered his lips to hers once more.

Cara melted into his kiss.

"Oh for god's sake!" William stomped over to the car with an umbrella and escorted Cara's mother to the front door.

Still grinning, James got to his feet, pulling Cara up with him. He helped her unload her grandmother's wheelchair while William returned with the umbrella. The three of them managed to get her grandmother indoors and then William and James went back for the bags. Waiting, red-faced and dripping in the entryway, her grandmother gave her a wink and Cara burst out laughing. James' sister handed her a towel and she dried off as best she could, mopping up the floor just as James and William trooped in, enlarging the puddle.

"That seems kind of hopeless," said James' mother. She gave Cara a hug. "Why don't you two go upstairs and get changed and I'll take care of this."

Cara thanked her and reached for her bag, but James already held it. He snatched up her hand, tugging her toward the stairs. Cara kept her eyes locked on him because if she looked at anyone else, especially her mother, she'd die with embarrassment.

"Every single person knows what we're about to do," she hissed.

"Then let's not disappoint them." Tossing her suitcase into his old bedroom, James swung her into his arms with a whoop. He kicked the door shut behind him.

James had forgotten to bring condoms. They searched through the drawers in his nightstand and came up with a pack that was at least ten years old. Cara stuck her head in a pillow to smother her laughter while James tried to put one on. It ripped in his fingers. Cara laughed even harder at James' profane response. After two more failures, he grabbed her shoulders and pulled her close.

"I want you, baby." His voice sizzled against her ear. "My hand has been a lousy substitute for three fucking months."

Cara smiled. "Why you poor thing. But what about me?"

"What about you?" His grin grew positively wicked.

Cara reached between their bodies to stroke him. She nibbled on the side of his neck. "There is no substitute for the real thing," she said, making her point as she tightened her caress, hearing James' low rumble of pleasure.

He lowered her beneath him on the small single bed, positioning her exactly the way he wanted her. He spread her legs and slid down her body to sample her.

"God you taste like heaven." He lifted his head for just a moment. "I was beginning to think I'd imagined you."

Cara couldn't manage a response. His tongue was persistent, causing her to arch against his mouth again and again as he brought her to one peak after another. By the time James covered her with his body, Cara felt like butter left out in the hot summer sun. She gasped the moment he entered her, the pleasure of his body moving within hers was so intense she nearly screamed. James' mouth descended upon hers, muffling her cries. He lifted himself on his elbows, withdrawing nearly all the way, driving deep inside her as she thrashed beneath him.

"That's it, baby, just like that. Come for me again just like that."

Cara's eyes locked onto his. "Oh yes." The rhythm of James' thrusts brought her to the brink.

He plunged stronger, harder, deeper, practically vibrating inside her, wild with need. His mouth sucked the delicate skin of her neck as her hands clutched at his buttocks, drawing him inside, holding him tight. At last James came, his mouth buried in her hair in an attempt to muffle his roar. It took several minutes for their hearts to stop pounding, for their breathing to slow.

James rolled onto his side, taking Cara with him.

"I can't tell you how much I've missed you." He smoothed her curls.

"I think you just showed me."

James' laughter shook her too. "You're right about that, honey. I hope you don't mind, breaking the condoms I mean."

"Our luck has held so far," she said, wrapping her arms around him. "It's not a big deal."

"Hey." They heard a voice from beyond the door. "I'm counting to three and then I'm coming in." It was William.

Cara ducked her head, as James scrambled to pull a blanket up over them while William counted to three. When he reached three, he flipped open the door, glaring in their direction.

"Shut the door," James ordered.

William shut it with a bang and strode into the room. Deliberately making a great deal of noise, he pulled a chair out from under James' old school desk, flipped it around backward and sat facing the bed.

"Look, do I need to call a minister? Are we having us a shotgun wedding? I had to turn the music way up downstairs to cover the noises drifting down the stairs."

"Will, get the hell out of here."

"Uh-uh, not until I know your intentions are honorable."

"You mean not until I ask you to be my best man."

"Hey, as far as I can tell, I'm the closest thing to a big brother Cara has, and yeah, that too."

Cara giggled, shaking the bed.

"He's been harassing me all afternoon," James muttered under his breath. "Okay, yeah, you can be my best man. Now get out so I can ask her to set the date."

William didn't move.

"What are you waiting for?"

"Isn't there some sort of custom about the best man seeing the bride naked before the wedding?"

Cara let out a shriek from beneath the covers.

"Oh hell no," James said. "Didn't you just say you were the closest thing to a big brother she has? Move it or you'll see me naked when I throw your ass out the door."

"Jesus, that's a scary thought." William unfolded himself from the chair. "All right, I'll go, but don't expect me to cover for you for the next two days." On his way to the door, he turned around again.

"Get out," James repeated.

"You're positive there's not some custom about naked brides and best men?"

James threw something. Cara heard it hit the door.

"Now where were we?" He reached for Cara.

"Setting a date."

"Later, I'm busy right now." James lifted the blanket over his head, diving beneath. Cara squealed as his mouth closed around her erect nipple.

Forty minutes later, they descended the stairs. Catching the cockiness in James' step, Cara held back her laughter. She, on the other hand, felt her face flush with embarrassment.

She disappeared into the kitchen to help James' mother prepare a light supper while her mother and grandmother conversed with James and William. Cara was delighted to hear her mother ask James questions about his cardiology fellowship. Her mother had changed over the past six months. It was as if she had been offered a second chance and she'd jumped at it. *Like mother like daughter?*

For the first time in memory, Cara's mother wasn't critical. She didn't fuss or complain. It made Cara wonder if her parents had been as united in their marriage as they'd seemed. In that instant, Cara remembered David Walker's accusations about her father and his secretary. She dismissed them once again, refusing to give his words any credence. Her mother seemed happy, she and James were happy, that's all that mattered.

Cara could hear James and William discussing football and medicine, in that order and she grinned. Another month or so and she'd be living with James in North Carolina. The idea nearly stopped her in her tracks. Cara felt like hugging herself, or maybe pinching herself. She'd never imagined her life could do such a one-eighty. Not in a million years.

Chapter 17

Three days before Christmas, Cara's grandmother passed away. She raced home to console her mother and help with the funeral, relieved to find that Phil Jackson was already there.

Cara stayed with her mother through the holiday, worried she'd fall into another depression like she did when Cara's father died, but instead her mother wanted to focus on the wedding and Cara's upcoming move to North Carolina. Odd as it seemed to her, Cara felt closer to her mom than she had in her entire life. Her mother, who had never wanted much physical contact with Cara, hugged her tight and kissed her before she left for Iowa City.

She said, "Drive carefully."

Cara wondered if this was Phil's doing, but truth be told, she didn't really care. Her mother's new and improved attitude caught her off-guard and Cara didn't quite know how to respond. Dropping her defenses with anyone besides James was not in her repertoire. It felt odd and unnatural to put her arms around her mom. Cara did her best to hide her discomfort, but still. . .

Perhaps her mother had forgiven her for not being the daughter she wanted. Perhaps it was time to forgive her mother for not being the mother she wanted.

Cara mulled it over as she white-knuckled it back to Iowa City on icy roads. She had a lot on her mind, and her stomach churned like crazy. First and foremost, she needed to finish packing and then check on James' flight. He was supposed to arrive in Chicago the next day, weather permitting. She'd be meeting him at O'Hare and they'd hit the road, driving as far as they could before stopping at a motel for the night.

She'd tried to reach James several times over the past few days, but she'd missed him. Of course she and her mother hadn't been home much either. She knew this was a busy time for him, especially since he would be taking a few days off to help her move. But James didn't know about her grandmother unless William had managed to reach him. She'd dropped by the hospital before driving home to tell him what had happened.

As soon as she hit Iowa City, she headed back to the hospital to see if William had heard from James.

William paced at the gate. The winds were so bad at O'Hare that James' plane had been held up several hours in Atlanta. According to the arrival board, the plane had just landed.

When James had called yesterday to find out why he hadn't been able to reach Cara, William filled him in and made arrangements to pick him up a day early. James didn't want Cara to be alone. William managed to get the day off, but the drive had been tough, and chances were they'd get back to Iowa City pretty late. He hoped Cara would already be off the road. William didn't want her driving home in the dark in this kind of weather any more than James did.

To his great relief, James was one of the first passengers off the plane.

He shook William's hand. "Thanks for doing this."

"Don't worry about it. I know how you feel. I don't like the thought of her driving alone in this weather either."

"Have you heard what time she expected to make it back to Iowa City?"

"No but I imagine she left early. Cara's no dummy."

The two men threaded their way through the holiday crowds.

James cleared his throat. "I'll be glad when the move is over. The separation has been hard on her, not to mention all the work she's had to complete this semester. I imagine things at home haven't made it any easier. I was sorry to hear about her grandmother. I wish she'd been able to reach me."

"She checked in with me at the hospital before she left. She seemed all right."

"That's good," said James. "Where Cara's concerned, everything happens at once."

"Yeah, well, don't worry. You'll see her in a few hours."

Cara parked in front of the Med Center and headed up to Orthopedics. Will might be in the middle of afternoon rounds, but she could wait. The nurses' station was crawling with staff, but no Will. Cara managed to attract the attention of one of the nurses, asking if she knew Dr. Donovan. The woman knew who he was, but she didn't know where he was. For a time Cara stood by the desk, searching for a familiar face. When no one appeared, she gave up and returned to the elevators. As she hit the down button, she felt a presence close behind her and she whirled around. It was Dr. Payne. Startled, Cara gasped.

"Sorry," he said. "I didn't mean to frighten you."

Cara wondered when Dr. Payne had learned to use the word *sorry*.

"No." She put some distance between them. "It's okay. I was just looking for Dr. Donovan."

"He's off this afternoon," Payne said. "He took the entire day off."

"Crap," mumbled Cara.

"Anything I can do?"

Cara looked at him, surprised. This was the first time Ezra Payne had ever spoken to her with any semblance of politeness. He'd been the only fly in her ointment all semester.

For some reason he'd stuck around the cholesterol screening project as a volunteer. Cara was convinced he'd done it just to make her miserable. He spent his time grousing and complaining about her management of the screenings, criticizing and insulting her every chance he got. When William found the time to join them, Payne kept quiet, but William could rarely make it. There were occasions when Cara got the distinct impression Payne was coming on to her. The thought seemed ridiculous since the man so obviously disliked her. He'd loiter near the vans until she climbed inside, then he'd follow her, making his usual snide comments. Several times she'd tried waiting for him to get in first, but he never did. He'd just wait to see which van she was riding in, climb in after her and sit right next to her. It had gotten so bad that Cara pretended sleep the entire way home. She felt sorry for him. Everyone else who worked at the screenings went out of their way to avoid contact with him. Cara tried to cut Payne a little slack. She'd lived on the periphery most of her life too.

Cara snapped back to reality. "No, thank you," she said. Then she reconsidered. "If you see Dr. Donovan, you can let him know that I'm back and I'll be in my apartment. I'd appreciate it."

"Sure. No problem," replied Dr. Payne. He continued to stand beside her as she waited for the elevator.

"Are you going down?"

"Yes, I'm on my way to the cafeteria."

They rode the elevator together in an uncomfortable silence. When the doors opened on the first floor, Cara nodded in his direction and headed to the exit.

Ezra Payne followed Cara. He watched her get into her car and pull away from the visitor's lot. He took his time walking to his car parked in the staff lot. He knew where Cara lived. He decided he'd give her some time to relax. There was no reason to rush. William Donovan had gone to pick up James Mackie in Chicago. He'd heard him tell the Chief of Staff early this morning that Mack was flying in and he needed the day off to meet his plane. Considering the weather, Payne doubted they'd make it back before late this evening.

He climbed into his car, started the engine. Payne tapped his fingers on the steering wheel, thinking. Cara Franklin had never really given him the time of day. If he went to her apartment to talk to her, she would. She'd have to. Payne had been obsessed with her for months, following her, fantasizing about her. When she showed up at the nurses' station asking for Will, he realized there was no one around to interfere. He'd have one last chance to be with her.

He'd already driven by her place earlier. All the cars were gone. The other tenants had probably left for the holidays and she would be alone in the house. It was now or never. Payne put his car in gear and drove to his apartment to change out of his scrubs. He wanted to look good for her.

Cara unlocked the front door, leaving it unlocked in case Will came by. The first thing she wanted was a nice hot bath, and she was afraid she wouldn't hear Will's knock.

She dragged her suitcase up the stairs, tossed it onto the bed. With a sigh, Cara gazed around the room. She was only half-packed. There was a hell of a lot to do before tomorrow.

Cara turned the two handles on the tub to let the water heat up while she pulled off her winter boots. She stripped off her jeans and the heavy sweater she'd worn for the drive home, reminding herself to give her mom a call when she got out of the bath. She'd promised to let her know she'd arrived safely.

Inviting steam drifted up from the water in the porcelain tub. Cara adjusted the temperature and sat on the edge while it filled. She felt her stomach clench with anticipation. Tomorrow she would be with James.

Cara wondered how he would feel when she told him she was pregnant. She couldn't help but laugh when she thought about Thanksgiving and the broken condoms. She hoped James wouldn't have misgivings. He was in the first year of his fellowship and she was reluctant to saddle him with a child so soon. It would mean an abrupt change in wedding plans and she'd have to put off her graduate studies, yet she couldn't help but wonder what a child of theirs would look like, be like.

Cara climbed into the tub, leaned her head against the back. She closed her eyes, allowing the hot water to soak away the chill she'd picked up on the drive back to Iowa City. James' face flitted before her. Just one more night apart, one more night.

It was late when they pulled up to the curb in front of Cara's apartment house. James breathed a sigh of relief when he spotted her car in the drive. For some reason, he'd been anxious during this trip, his stomach churning all the way from Chicago.

"I'm going on up," he said. "I'll be back for the bag in a minute."

"I'll get it. Go see Cara."

James nodded and strode to the front door, surprised to find it wide open. The front hallway was freezing. Maybe Cara was already moving a few things into her car. He called out to her, but there was no answer.

"Cara," he yelled again, taking the stairs two at a time. "I came in early."

She didn't reply. As James reached the landing below her apartment, he could see that her door was ajar.

"Cara?"

James pushed open the door. His eyes fell on her where she lay on the floor beneath the ceiling light, naked and bloody and broken. For an instant the scene didn't register, and he stood, frozen, wondering if he imagined the sight before him. Then, chest heaving, he knew it was horribly real and he felt like a wrecking ball had slammed into his gut. He shouted for Will, as he dropped to his knees at her side, checking her neck for a pulse.

"Jesus Christ." Will's voice came from somewhere behind him.

"Find a phone," said James. "Find a phone now."

Will raced from room to room, searching for a phone. "Her phone's been ripped from the wall," he yelled.

"Downstairs, there's a phone in the kitchen."

"Is she breathing?" Will shouted.

"Yeah, get me a blanket." James voice shook. Cara was breathing, but just barely.

"Hold on."

James could hear Will giving their location to the 9-1-1 dispatcher. Within a few moments he was back. He grabbed a blanket from the bed and covered Cara's body, James pressed his shirt against the side of her head, attempting to stanch the bleeding from a large gash. There was blood on his hands, blood on her thighs, her face, matted in her hair. Her fingernails were torn and bloody.

"What can I do? What do you. . .? What do you want me to do? What can I do to help?"

"Meet the ambulance out front. Just, oh god, just meet them out front. Get them up here as quick as you can."

James heard Will's boots thudding down three flights of stairs. He stared down at Cara, his heart filled with fear. He couldn't begin to imagine who would do such a thing, how such a thing could happen. He'd dealt with stuff like this before in the emergency room, but never with someone he knew; never with someone he loved.

Dear God let her live. I'll give up anything if you'll just let her live.

James knew he would remember the sight of Cara's battered body until the day he died.

"Cara. Cara, sweetheart, Cara, open your eyes. Please darling, open your eyes. Jesus, Cara, please. Cara, come back to me. Please. It's James, honey, it's James. I'm here. I'm right here. Please baby, open your eyes." He rocked her as he spoke, his hand pressed to the side of her head. "Please honey, wake up."

Cara's eyelids fluttered, the movement so delicate that at first James thought he'd imagined it. Her mouth moved, forming a word.

"It's okay, honey, the ambulance is on its way. You'll be all right. You're going to be okay."

She moved her mouth again. He could just barely read her lips. It looked like she said, "Pain".

"I know it hurts, honey. I know it hurts. It will be better soon. It will be better."

James heard her voice again. This time she tried to make her words clear.

"No. Ezra Payne."

And he knew.

James sucked in a harsh breath, his entire body trembling with suppressed violence. He ordered himself to stay under control for her sake. Now was not the time to think about what he would do to the man. Now was about Cara, about keeping her alive. He couldn't let her slip away from him.

"I heard you honey. I understand." James tightened his hold on her. "Stay with me. Just stay with me and I'll take care of everything. I'll take care of it. All you have to do right now is stay with me."

He heard approaching sirens. *Please god, let them hurry.*

James stood in a daze, listening to the surgeon's words - internal bleeding, ruptured spleen, three units of blood, broken ribs, fractured skull, concussion, multiple fractures both hands, abrasions, contusions, lacerations, rape, miscarriage. His brain knew exactly what the man was saying. As a physician he knew it by heart. But despite the fact that he heard every word, his heart couldn't make sense of a single one.

Will stayed with him the entire time, doing his best to interpret. James managed to pull himself together long enough to hear Dr. Peterson say, "Cara is in the Recovery Room. You can see her as soon as we're sure she's stable enough to be moved to Intensive Care."

How could something like this happen? How could this happen?

"I should have known," muttered Will. "I should have seen it coming."

James stopped pacing long enough to glance at his friend. "It's not your fault."

Will stared down at the floor. "One of the nurses told me weeks ago that Payne had a serious thing for Cara. That he'd stayed with the research project so he could be near her. I thought she was exaggerating and even if she wasn't, I didn't think it mattered. Cara was done with her job. She was moving away. I figured him for your run-of-the-mill asshole, not some fucking depraved freak."

"How could you have known? Shit, I worked with him for two years. I hated his guts, but it never occurred to me that he was capable of, of something like this." James ran a hand through his hair, distraught. "What am I going to do, Will? What am I going to do? What if she doesn't survive? I don't think. . ." James' voice failed him for a moment. "I don't think I can live without her."

Will was silent.

"He killed my kid. The goddamn son of a bitch killed my kid."

"I know."

"She didn't even get a chance to tell me."

The double doors to the Recovery Room swung open and a nurse appeared.

"Dr. Mackie? You can come back now. Miss Franklin's condition seems to be stabilizing. We'll be moving her to Intensive Care in a few minutes."

James looked at Will. "Let me know when they find him."

Will nodded.

James followed the nurse to Cara's bedside. Despite the fact that he'd already seen her injuries at the apartment, the sight of her pale battered face felt like a knife in his heart. Both her eyes were purple and swollen shut. The left side of her head had been shaved and the superficial damage repaired, but he knew beneath the repair was a fractured temporal bone and she was suffering from closed head trauma.

Her left cheek was bruised, her neck and shoulders battered. Both hands were wrapped with thick dressings. A hand surgeon had been called in to place pins in the delicate bones of her hands and fingers.

James wondered briefly if Cara would ever paint again, but he dismissed the thought. That was the least of his worries.

The nurses had laid a gown over Cara's beaten torso. James moved it aside. He swallowed hard, forcing himself to look at the damage done. There was a six-inch incision on the left side of her abdomen where the surgeons had removed her spleen. The wound was bloody, red, raw. Her fractured ribs were taped. Fortunately there had been no jagged edges to puncture a lung.

James replaced the gown. He didn't want to see any more. He covered her with another warming blanket. He dreaded the next few months. He feared what this would do to her. Not just physically. If his beloved Cara survived the next few days, her body would heal. What about her other injuries? There would be a heavy emotional price to pay, and he was afraid for both of them. He loved her. Nothing could change that, but he didn't see how either of them would manage to get through this unscathed.

His very first encounter with Cara was crystal clear in his mind. He'd witnessed firsthand what happened when she'd been traumatized. He'd seen how Cara withdrew from everyone and everything. It could happen all over again, and he wasn't sure there would be a damn thing he could do to stop it.

For ten days, Cara drifted in and out of consciousness. James sat by her side, relieved only by Cara's mother and Will. Despite the fact that he didn't need to hear the words uttered aloud, her doctors warned them she could wake up with some gaps in her memory, possible visual deficits, personality changes, all of which had already occurred to him. On those nights when he managed to get a little sleep, the awful possibilities gave him nightmares.

Until ten days ago, what James Mackie wanted, James Mackie got. A lot of his friends believed he'd led a charmed life. That wasn't entirely true. Christ, his father had died when he was just ten years old, but his mother and his older sisters had managed to cushion the blow. Keeping him safe from harm, protected and loved, he'd emerged unscathed, growing into a confident, strong, determined man.

Cara had never had anyone to cushion the blows for her, not even him, not even now. He hadn't been here. He hadn't been here when she'd needed him most. God, if his fucking plane had left on time this never would have happened. He would have gotten to her apartment before she did. He would have been waiting for her. The thought ate him alive.

Ezra Payne sat in jail. He'd been arrested in his own apartment, in the bathroom, trying to shower away the evidence. It was hard to shower away a broken nose and the deep red scratches Cara had left on his face and chest. James was sickened beyond words, horrified to the depths of his soul, when he'd learned that Cara's blood and hair were found on the toe of Payne's right boot. His response was savage. James had been at the police station giving his statement when they brought Payne in. He tackled him, determined to beat him to death. It took four police officers to stop him, but not before he'd turned the man's face into a bloody pulp. Every fiber of his being wanted the man dead. James was damn lucky Payne's family didn't insist the police file assault charges against him.

By the end of the day, the police had a confession and plenty of evidence. They were simply waiting to see if they'd be filing rape and assault charges or murder charges.

James pressed a hand to his chest, trying to rub away the persistent ache. There were moments at Cara's bedside when he thought he'd simply forgotten how to breathe. When he wished to God he could forget how to breathe. Never much of a praying man, James prayed constantly. He bargained, he begged, he pleaded, he cajoled. *Just let her live. Please God, just let her live.*

On day eleven Cara woke up.

I don't want to be here. I don't want to be here. I don't want to be here. Why didn't Payne kill me? He should have killed me.

Cara knew where she was. She knew why. And she knew who sat beside her. He'd seen her. Oh God, he'd seen the awful things Payne had done to her. Cara couldn't bear it. Not now. Not ever. She kept her eyes closed.

"Go away," she hissed through gritted teeth. "Go away."

"Cara, sweetheart, Cara, it's me, James. You're going to be okay. Cara, it's going to be okay. It's all right, sweetie. Oh God, honey, everything is going to be okay."

Cara heard the tears in his voice.

"Go away," she repeated. The sound of her own voice made her head hurt. "Leave."

"Cara. . ."

She felt a hand on her arm. She moved away from his touch.

"I'm not going anywhere Cara. I love you. I'm not leaving you. It will be okay. I swear it will be okay. We'll get through this."

"My head hurts."

"I'll get the nurse," James said. "I'll only be gone for a second. You'll be okay, I promise."

No, Cara wanted to say, *It won't be okay James. It will never be okay.* She heard someone else enter the room. Within minutes Cara found herself drifting and she realized a nurse must have given her something for pain. *Yes. That feels better. That feels very good. I can go back to sleep.*

"She won't talk to me," said James, pacing in the hallway outside ICU, distraught. "She won't see her friend, Jeanie. She won't see Dr. Marsh. She won't see anyone but her mother."

"I know," said Will. "If it makes you feel any better she won't talk to me either."

James stared at his friend. "It doesn't make me feel any better."

"At least she finally agreed to an interview with the police," said Will. "It's a start."

Cara had told the police what happened, but she'd refused to allow James to be there for her to help her through the ordeal. Instead, she'd sent him out of the room, asking him to close the door behind him.

Today when he'd arrived, the charge nurse in ICU greeted him with the news that Cara was refusing all visitors, including him. He didn't know what he was going to do. He had no idea how to bring her back, how to get the Cara he loved to come back to him. When he'd spoken with her neurosurgeon Dr. Peterson repeated his warning that sometimes patients who had suffered traumatic brain injuries experienced personality changes. James already knew that. He didn't think this was a personality change. This was Cara's response to the attack, withdrawing from everything and everyone. This was Cara blaming herself for Ezra Payne.

"Do you know when she will be released?"

"Sorry." James had been lost in thought. "What did you say?"

"When will she be released?"

"Dr. Peterson is talking about moving her to a rehab unit. She needs therapy for her hands and she's a little unsteady on her feet."

"What about the left eye, any improvement?"

"She's lost some peripheral vision. It may be permanent. I don't know. She won't talk to me about it. Any information I get comes from her mother."

"It seems odd that her mom is the only person she'll talk to. I remember you telling me the two of them didn't get along very well."

"Yeah," said James. "Once upon a time they didn't. That's one good thing, I guess."

"Does she know you need to decide about the fellowship?"

"No, I haven't wanted to bring it up. To tell you the truth, I haven't had an opportunity to bring it up. Even if I did, I'm not sure I want to lay that kind of pressure on her. I want to stay with her, but I don't think. . ." James paused, "I don't think she wants me around."

"Maybe it's just shock, you know, the shock of everything, kind of a temporary setback. Maybe if you give her a few months she'll be back to normal."

James cleared his throat and stopped his pacing. "You don't know Cara like I do, Will. I keep trying to convince myself that this is temporary, that she'll snap out of it, but the truth is I don't know if she can. I'm scared to death, man. I am scared to death that this is as good as it's gonna get. That fucking Payne. That mother fucking Payne."

Chapter 18

February 1977

Cara had herself admitted to the University's inpatient psychiatric ward. She felt much safer there than she did on a medical unit, and she could restrict her visitors. Reliving the attack for the police had been brutal. Ezra Payne had entered her bathroom as she dozed in the tub. He'd talked to her, tried to tell her how much he cared about her. She'd shouted at him to get out of her apartment, to leave. She fought to climb out of the tub and get away from him, but he'd been too strong and he dragged her into her bedroom. She'd managed to grab for the phone, smashing it across his nose, but he threw her to the floor, ripped the phone from the wall.

She'd almost gotten away, making it to the door of the apartment before he'd tackled her, knocking the wind out of her. She remembered him punching her, kicking her in the side, in the ribs, in the stomach. The last thing she recalled was a vicious kick to the head. After that, she drew a blank. She didn't remember the rape. She didn't remember losing the baby.

Payne plea-bargained. Cara didn't have to testify in court. Because of the vicious nature of the crime, he was sentenced to forty-five years in the state penitentiary.

James had returned to his fellowship in North Carolina. Before she'd been discharged from the ICU Cara bluntly informed him that they had no future together she called off the engagement. She'd been cold, cruel. She'd broken him, watching him shatter as she spoke the words. But she'd hardened her own heart. It was for the best. James needed someone else in his life, a nice woman, not a train wreck, not her.

On his way to the airport James had stopped by her room one last time to tell her he wasn't giving up on them.

"I will always love you," he'd said. "I'll wait for you."

"Don't," Cara had replied. "Don't waste your time." Then she'd turned her face away from him.

She'd held her breath until she heard him leave the ICU. When his footsteps finally faded away, she'd begun to cry. Once she opened the floodgates Cara was unable to close them again. She'd climbed out of bed and stumbled toward the door, trailing IV lines behind her, intent upon throwing herself down the stairs. When the nurses finally managed to stop her she'd begged them to sedate her, and the staff had complied for her safety.

Circumscribed was the only way Cara could describe her life in the psych ward. It was exactly as it had been years before when she'd been hospitalized. She met with her psychiatrist or one of the psychiatric residents daily because that was expected of her. Three times a week she sat in silence through group therapy sessions. She left the ward every afternoon for an hour of hand therapy. The physical therapist remained optimistic that Cara would regain most of the dexterity in her hands, but her hands and fingers were badly scarred from the initial injuries and the surgical repairs. No matter how diligently she worked them, her fingers continued to feel stiff and unwieldy. She doubted she'd ever paint again, but then, Cara didn't really care.

She met with the ophthalmologist once a week for a recheck of her vision, and with her neurologist every two weeks so he could assess her progress. The ophthalmologist gave her exercises to compensate for the continued lack of peripheral vision in her left eye, telling Cara she could expect only a slight improvement. Her neurologist continued to reassure her that she would feel more normal as time went on. Cara laughed at him. This was *normal.*

Her mother visited regularly, bringing her flowers, cookies and letters from James. Cara gave the flowers to the nurses, the cookies to her fellow patients, and she stuffed the letters from James, unopened, into the shoebox where she kept the letters he'd sent from North Carolina. Aside from a few necessary articles of clothing, the shoebox was the only thing she'd asked her mother to bring her from the apartment.

Her mother and Phil Jackson had packed up her possessions and her artwork, hauling everything back to her mother's house. Phil had somehow gotten permission to leave Cara's car parked in the patient lot. She told him she wanted it left there in case she decided to check herself out and come home. In reality she wanted it there in case she decided to disappear. She had no idea where she'd go, but the idea of vanishing off the face of the earth appealed to her.

In early April, Cara's mother arrived for an unplanned visit. She told Cara she and Phil had gotten married. Cara wasn't surprised. She'd expected the news for some time. Her mother had already put Cara's childhood home on the market and moved into Phil's larger house, assuring Cara she'd continued to store her things.

"You're very young and you have so many options, dear," her mother said. She added with obvious hesitation, "You can always call James, you know. He and I talk at least once a week. He loves you Cara. He wants to be with you. You don't have to think about marriage, you know. Why not talk to him? What would it hurt?"

What would it hurt? Him. Me. My heart bleeds when I think of James.

"Maybe I'll consider it, Mom," she said, knowing she'd do no such thing.

"Good. That's good. That's progress," said her mother with a smile, giving Cara a pat on the knee. "Here." Her mom reached into her purse. "Here are some letters. They're from James. Oh, and there's one from Park City, Utah. Who do you know in Utah?"

Curious, Cara reached for the letters. She set those from James on the bed, but held onto the letter from Utah, turning it over in her hand. She glanced at the front of the envelope. There was no name on the return address, but the messy scrawl looked familiar. As she stared at the envelope Cara felt something stir inside her, something she hadn't felt in many months, interest. Reluctant to read it in front of her mother, she set the letter aside.

"I'll read it later. I don't know anyone in Utah. It's probably something to do with school."

Cara's mother shrugged, the letter forgotten. She ran a cautious hand over Cara's shorn head. "I wish you hadn't asked the nurses to chop off your beautiful hair."

Cara raised her eyebrows. *Beautiful hair?* "I didn't have much of a choice. A third of my head was already shaved."

Her mother sighed. "Do you think you might come home for your birthday? Are you feeling well enough? You know, well enough to check yourself out? You can always see Dr. Bowman if you need to talk to someone."

Cara looked into her mother's eyes, hating the hope she saw there. "Maybe," she replied with a forced smile.

"So have you done any painting? Anything in therapy you want to show me?"

"No. I don't paint. Remember, my hands?"

"Well, what about clay? Are you working with clay? I would think that would be good for you."

"No, Mom. I'm not working with clay." Cara changed the subject. "Can you stay for lunch?"

Cara's mother looked her up and down. "I'd love to stay for lunch. That way I can make sure you eat something."

Cara had lost a great deal of weight since the attack.

"Yes, Mom, you can make sure I eat." Cara glanced once more at the letter from Utah. She walked with her mother to the cafeteria, her stomach turning somersaults. Something was coming. Cara didn't know if it would be something good or something bad, but she sensed a subtle change in air pressure, like the feeling she got when storm clouds began to build in the distance. It was almost as if she could smell the ozone from a nearby lightning strike. Cara couldn't hear thunder, but she could feel its rumble all the same.

Cara returned to her room after therapy, still obsessing about the letter from Park City. She didn't know anyone who lived in Utah, yet the letter had practically crackled with electricity in her hands. When she picked it up again, she did so gingerly, holding it by the edges, fearful she might feel the thing pulse beneath her fingers. She didn't know whether to open it or not. She considered tossing it in the trash, yet that felt wrong. Cara got a feeling she was supposed to open it, as if the letter had arrived at this particular juncture for a reason. Yet still she hesitated.

After staring at the letter for fifteen minutes, she ripped open the envelope. Inside was a simple sheet of yellow notebook paper folded into thirds. Cara unfolded the sheet and she began to read. The letter was short.

Dear Cara,

I haven't talked to you in a long time, but for some reason you popped into my head the other day. I wonder what you're doing now. Do you still live in Iowa? I no longer live in California. Two years ago I moved to Park City, Utah. I'm a ski instructor during the day and I wait tables at night. The skiing is great and the restaurant business is big here. If you ever want to visit, here's my address, 1616 Kearns Boulevard. My phone number is (801) 435-5210. If you get this letter and you feel like it, give me a call sometime. Spring skiing is great! You'd love it!

Yours truly, John

Cara realized she'd been holding her breath. She blew it out in a whoosh. Flopping down onto her bed, she re-read the letter twice, considering. *John. Utah. Skiing.* She hadn't thought about John since high school. What would it hurt to call him tomorrow? She had checked herself into the psych ward, she could check herself out. She had her car keys, enough clothes for the time being, and plenty of money in her savings account.

Knowing John, he wouldn't care if she showed up out of the blue and he wouldn't care why she showed up. She doubted he'd ask her a single question; he'd just open the door and let her in.

Yes, this is exactly what I've been wishing for. The chance to crawl out of my own skin and be somebody else, go somewhere else. The timing could not have been better. Even if the devil himself waited for her in Utah, that's where Cara would go.

"She's gone." Louise Jackson buried her face in her hands and sobbed. "What do I do Will? What do I do?"

Will helped the distraught woman into a chair.

"Cara?" He was incredulous. "Gone? I just talked to one of the nurses over the weekend."

"No, she checked herself out, on Monday. She checked herself out. What do I do? Should I call the police?"

Will ran a hand through his short hair. He didn't know what to do. In the state Cara was in. . .God, he didn't even want to think about it. Cara's mother clutched a piece of paper in her hand.

"What's that? Is that a note? Did she leave a note? Let me see it."

When he reached for the piece of paper Cara's mother didn't resist. Her empty hand flopped onto her thigh.

The note was terse.

Mom, I've gone to visit a friend. I'm safe. I have plenty of money. Please try not to worry. I promise to contact you soon. Cara.

The first time he read it through, Will saw only letters of the alphabet. The second time he read the words. *What the hell?*

"Who is she talking about?" Will asked. "Do you have any idea who she's visiting?"

"No, no idea whatsoever. I don't know anyone she knows other than you and James and some of the people from her work."

"What about the staff? Do they have a clue where she went?"

"No." Mrs. Franklin rubbed her eyes. "They just said she checked herself in so she could check herself out." The woman paused. "You don't think, oh my god, you don't think she'll hurt herself, do you?"

Will shook his head. "No, I don't think so. This isn't a suicide note. I don't think Cara's the type. I mean— if she was inclined to do something she would have done it months ago."

Cara's mother let out a heart-wrenching cry. Will knelt down beside her. He put an arm around her shoulder.

"Look, I'm not quite sure what to do, but I don't think you can send the police after her. Cara's an adult. Do you have any reason to believe she might be in danger? Did she say anything to you, anything at all the last time you were here?"

Mrs. Jackson began to hiccup. "No, she seemed. . . She seemed okay. We had lunch together. I brought her a couple of letters from James and she probably stuck them in the box, the shoebox where she keeps them."

"Did she leave the box? Did she leave anything? You're her mother. If she left something behind, the nursing staff should give it to you."

"No, I asked. There's nothing in her room. All she left was the note. It was at the nurses' station."

Will was stumped. "Is there anything else you can remember, anything at all?"

"No. Yes. There was a letter, another letter, from Utah. I don't know who sent it. There was no name on the return address. She didn't open it while I was there. She left it on her bed."

"Did she say anything about it?"

"No, just that she didn't know anyone in Utah. That's all she said."

"Okay. Let's not jump to any conclusions. She may be in Utah or she may be here in Iowa City, staying with a friend from the Art Department. I don't know. I'm pretty sure you can take her at her word. She's safe. She's not going to hurt herself. Let's wait for her to call. She said she'll get in touch with you so let's assume she's telling you the truth."

"But, Will, how do I tell James? How do I explain this to James? He's still hoping she'll change her mind about the two of them."

"I'll tell him," said Will. "You don't have to worry about it." He took her arm and helped her to her feet. "Let's get you something to eat. I don't want you driving home until I know you're feeling calm."

"But. . ."

"I'll take care of it, Mrs. Jackson. I'll deal with James."

Cara's mother laid her hand on Will's arm. "You've been a good friend to her, Will, to both Cara and James. Thank you."

Will called James that night. Within two words, James had things figured out.

"Cara's gone, isn't she?" James' voice sounded tired, defeated.

"Yeah, man, she's gone."

"Where'd she go?"

"I don't know. She took off on Monday morning, I guess. She left her mom a note. She said she was safe, that she had enough money. She said she'd call."

After a long moment of silence, James spoke up.

"That's it, then."

"What do you mean, that's it? You're not going to wait to see where she is and go after her?" Will couldn't believe what he was hearing.

"No."

"But Mack, you love her. She loves you. I mean, you two fit together like. . .like puzzle pieces. You can't just let her go."

"What the hell do you expect me to do, Will? What the hell can I do? She doesn't want me. She's done with me."

"No, you know that's not true. Cara doesn't know what she wants. Wait until she calls her mother and then go after her. Make her listen to you. Make her come back to you. Don't let her get away with this."

"Don't let her get away with what?" James asked.

"Blaming herself. Do you hear me? Blaming herself," Will shouted, unable to hold back his frustration.

"I can't stop her." James was yelling now. "Goddamn it, Will, I can't stop her. I can't make her do a fucking thing. Cara has to want it. She has to want me and right now she doesn't want anything to do with me. It wouldn't matter what I said to her. Don't you get it? Do you think this is easy? You think this is easy for me? It's killing me, man. It's fucking killing me!"

"But. . ."

"No. I can't do this anymore. I won't do this anymore. I can't live this way. I'm done. Got it? I'm finished with all of this."

The phone clicked off. Will stared at the receiver like it had just bitten him.

James ripped the phone from the wall and hurled it across the room. It smashed into a lamp, a stained glass lamp Cara had purchased for him at an antique store in the Amana Colonies. They'd spent a weekend there last summer, staying in a homey, old-fashioned inn. They'd bicycled, gone sightseeing, shopped, sampled dandelion wine and homemade cheeses. He stood in his kitchen, reliving their joy in each other, their play, and their wild lovemaking in the big canopied feather bed.

Staring at the shards of colored glass scattered across the floor of his living room, his eyes caught on the deep red pieces. He pictured Cara's thick braid weaving and bobbing behind her, hanging nearly to her waist, shining like polished mahogany in the sun as she peddled down the hill to the inn. He heard her bubbling laugh.

So this is a broken heart, James mused. *I've never had one before. I don't ever want to feel like this again.*

James turned towards the kitchen to get a broom and a dustpan. He swept the pieces of broken glass into the dustpan, dropping them into a paper bag. Grabbing the metal lamp stand, he carried the bag and the lamp out to the trash bin. He lifted the plastic cover and dropped the broken lamp into the bin. Cara was gone. She wasn't coming back. She'd left James no choice. He had to let her go.

Chapter 19

Cara drove straight through, stopping only for gasoline and an occasional bathroom break. Considering the fact that Cara had never been any farther west than Omaha, the ease of the trip surprised her. All she had to do was head west on Interstate 80 and then watch for the signs to Park City.

John lived on one of the main streets. When she'd called him, he'd said exactly what she'd expected him to say—*come on down*, offering her his extra bedroom. He claimed he needed help with the rent anyway. It sounded like he could get her a job too since a hostess had quit at the restaurant where he waited tables. He offered to speak to his boss on her behalf. John said if Cara could get there fast enough he was pretty sure the position would be hers.

It seemed as if a great weight lifted off Cara's chest. During the drive, she'd actually flipped on the radio to listen to some music. She was a little concerned about her lack of warm clothing—her mother had taken most of her things back home—but she had plenty of money and she figured she could purchase some stuff when she got to Park City. She'd need some nice things too, if she was going to work as a hostess. Cara tried to recall what she'd left in her suitcase. She'd never unpacked it in the hospital. Maybe her mother had thrown in a couple of her skirts and blouses.

The suitcase was in the trunk of her car, along with the shoebox containing James' letters and the cassette tapes he'd made for her. She'd planned to leave the shoebox behind, but at the last minute she was unable to part with it.

What would she do with it? She didn't even know if she'd ever open it again. All Cara knew was that something had tugged at her when she'd set the box on the bed and walked out the door. She had to go back and get it.

Cara shrugged. It was better not to dwell too much on James, but she decided it didn't hurt to bring his letters along. The letters and tapes were mere keepsakes, nothing more than mementos of her old life.

Cara drove up Kearns Boulevard, appreciating the gorgeous views while keeping an eye on the road. She'd never seen mountains this close before and here she was, in the middle of a rustic mining town, now an up and coming skiers' paradise.

Snowfields lingered on the mountains, glistening white in the sun. John had mentioned that if conditions were good, he'd be skiing all week. Cara couldn't imagine herself skiing. She opened the driver's window wide so she could taste the breeze. The air felt cool and dry against her cheek. It smelled crisp as a just-picked apple, fresh and light, different from the thick, dark, loamy Iowa smell Cara was accustomed to.

Cara found the house easily enough. The place was pretty much what she'd expected. It was shabby, more like a shack than a house. John had been upfront about the fact that he lived from month to month. He needed someone to share expenses.

Cara parked her car and climbed out, stretching muscles cramped from the long drive. She wondered if John would recognize her. He'd never seen her without long hair. Now she wore it cut very short. It curled tightly around her cheeks and along the back of her neck. She tucked a few loose stands behind her ears. It had just barely grown long enough to do that.

John said he'd leave a key under the mat. After knocking to be on the safe side, Cara turned over the ragged doormat, found the key and unlocked the front door. The interior of the house wasn't much better than the exterior. The place smelled of dry rot, but as Cara walked from room to room, she noted that John kept things reasonably clean. The sitting room contained a ratty old couch, a vinyl beanbag chair and a faded throw rug. Cara checked out the first rate stereo system. That was typical of John and his misplaced priorities. The kitchen was small, the appliances ancient. The kitchen table was nothing more than a large wooden crate with two mismatched chairs. She could tell the crate doubled as a counter top. Making a mental note of dishware, cleaning supplies and pantry staples she'd need to buy, Cara scanned

John's bedroom and the single bathroom. She wrinkled her nose a little. It was obvious a guy lived here.

Cara found her room in the back of the house. At some point in the distant past, someone had added on a sun porch with a separate door so it could be closed off in the winter. There was no heating duct. The room came furnished with a futon on the floor and a small chest of drawers. John had thought to toss a sleeping bag and an old pillow onto the futon. That would have to do for the time being. Cara hadn't seen anything resembling a department store on her way into town. If she wanted warm quilts, clean linens and towels, she was going to have to make a trip into Salt Lake City as soon as possible. At least the room had a lot of windows.

As she headed back to her car to unload her few possessions, her chest began to ache. She automatically tried to rub the pain away, but it didn't work. It never worked. A sudden vision of her cozy bedroom back in Iowa City assailed her.

She remembered James sprawled across her bed on his stomach, sound asleep. The sun from her open window skimmed his naked back and muscular buttocks, dusting his skin with gold.

Tears filled Cara's eyes and she covered them with her hands.

He was beautiful. James was singularly beautiful inside and out. He would never be a part of her life again, and it was all her fault. She had been so stupid. She was the one who told Ezra Payne she would be alone in her apartment. She'd left the front door unlocked. She'd fallen asleep in the tub. She, of all people, should have known better.

I can't keep doing this. I can't think about this anymore. James is gone because I made him go. I didn't want him to want me.

"Get your things. Forget him. He's not for you."

Cara tripped on an uneven patch of gravel as she turned back toward the car. She fell to her knees, scraping them both beneath her jeans.

James, it hurts so much to leave you behind. Oh god, it hurts so damn much.

Three weeks later, Cara had yet to get a job, but the situation in the house was much improved. She'd tidied up the bathroom, installed shelves and hooks and bought new towels. The kitchen now had a real table. The floors had been scrubbed and the cabinets had been cleaned and stocked with staples. She'd organized the pots and pans and kitchen utensils, bought some inexpensive kitchen towels and they now possessed more than one place setting. She'd single handedly wrestled the futon in her bedroom onto a raised platform. She now slept between nice cotton sheets and beneath several warm quilts, because the nights were still quite chilly. Although the shopping in Park City was quite limited, the town did support an excess of sporting goods stores. Cara picked up a windbreaker and a parka, a wool cap and a pair of thick gloves. She also found a sturdy pair of hiking boots and some fleece-lined snow boots.

John was away most of the time, either working or hanging out with the other ski instructors. When he was around, he was usually stoned. He was generous with his dope and he urged Cara to join in, but she wanted to try to make it in her new life without resorting to the numbing effect of drugs.

Cara took every opportunity to find out about the hostess job, but for some reason John was evasive. Finally, at her wit's end, she asked him flat out why he hadn't introduced her to his boss as he'd promised. He couldn't meet her eyes.

"What?" she asked. "What is it? Am I so offensive that you're afraid to be seen with me?"

John's turned towards her, red-faced. "No, it's not that. It's, well, Cara, look at yourself. You aren't *cool*. I mean, I work for a pretty high-class guy. Have you looked in the mirror lately? Your hair's all ragged, your jeans hang on you. All you wear are baggy tee shirts. I can't take you in to meet him looking like this. You gotta clean yourself up, you know, fix yourself up, get some style. You used to be real pretty. Now you're just sort of, I don't know, sort of messy."

Cara felt as if all the air had just been sucked out of the room. She turned around and headed for the door. She heard John call her name. She ignored him.

You used to be really pretty. Now you're just sort of messy.

Messy. John had her pegged. She wondered what he'd say if he knew exactly how much of a mess she truly was. Cara forced back tears. *Uh-uh, no crying.* She'd promised herself after that first day in Park City there would be no more crying.

Cara hiked up the hill through the center of town. She turned right, striding past the last of the buildings, continuing on toward the ski slopes. When she entered a copse of trees she stopped to perch on a rock outcropping. Dusk had fallen, painting the sky a pale rose. The wind whistled as it brushed through the pines. Cara heard the occasional chirp of a bird bedding down for the night.

John was right. He couldn't introduce her to his high-class boss and expect her to impress him. How could she start a new life when she still clung to the old? She needed to step it up. When he was stoned John waxed on and on about the wealthy Hollywood-types who patronized the restaurant, the movie stars to whom he gave ski lessons.

That was the world she needed to fit into. She still had enough money. A visit to a salon and a little shopping wouldn't break the bank. She could leave early in the morning for Salt Lake City. If she didn't get everything done in one day, she could afford a night or two in a motel.

Cara shook her head, surprised she'd forgotten the lessons Jeanie had taught her, *look the part even if you don't feel it.* Jeanie used to say, *the outside affects the inside and vice versa.* It had worked once before. Cara needed to get the outside fixed as soon as possible and hope maybe that would help fix her inside. She didn't want to see John again tonight, preferring to wait until it grew so late John would either be gone or passed out in bed. She'd see him when she felt ready.

"Holy shit." John gave a whistle as Cara strolled out of the bedroom. "That's what I'm talking about."

Cara twirled for him, giving him a three hundred and sixty degree view of her makeover.

"Much, much better. You are hot Cara. You are sizzling. Damn." He circled her, checking out the hair and the outfit. "Now you can come to work with me. My boss will be in tonight. He's hosting a private party for a few of his friends in the back room. Come, and I swear you will get that job. Goddamn, you look good enough to eat."

Cara almost smiled. She'd better look good. She'd spent hours in an expensive salon in Salt Lake City the day before getting the works—hair, nails, a pedicure. The stylist had trimmed her unruly hair, teaching Cara how to slick it back with gel and curl the ends. The cut was stark, sleek and sophisticated, drawing a man's gaze to Cara's lush red lips, her high cheekbones and her wide-set, almond-shaped eyes.

Cara had made judicious use of a dark gray eye shadow, the way Jeanie had taught her, to bring out the violet color in her eyes. She had such naturally thick lashes that she'd skipped the mascara, but she'd touched her lips with a deep, dark red stain, almost the same color as her hair. She didn't use much but, as the girl at the makeup counter had teased, just enough to make a man salivate the moment he met her.

She wore a fitted black skirt that fell to mid-thigh, exposing what her mother would consider an indecent amount of her long legs. The blouse she'd donned was a pale, mint-green silk. The color emphasized her creamy complexion and pulled out the mahogany highlights in her hair. She'd unbuttoned the top button.

Studying her, John reached over in a friendly fashion and unbuttoned her second button. The lace edge of her new black bra just barely peaked out, giving anyone who might be interested a tantalizing taste of what lay beneath her clothes. John checked out her shoes. Cara had slipped her bare feet into black stiletto heels. She'd forgone the stockings, her dislike of stockings a persistent holdover from her previous life.

The only jewelry Cara wore was a pair of simple gold hoop earrings. She'd learned from Jeanie that a woman should never overdo the jewelry. She should wear just enough to draw the eye to the body part she wanted another person to appreciate. Cara wanted John's boss to look at her face. She didn't want him to focus on her scarred hands. But what would it hurt if he looked at a few other parts of her too?

Two nights in a motel, two days of shopping and the salon makeover had used up a sizeable chunk of her cash, but Cara hoped to make it back quickly. Her portion of the rent was only ninety dollars a month and she spent little on food. If she had to she could last six months or more on her savings. Cara's mother had offered to send money when she'd called her ten days ago, but Cara had turned her down. She didn't the obligation. This was her new life. It was better to make a clean break.

Her mother had cried during the phone call, begging Cara to come back home, but Cara had held it together. She was fine, she had a nice place to live, she was perfectly safe, and she would soon have a job. After some wrangling, she'd reluctantly agreed to call home every two weeks to check in, and she left her mother with John's phone number and address in case of an emergency.

Her ability to resist that nagging inner voice, the one that demanded to know if James was all right, pleased Cara. Her future didn't lie with him. It was better not to look back, just like it was better not to look too far ahead. Thinking about her past and wondering about her future didn't pay. Maybe John had the right idea. Hang out, party, work a little, party some more. What had all her hard work gotten her in the end? The same as always, not a damn thing.

It was better not to get attached. Not to make plans. Not to fall in love. If you had nothing to lose then there was nothing to miss when it was gone, right? That had been her rule until James had appeared at her office in the med center. Never let yourself fall in love. Well, she broke her own rule and look what happened. For an instant Cara felt sick, as memories flooded back of that night, memories of Ezra Payne. She shoved them into a corner of her mind, ordering them to stay put.

"I'm gonna get changed," John said, interrupting her thoughts. "Then we can go. Do you mind driving? My car's out of gas."

"Not at all," said the new Cara. "You think this will work? You think I'll get the job?"

"Oh, hell yeah. You're exactly what he's been looking for. You look just the way I described you. Better." John disappeared into his room.

"But I thought you didn't talk to him about me yet. You didn't tell me that you'd already. . ." Cara's voice trailed off. What did it matter if John had been withholding information? Once he got a look at her he'd probably realized he couldn't bring her by the restaurant, but he was afraid to tell her, afraid of hurting her feelings. Obviously this was a classy place.

Ten minutes later, John reappeared. Cara grabbed her new leather clutch and they walked to her car. As he opened the passenger door, John cleared his throat.

"Uh, one more thing," he said, looking across the roof of the car, a sheepish expression on his face. "I, uh, told my boss you're twenty-three. It's kind of a Utah thing. The liquor laws and all that. The older you are the better. He thinks I'm twenty-three too, so let's just keep that between us, okay?"

"I'm not sure I understand," said Cara. "What liquor laws?"

"Utah liquor laws are kind of weird. You can't sell liquor in a restaurant, only in a private club. You can't even sell wine unless you have some kind of special license, I think. You can serve wine if the customer brings it, you just can't sell it."

Cara looked at John, confused. "What does this have to do with me?"

"Well, my boss runs a, well, it's kind of like his own private club in the back. He serves alcohol and he won't let anyone under twenty-one work there. I mean, sometimes even twenty-one isn't old enough for him, so I fudged a little. Do you mind backing me up?"

"Yeah, sure." Cara shrugged. "No problem. It doesn't matter anyway. I turned twenty-one a while ago.

"Good, thanks. I just don't want any misunderstandings. And I'd like to keep my job."

"Will your boss need to check out my driver's license?"

John winked at her. "I doubt it."

Cara developed a bad case of the jitters during the short drive. This was not her forte, a restaurant and private drinking establishment. What did she know about food and alcohol? She didn't eat much and she didn't drink. She lagged behind John.

John turned back towards her. "Relax," he said. "You'll do fine. It's no big deal. You're just meeting him tonight. That's all. Don't sweat it. And Cara," he added, "Whatever you see, keep it to yourself."

"Pardon me?"

"Nothing." John held the door open for her.

The minute she stepped inside, Cara was wrapped in scent. She smelled roasting meats, the yeasty aroma of warm bread, the spicy tang of garlic and tomatoes and the light, salty, slightly sweet fragrance of fresh fish. The restaurant delighted her. Glass on three sides provided lovely views of the town and the ski slopes. The windowless side was taken up by an old, heavy wooden bar. It looked like something straight out of a western saloon. As John had explained to her, the bartender was only allowed to serve low alcohol beer.

Cara watched waiters bustle back and forth between the tables, the bar, and a door that she assumed led to the kitchen. She didn't notice any waitresses. John escorted her to the bar, and sat her on a stool. "Wait here." He motioned to someone. A man stood up from behind the bar. Despite her height in the high heels, Cara had to lift her head to see his face. He looked like an athlete, a boxer or a football player.

"Jerry," John said to the bartender, "this is my friend Cara, the girl I told you about. Cara, this is Jerry, our bartender."

"Hello." Still sensitive about her scars, Cara kept her hands at her sides. She'd told John she'd been in an accident.

Jerry gave her a slow once-over, his eyes sliding from her head to her toes, before he shot her wide, white smile.

"You were right, man," he called after John. He poured Cara a beer. "On the house."

"Right about what?"

"That you would be perfect for the job. What did you say your name was?"

"Cara. Cara Franklin."

Jerry stuck out a big hand. "Well, Red, you are a real beauty. Welcome to Park City. I'm Jerry Mitchell. I tend bar and I'm the bouncer on the weekends. Anyone gives you any trouble, you come see me."

Cara hesitated as she laid her hand in his. He squeezed hers, making her wince. He glanced down.

"What the hell happened to you?"

"A car accident," she said. "It happened last December."

"Both hands, or just the one?"

She showed him her other hand. He held them both in his for a moment, studying her scars.

"Rough." He released her hands with a gentle motion, turning to pour a couple beers for one of the waiters.

Cara sat on the barstool and looked around. For a Wednesday, the place was busy, but not packed. John had told her that the big crowds came in on Friday and Saturday nights. The restaurant was closed on Sundays except for private parties. To Cara's eyes, the patrons appeared well-off, the wait staff professional and unobtrusive. She watched a waiter wheel a cart to one of the tables and, with almost comical theatrical gestures, make a Caesar salad for two. A smile tugged at the corners of her mouth and she would have laughed out loud, but for the fact that everyone else in the restaurant seemed to take the matter quite seriously.

"You gonna drink that?"

"Oh, sorry." Cara smiled at Jerry. "I don't drink much. Thank you though, I do appreciate it." She took a sip.

"Kind of like water, isn't it?"

"Sorry?"

"Utah beer. It's kind of watered down."

"Oh, John mentioned something to me about the liquor laws here."

"Yeah, they're pretty strict. But there are ways to bend them without breaking them. Just like back in the days of Prohibition. People will always find a way to buy alcohol." Jerry grinned at her. "You're not quite what you seem, are you, Red?"

Cara's eyes opened wide. "What do you mean?"

"John's a flake. He shows up to work on time, but he's still a flake. Stoned on his ass is more like it. He tells us about this friend of his who's coming to room with him, this beautiful stoner, and he asks the boss if he can give you a job. Knowing John, I figured you'd be just as flakey as he is, maybe some empty-headed bimbo, but you're not. You graduate from college?"

"Yes."

"What's your degree in?"

"I was a double major in Art History and Painting."

Jerry whistled. "Then what the hell you doing here?"

"Taking a break."

"After your accident, huh?"

Cara nodded.

Jerry said, "Well, you have what I call the three 'Ls'."

"The three 'Ls'?"

"Long, leggy and luscious."

At his words, Cara did laugh out loud.

Jerry grinned at her again. "I was wondering what it would take to get a laugh out of you, Red. You look so serious." Then he said, "The boss is coming. Watch yourself. Remember, if you need anything I'm your guy." He busied himself pouring beer for another waiter.

Cara felt her stomach twist as she rose from the stool and turned to meet the man who might become her employer. She spotted him across the restaurant, a tall man standing just in front of John. Brown eyes, hard eyes, locked upon hers. It almost as if he was a predator and she his prey. Cara sucked in a breath. The man was beautiful. He looked exactly like an older version of James.

The moment Micah Welsh laid eyes on the young woman sitting at the bar, he determined to have her. She was breathtaking. He stood still, eyes narrowed, watching as she chatted with Jerry. Jerry obviously appreciated the same things he did. When Micah saw Jerry say something to her, and she tossed back her lovely head and laughed, he decided he'd had enough. Just as he stepped forward, one of the waiters moved into his path. Irritated, Micah walked around him. The young man mumbled something, but all Micah's attention remained riveted on the woman. As he approached, she turned towards him and rose from the stool. The look on her face intrigued him; she seemed startled at the sight of him, as if she recognized him.

Impossible.

Micah would never have forgotten a woman like this one. God, she was stunning. Her lips alone could drive a man insane. He took in her long, shapely, bare legs, the skirt that hugged her hips like a second skin, the taut waist, the perfect silk blouse, unbuttoned just enough to expose the rounded slope of her high, firm breasts. She was not for Jerry, or any other man. She was his.

The waiter kept pace with him. Micah finally stopped to pay him some attention. "What is it?" He kept the annoyance out of his voice. It wouldn't do to make a bad first impression on the woman.

"I just. . .I just. . .I want to introduce you to the friend I told you about."

"What friend?" Micah considered firing the idiot on the spot.

The waiter turned and motioned to the woman. She walked towards them, her violet eyes questioning, never leaving his face.

"Cara, this is my boss, Mr. Welsh. Mr. Welsh, this is an old friend of mine, Cara Franklin."

Micah took her hand in his and brought it to his lips. "Micah," he murmured, "call me Micah. I'm delighted to meet you, Miss Franklin."

The woman appeared flustered at his display of courtesy. "I'm sorry to be so impolite," she said in her soft voice. "I didn't mean to stare, but you look like someone I used to know. You've caught me a bit off guard."

"Not in an unpleasant way, I hope," he replied, giving her his most disarming smile.

"No." She shook her head. "Unexpected would be a better word."

Micah could hear the waiter prattling on. "I told Cara that maybe she could talk to you about the hostess job, you know, since Beverly quit."

"Yes," said the woman. "I recently moved here and I was hoping..."

Micah tucked her arm into his, drawing her towards the private room in the rear of the restaurant. "I'm certain we can work something out, Miss Franklin. Why don't you come with me to the club? It's much quieter and we'll be able to talk, if you don't mind waiting for me to finish up a little business, that is?"

"That sounds fine." She shot a glance at John. He nodded and she allowed Micah to lead away from the bar.

This one is a bit skittish. Micah realized he'd have to take his time. This wouldn't be a quick fuck and a *see ya later, doll.* His grin widened. It had been quite a while since a woman had intrigued him. There was an innocence about Miss Cara Franklin, a vulnerability despite the way she looked. He doubted she had any idea of the effect she had on every man in the room. If he played his cards right, he could keep her around for a while. A woman like this could be very, very good for business. And to think, that little prick, John, found her for him. He'd have to remember to thank him, later.

Cara sat alone at a corner table nursing a glass of champagne. Mr. Welsh, Micah, chatted with two men near the rear exit. Despite the fact that he turned his head in her direction every so often, he seemed engrossed in his discussion.

Before he'd excused himself, Micah had waved off the waitress and poured the champagne for her himself, insisting she wait for him to finish up his business. Cara took the opportunity to study him. The man was tall, broad shouldered and narrow hipped. His thick hair, with its neat cut, shone a rich, dark brown in the warm, muted glow of the candle-lit room. Cara hadn't missed the muscular feel of his arm beneath her hand when he'd escorted her to the private club, nor could she ignore the perfect fit of his tailored slacks and the crisp white of his shirt.

There was no sense denying it, Micah Welsh intrigued her. Knowing where that might lead, a small voice in her head whispered, "run." Cara ignored it. She wanted to know what sort of job he'd offer her. Besides, how could she help but be fascinated by a man who looked exactly like James, yet was nothing like him at all?

Micah was older, charming, seductive, sophisticated. Cara assumed he got whatever he set his mind to. In that respect, he reminded her of James. In all other respects he was James' cracked mirror image. Out of the blue, Cara was struck by an intriguing notion. Perhaps she could have James, or someone like him, without the painful burden of love. As she sipped her champagne, speculating about the man who might become her employer, thoughts roaming in disparate directions, she reminded herself that this was not about James. This was about leaving him behind.

Micah Welsh couldn't believe his good fortune. Of all the nights for a doll like her to walk into his place. . . Here he was, meeting with his two biggest buyers, one from Los Angeles, the other from New York, and there she sat, looking like a birthday cake. It hadn't escaped his attention that both men had licked their lips when he strolled into the room with Cara on his arm. A beautiful woman was always good for business. But nobody was getting their hands on this one, at least not without his say so.

When they'd concluded their discussion, Micah set the two men up at a table. One of them asked if the redhead was available. Micah made it clear she was off limits. Instructed two of his waitresses, Charlene and Donna, to get his associates whatever they wanted.

These two gentlemen knew when a line had been drawn and they wouldn't dare cross it. There were others though, who would challenge him. If he was going to keep this woman for himself, he'd have to be prepared to battle now and again.

Good. Life had been a bore of late. Micah enjoyed a good fight, but more than that, he was fond of the chase. He glanced at Cara Franklin. She sat still, like a young doe hiding in the bushes, and he was the big bad wolf. He'd begun his pursuit the instant he'd caught her scent. She would belong to him if it was the last thing he did.

Chapter 20

Micah treated her to a delicious dinner of Caesar salad, steak au poivre with a Dijon cream sauce, roasted fingerling potatoes, tender-crisp steamed green beans and a shared crème brûlée for dessert. He offered to drive her home. The two of them had split a bottle of Bordeaux. Although the wine didn't seem to affect Micah, Cara wasn't accustomed to alcohol and she didn't feel right about driving.

Cara thanked him for both the dinner and the kind offer, but she kicked off her high heels and handed her keys to John. "Please don't trouble yourself. I'll walk home."

Cara smiled one of her rare smiles. "I really can't impose upon you. You've already been so generous with your time." Cara didn't mention that they hadn't gotten around to discussing a job.

"I insist," said Micah. "I can't let you walk alone in the dark. I'd never forgive myself if anything happened to you. Please, it's the least I can do."

"The least you can do? You've done more than enough, Mr. Welsh."

"Micah, remember? You promised to call me Micah."

"Yes I did, Micah."

"You've allowed me to enjoy the pleasure of your company, Miss Franklin. Please, I insist."

Micah pressed a hand against the small of her back as he steered her out the door towards his Jaguar. The act was possessive, proprietary, the simple act prompting Cara to remember another hand.

She shoved the memory away, willing herself to relax into Micah's touch. Over the past three hours Cara hadn't learned much about the man, but what little she had managed to ascertain gave her pause. He had been unfailingly polite and considerate. She'd watched him firmly rein in the sexual hunger she saw in his eyes. Despite that evidence of control, she realized Micah Welsh wasn't a man to be trifled with. He was the kind of man people respected, even feared. To tell the truth, Cara felt a little afraid of him. The marvelous dinner he'd just treated her to had strings attached. He would eventually expect to be paid back, and not in kind.

Cara reclined in the soft leather seat and closed her eyes. She wondered how long she could stall him. Yes, she would go to bed with him in the end. There was no point pretending she wouldn't, just not tonight. *Please God, not tonight.*

It didn't occur to Cara to be self-conscious about the dilapidated condition of John's house until Micah had already walked her to the front door. By then it was too late. There was no way she could let a man of his sophistication inside. She doubted he would understand, and he might be tempted to ask why in the hell she was living like this. And he might suggest she come home with him. Thank god there was no porch light.

She turned to face him, extending a hand.

"Thank you," Cara said. "I had a delightful evening. I'm afraid we never got around to discussing that job."

Micah took her hand in his. He leaned over to give her a gentle peck on the cheek.

"We'll have plenty of time for that," he said. His lips just barely brushed her ear.

Cara held very still, afraid to encourage him, yet just as afraid to discourage him.

Micah straightened up, her hand still in his. "Come with me tomorrow."

"Where?"

"Just come with me. I'll pick you up at noon."

Cara laughed. "I need to know where we're going so I'll know what to wear."

"Shorts, and bring a bathing suit."

"A bathing suit? That's one of the many things I neglected to pack when I moved here."

"I'll find a suit for you. You must be. . .? His eyes traveled her torso. "What, a size two?"

Cara raised her eyebrows. "Yes. How did you know?"

Micah shrugged off her question. "Be ready at noon."

"All right, thank you," Cara said. "Good night, Micah."

"Good night." Micah continued to clasp her hand with his own.

With a gentle motion, Cara disengaged her hand and unlocked the front door.

"Hey, uh, John, come with me." Micah headed to the stairs that led to his private office.

Micah walked to his liquor cabinet and reached for a bottle of single malt scotch. He poured two glasses, handing one to John. "Have a seat," he said, in a cordial fashion.

John sat.

"Tell me about this friend of yours. Tell me about Cara."

This was exactly what John had been hoping for. That Cara could get him an in with the boss, get him into some of the backroom business. That's where the money was, not waiting tables and selling penny ante homegrown weed to the local high school kids who didn't know any different.

Deciding to play it cool, John leaned back in his chair and sipped his scotch. The liquor burned his throat, but he pretended he'd been drinking it all his life.

"What do you want to know?"

Micah didn't mince words. "Are you sleeping with her?"

"Hell no." John choked on the scotch. He coughed and sputtered and tried to catch his breath. "Cara and I are friends, that's all we are."

"How do you know her?"

"I lived in Iowa for a few years when I was in high school. Like I said, she was a good friend of mine."

"Why did she decide to come out here? Why did she move in with you?"

Jeez, John thought, *what the hell is this? An interrogation?* "I don't know," he said. "I got back in touch with her and she was at loose ends, so she came out. It was no big deal."

"At loose ends? Why was a woman like Cara doing nothing?

"She'd graduated from college and she had some plans, but I guess something happened. An accident or something. She had to change her plans."

"What kind of accident?"

John shrugged. "Didn't you notice her hands, Mr. Welsh?"

"What about her hands?"

"The scars, they're scarred. She broke a lot of bones in her hands. She used to be an artist, a real good one. I don't know if she can paint anymore."

John watched Mr. Welsh fiddle with his drink.

"Did you tell her I had a job for her?"

"I mentioned, yeah, I just mentioned there might be a job available that she could apply for. That's all I said. Was that okay?"

Micah waved off the question. He twirled the glass of amber-colored liquid.

"Do you trust her?"

"Cara? Shit yeah. She's smart. She keeps her mouth shut. She watched out for me when nobody else at that damn high school would give me the time of day. She was always one step ahead of the narc assistant principal. She drove him insane for three years. He never figured out how she knew where he would be before he even knew it himself." John paused. "Trust Cara? I probably trust her more than I've ever trusted anyone. Besides, she's pretty. I always thought she was the prettiest girl—woman—I'd ever seen."

Micah tossed back his scotch and narrowed his eyes. "There is that," he agreed. "She is most definitely very, very pretty. Thank you, John. We're done here."

John set his empty glass on the desk and rose from the chair.

"Oh, John, by the way, make sure you don't fuck Cara. Make sure you don't even think about it."

John kept his expression blank. "Don't worry, Mr. Welsh, we're friends, that's all we are, just friends."

"Keep it that way."

When he heard the door close, Micah walked over to the bar and poured himself another drink. He'd get Cara Franklin out of that house as soon as possible. He didn't trust the little shit around her. Even if

John didn't want her for himself he'd probably pimp her out to one of his ski buddies for an ounce of weed.

Micah took a sip of his scotch and sat down behind his desk. He put his feet up and leaned back in the leather chair, closing his eyes. He'd have to take it slow with this one. If he came on too strong she'd bolt. He could sense it. He'd need to work his way past her defenses, get her to trust him, let her guard down.

Micah felt like rubbing his hands together with glee. The thought of a new conquest excited him. He hadn't been this interested in a woman since his second wife. He wondered if Donna was still downstairs or if she'd gone off with one of his associates. He picked up the house phone and called down to the bar to ask about her. Jerry said she was still serving drinks in the back. Micah asked Jerry to send her up. He could work off some steam with her.

Cara was up early the next morning. By eight o'clock she already had a nine-thirty appointment with a local doctor. She didn't care who he was or if he was any good, she wanted a prescription for birth control pills. It was a perfect time to start them. Her period had just ended the night before. She didn't kid herself. Staying out of Micah's bedroom wasn't going to be an option. He hadn't pushed her last night, but she knew exactly where they were headed.

When Cara returned from the drug store she found John sitting in the living room, looking like the proverbial cat that had swallowed the canary.

"What?" She was surprised to see him awake before noon on a day off.

"Go look in your room."

Cara pushed open the door to her small sun porch. At least a hundred red roses filled the room. John had set the vases everywhere. She threaded her way around the bed.

"My God."

"Yeah, no shit!" "You made quite an impression on him."

She drew her finger across one of the velvety petals.

"The man is seriously interested, Cara. If you play this right, you could go places. I mean, really go places."

"I'm not playing a game, John."

"Well yeah, I know but, well, you know what I mean. He is really into you. Use it. He's fucking loaded. He owns two other restaurants in Salt Lake and one in Sun Valley. He's got three private clubs. Besides he's got other, uh, investments. You know, other stuff going on."

"Stuff?"

"Yeah, Mr. Welsh has a lot of business interests. Here, on the East Coast, in Los Angeles. I don't really know much about it. But hey, he's been around long enough that he's made plenty. He must be, like, thirty-eight or forty or something. Besides, if you get in good with him, then that's good for me." John winked at her. "I don't want to be a waiter the rest of my life."

Cara lifted one long-stemmed rose from a vase and brushed the flower over her lips. She couldn't deny that Micah Welsh was a very impressive man, but neither could she lie to herself. He meant nothing to her.

"I need to change clothes John. He's picking me up at noon."

"Yeah, okay." John backed away from the door. "Hey Cara. . ."

She turned towards him.

"Don't hold out too long. He's not a patient man."

Cara frowned, acknowledging John's words with a slight nod of her head before she closed her door. Who was she kidding? What was she holding out for? She didn't like her life anyway. If Micah Welsh could reshape it in his image, would that be such a terrible thing?

Over the next six months, Cara began to forget that she once painted beautiful pictures. Instead, she allowed her body and her mind to become a blank canvas for Micah. If he said, "Straighten your hair", she straightened it. If he said, "Wear it natural today", she curled it with her fingers. He didn't like the way red looked against her skin so she never wore red. If he bought her a necklace, she put it on. If he preferred her long neck bare, she left it bare of adornment. If Micah wanted her skirts shortened, Cara made a trip to the dressmaker, at his expense, to have them shortened. She let him shape her into his perfect accessory.

She played her part in the bedroom too, putting into practice Rick's detailed lessons on how to please a man. She knew how to give Micah pleasure and she knew how to leave him wanting more.

Sex made a sound. Cara had no problem faking it. Her only goal was to ignore the self-loathing she felt during and after each and every encounter. She decided life was a trade-off. There were advantages to being with Micah. For one thing, she wasn't required to make a single decision. He managed her affairs completely and he asked very little of her. Simply that she be his fantasy and do as she was told.

Sometimes Cara felt like a character on a movie screen, flat, two-dimensional, make-believe, as if she was nothing more than a projection of Micah's imagination. When she allowed herself to think about the situation she found it disconcerting, yet at the same time, she felt peaceful, at rest. For once she lived her life in neutral, content to drift, aimless, unfettered by attachment to anyone or anything.

At long last she was free of sadness, joy, anticipation, fear. She'd let go of memories, good and bad. Her only obligation was to please Micah. Occasionally she noticed him watching her, an odd look in his eyes, as if he wished for something more. Probably love, Cara thought, the one thing she wasn't able to give him. She had already loved a man, a real man. She would never fall in love again.

Micah slipped a possessive hand beneath the strap of Cara's dress, resting his palm on her naked, perfect shoulder. He moved his fingers in slow motion, subtly caressing the back of her lovely neck. He knew very well he was the envy of every man in the club and his eyes issued a challenge no one dared answer. Cara's presence had become invaluable. She attracted attention without even realizing that was exactly what he wanted her to do. With a shy toss of her head and one glance from those soft violet eyes, she was able to coax the most reticent of men to do business with him. What man worth his salt could say no to a beautiful woman? Especially one so attentive, articulate and genteel?

They'd caught a late afternoon flight into Los Angeles and he'd brought her to a club he owned in tandem with his nephew, Frederick. It was her first time in L.A., and Micah could feel her innocent astonishment at the lively city with its interminable traffic jams and its unabashedly narcissistic residents.

His associates were eager to know about his new plaything, wondering discreetly when he would share. Micah shared his women when it suited him, when he had something to gain from their liaisons.

When they'd arrived and he'd watched Cara work her way through the room, her sweet hips swaying in the bronze silk dress he'd bought her, her cheeks flushed from the champagne his nephew had poured for her, he'd suddenly realized he didn't want to share her. He wanted to own her. When he'd motioned to her, she moved to his side without hesitation.

Now he deliberately toyed with her hair. He moved his fingers down her neck, over her shoulder, along her spine, finally resting his hand on her thigh, making sure every man in the room watched. There would be no question as to whom Cara belonged.

He'd moved her into her own town home in Park City, but lately he found himself jealous of every moment she spent there without him. It was one of the reasons he'd brought her with him to Los Angeles. It was either bring her or insist that Jerry watch her again. Jerry had standing orders to keep tabs on her whenever he left town. Jerry had protested that he wasn't a damn babysitter, that he had too much work to do at the restaurant already, but despite his complaining, the man did as he was told. He grudgingly reported her every move. Other than hiking in the mountains and running an occasional errand, Cara stayed put.

Micah was surprised at how little Cara seemed to expect out of life. At times it bothered him and he wondered, with a vague sense of unease, if he was being set up. In Micah's opinion, a beautiful woman should expect a lot, should demand a lot. Always gracious, Cara accepted everything he gave her yet she demanded nothing of him. More often than not, she'd just smile one of her rare, enigmatic half-smiles before she'd take him to bed. Only one other thing triggered a tiny alarm bell, for all her seeming inexperience, Cara was the best lover Micah had ever had.

The last time he'd left her alone that little weasel, John, had sneaked by to see her. Jerry mentioned it in an offhand way. Furious, Micah had confronted Cara, demanding to know if John had been there. He'd grabbed her arm, hard, leaving a bruise. Caught off-guard by his overt show of anger, she admitted that she'd seen him. She said John was hoping she could intercede for him, help him get him a better job.

That prick was becoming a constant irritant. Behaving as though Micah owed him, *owed him*, for finding Cara. He kept asking to work in the back. Something would have to be done about him, but not just yet. Not when Micah still had questions about Cara's feelings. She'd never once said she loved him. He obsessed about it, waiting to hear those words spoken from her lovely mouth.

He'd toyed with the idea of moving her out to his ranch or taking her to his apartment in New York, but he wasn't quite sure he was ready to give her access to all his secrets. The ranch would be the best option. She'd be isolated there. The club scene in New York was rapidly picking up, demand for cocaine was increasing, and it would be hard to keep her from learning about his backroom business deals.

As far as Cara was concerned, he was a successful entrepreneur, pure and simple. She didn't seem to look beyond that. He could ask her to marry him, but that would be a big risk, an enormous risk. His previous marriage had nearly ruined him. Fortunately Dominique had seen the error of her ways and she'd been persuaded to keep her mouth shut. His ex-wife was a fucking cunt and Micah didn't want to have to deal with that shit again.

Cara had withdrawn a bit, grown a little quieter since he'd confronted her about John, despite his apology and two dozen red roses. It wouldn't do to lose her now. He wondered if he should reconsider a marriage proposal.

Micah watched his nephew approach. He knew the young man wanted to talk business. Cara must have recognized it at the same time he did. She rose in one fluid movement and excused herself, asking for directions to the powder room. Eyes riveted on her face, his nephew obliged, turning to watch her walk away.

"Where the hell did you find her?" He whistled through his teeth. "She's a beauty."

Micah growled. "Don't even think about it."

The man laughed. "Uncle, I wouldn't dream of it. I'm happily married and I know which side my bread is buttered on. I'm just pointing out the obvious. You plan to keep this one?"

"I haven't decided yet," Micah said, irritation making his voice hoarse.

His nephew turned to look at him. "You've got it bad," he said. "Maybe you should make an honest woman of her. My mother would be thrilled if her little brother remarried."

Micah sipped his scotch. "I had problems the last time."

"Ah yes, my dear Aunt Dominique. As I recall, Dom was, how shall I put it. . . In your face? Flamboyant? Not like this one. If I'm any judge of women, this one's a class act."

A class act, Micah thought. That was Cara to a tee.

"Is she discreet?"

"The subject hasn't come up."

"Does she suspect?"

"Not so far as I can tell."

"If you plan to keep her around for a while perhaps you should marry her. If she becomes your wife we can minimize our risks. Limit any potential damage. It's not hard to end a marriage. If worse comes to worse, I mean. Marriage has some definite advantages."

Micah stared at his glass. "I'll consider it," he said. "Now, tell me about this new plan of yours to expand our distribution on the East Coast."

As usual, Cara's sleep was disturbed. She lay on her side, a hand beneath her cheek, trying to focus on the regular rise and fall of Micah's chest.

The early hours of the morning were agony for Cara. It was in the dark that she recalled who she was and where she'd come from. In the quiet, she remembered she hadn't emerged, fully formed, from the top of Micah's head. In the darkness, Cara fought back tears. James wasn't beside her and he never would be.

Showing any emotion in front of Micah wasn't an option. If she was lucky, it would merely make him uncomfortable. If she was unlucky, it would make him angry and he'd demand to know why she was crying. He wouldn't be happy if he learned the reasons, all the many reasons.

His vicious response to an innocent visit from John had unnerved her. She'd been stunned. Micah had never before laid a hand on her in anger, or even raised his voice to her. How had he known John had dropped by? The only explanation she could come up with was that John had mentioned his visit.

After that incident, Cara concluded she should pull back a little, perhaps begin a gradual disengagement. In the dark, she could allow her doubts to surface. Micah Welsh was a complicated man. Perhaps it would be better if she knew how complicated, but Cara's instincts told her not to question him. For one thing, she wasn't certain how he'd react. For another, he'd been generous to a fault, with his time and his money. He'd provided her with everything a woman could ask for.

He'd provided her with a life. What difference did it make that it wasn't her life? She was better off. Micah protected her. No one dared hurt her because they knew she belonged to him. Cara couldn't even fault Micah as a lover. He was skilled, and Cara might have enjoyed herself if she wasn't numb to his touch, to the touch of any man. But that fault lay with her, not him. She was the one who was deficient.

Where would she go if she left him, back to Iowa? Would she move in with her mother and Phil? Work as a waitress? Keep company with regret for the rest of her life? Grow old all alone? Cara shuddered at the thought. She'd be better off dead. It occurred to her that there was the very real possibility she wouldn't be the one leaving. Micah might become bored with her. He'd created her with a casual snap of his fingers and he could destroy her just as easily. Cara's heart began to pound in her chest as a wave of pure panic washed over her. She couldn't bear to be alone in the dark with her thoughts.

"Micah," she cried out, clutching at him. "Micah. . . Oh God Micah. . ."

"Wha-what-what is it?" Micah bolted upright. "What is it? Cara? What is it?

"Oh, God. Oh, God, Micah. Don't leave me. Please, don't leave me. . ."

Micah might have been half-asleep, but Cara's words registered. Yes. He rolled them around in his head, triumphant. This was the first time he'd ever seen Cara lose her composure. And it was because she loved him, because she didn't want to lose him. He turned to her, gathering her in his arms. He could feel her heart pounding in her chest. She gasped for breath.

Micah laughed. He had her. By God, he had her!

"Don't worry, darling, I'll take care of you. You belong with me. You're mine. I'll never let you go. Never."

He laid her down and fucked her, showing her just what he meant. He knew she loved him now, because she cried while he did it.

The next morning he flew with her to Vegas. They were married in a small chapel on the strip. The ceremony was witnessed by an Elvis impersonator and a drag queen. What did it matter? The marriage was just a formality to be gotten out of the way as quickly as possible. Within the hour they were back on a flight to Salt Lake City. Micah had called ahead to the restaurant in Park City to give Jerry the news. He told him he expected a wedding cake and plenty of iced champagne on their return. As usual, Jerry grumbled about the extra work, but nothing could dampen Micah's mood. In a cheerful voice he told Jerry to go to hell. Now he could sell that damn townhouse and move her into the ranch. He wouldn't have to worry about John or any other rat-faced son of a bitch sniffing around her. As far as the business went now wasn't the time to think about it. Now was for celebrating his beautiful young wife.

The deed was done. Once Cara had spoken with her mother, said the words aloud, the act became real. She was a married woman, Mrs. Micah Welsh. Even as she smiled at Micah sitting next to her on the plane, even as she reached for his hand, she felt herself retreat inside. Breaking down last night had been a terrible mistake, and now she'd compounded the mistake by marrying him. But she couldn't let Micah know how she felt.

It will be all right, she told herself. *Micah will manage everything and I can stop thinking. That is what I want, isn't it?*

Chapter 21

Thanksgiving 1977
New York City

James laughed out loud. "You've got to be kidding. Cara? Married? If this is your idea of a joke, it's not funny."

"No Mack," replied Will. "I'm not joking, and I don't think it's funny either. I spoke with her mom last week. Cara's married, to some rich guy out in Park City, Utah. She just did it, in Vegas."

James practically fell into a kitchen chair. He felt like someone had kicked him in the gut. The news had knocked the wind out of him. "It's been nearly a year. It was just last Thanksgiving we were at my mother's house, that we set the date. That she got pregnant with my child."

"It's not getting any easier, is it?" Will pulled out a chair and sat down across the table.

"Hell. No. Who did you say she married?"

"Some rich guy. Louise said he's older, early forties maybe. Owns a couple of restaurants or something."

"Has Louise met him?"

"No," said Will. "She hasn't even seen Cara since she moved out there. I got the impression Louise thinks the man's, well, controlling, for lack of a better word."

"What's his name?"

"What difference does it make?"

"What's his name?"

"Micah Welsh. Why?"

"So I'll kill the right man."

"Hold on, Mack, this was Cara's decision. Nobody held a gun to her head."

"The hell it was." James growled as he rose from his chair, giving it a kick, sending it crashing to the floor with a loud bang.

"Hey!" Will jumped up. "Where are you going?"

"Utah."

Will hurried to step in front of him, block his way to the door.

"Move out of the way, Will. Get out of my way."

"No Mack. I can't let you do this."

"Get the fuck out of my way, Will!" James shouted at him, his right hand clenched into a fist.

"Six months ago I told you to go after her. Do you remember? I begged you to go after her before she did something stupid, something like this. You refused. Remember? You refused. And now you have no right to interfere. You have no right to go after another man's wife. Do you hear me? It doesn't matter that you love her. It doesn't matter. She's married Mack. She's married, and there's not a damn thing you can do about it."

"Move away from the door, Will."

"No, I won't. Go sit your ass down and cool off. There's nothing you can do, Mack. There's not a damn thing you can do."

James turned on his heel and strode to the closest window. It overlooked a busy street, but when he stared down he didn't see a damn thing. Somehow he had imagined. . . James didn't even know what he'd imagined. That Cara would come to her senses one day? That she'd come back to him? That some spring morning he'd open the door to his apartment and there she'd be, waiting for him? Her arms open wide, welcoming him?

He'd been a bloody fool. Will was right. He should have gone after her when he had the chance. He should have made her listen to him. He'd known, better than anyone, how fragile Cara was, how Ezra Payne had broken her. The only excuse James could come up with, and it was pretty meager, was that he'd been hurting too. He'd blamed himself for Ezra Payne as much as she'd blamed herself. He hadn't been there when she'd needed him the most. He felt as responsible as Payne for her suffering.

James had been aware, even when he'd walked out of her hospital room, that Cara still loved him the exact same way he still loved her. But now, to hear that she'd married another man? James knew to the depths of his soul that another man would never make her happy. Another man could never take his place. Yet Will was right. He didn't have a choice. He had to let her go. If it was possible, if he was ever going to find any happiness for himself, he needed to let Cara go for real this time.

How the hell am I going to do that?

Chapter 22

February 1978

"Get rid of him," Welsh said. "I don't want him around Cara. He talks too much and I'm sick of his whining."

Jerry sighed. He'd seen this was coming. The kid was a royal pain in the ass. When Micah had called him up to his office, he'd been hoping it had to do with the raise he'd requested. No such luck.

Jerry didn't mind playing the role of enforcer on occasion. He didn't take it too seriously. He'd never caused anyone a permanent injury. As bouncer he'd tossed out drunks and he'd protected the girls in the back from abuse, unless the abuse came from Micah. There wasn't much he could do about the stuff Micah dished out, except offer a shoulder to cry on and suggest that a girl find another job.

Micah had more or less left the girls alone since Cara showed up in Park City. Now she was the one Jerry worried about. He hadn't noticed any obvious bruises, but if he knew Micah, it was only a matter of time. One day Cara would say no. Micah would show his true colors and blow his stack. Some of the girls could handle Micah, a couple even liked it. Jerry didn't think Cara could survive him.

It was a dangerous thing, to care about the boss's wife. Jerry was convinced Cara was more than she pretended to be, a whole lot more. He'd recognized it the first time he'd looked into her eyes. It seemed to him that something had happened to her and she was running from it. Whatever it was must have been pretty bad. She was a classy girl with an education. She was as smart as a whip and those eyes of hers missed nothing. In Jerry's opinion, Micah underestimated her. Jerry figured that either Cara was a great actress or she was heavy into denial. She had to know Micah Welsh wasn't on the up and up.

Jerry prided himself on his ability to read people. It was one of the reasons he was so valuable to Micah. Jerry could spot a cop a mile away. He could smell an alcoholic before a man even ordered a drink. He knew which patrons would be trouble before they lifted a finger. Jerry saw Micah Welsh for what he was—a cruel, heartless, son of a bitch, narcotics distributor who liked to beat on women.

He'd heard the rumors about his ex-wife, Dominique. How after one particularly rough night that landed her in the emergency room she'd threatened to rat Welsh out. Welsh sicced one of his goons on her and the man shredded her pretty face. After that, she'd agreed to a quiet divorce quick enough. Jerry hoped she'd at least gotten a big settlement, but he had his doubts.

Jerry had never laid a hand on a woman and he never would. That was where he drew the line. He wished he'd had an opportunity to warn Cara. Right before she'd left with Welsh for Los Angeles, she seemed to be pulling away. Jerry hoped she was reconsidering her situation and she'd take off before it was too late. But then she'd come back married to the bastard. Damn. If things went bad, Jerry could maybe help her disappear, if he could get to her in time, but that was about all he could do.

Welsh waited for an answer.

"I do it my way," said Jerry.

"Do whatever you like. Just make sure he doesn't come around here anymore."

After they closed the restaurant, Jerry asked John to take a ride with him. "Let's go someplace we can talk," he said.

Yes, I'm finally getting what I deserve. John was excited. He'd wanted a piece of the action ever since he figured out how the boss really made his money. That's why he'd put up with the waiter bullshit for over two years. Because of Cara, he finally had his opportunity.

Caught up in thoughts of his good fortune, John didn't stop to wonder where they were going. When Jerry merged onto the freeway and headed towards Ogden, John figured they must be going to see someone else, someone outside the restaurant. He leaned back in the seat and relaxed. His life was about to get interesting.

Jerry pulled the car down an alleyway near the railroad tracks and parked. Ogden was about as rough as it got in Utah, which wasn't saying much. It was a former railroad town and people from all over the country had settled there. Jerry figured a mugging would be more believable if it happened in Ogden. Park City was out of the question. The place was as quiet as a tomb.

"All right kid, we're here. Let's go." Jerry climbed out.

"Great," said John. He opened the car door with enthusiasm. "So who are we meeting? You gonna hook me up with distribution or sales or what?"

"Neither. Let's talk for a minute."

"Yeah, sure." John walked over to Jerry's side of the car.

"Look kid, it's nothing personal. I just want you to know that. And I want you to know something else. If I don't do this now, tomorrow or the next day or the day after that someone will show up at your door and it'll be a whole lot worse."

"What the hell are you talking about?" The kid looked confused.

"Welsh doesn't want you around anymore. You show your face again and he'll mess you up. You rat him out and you're a dead man. Listen to me. This is important. When the cops ask you what happened, say you don't remember. You got it? Do you understand what I'm saying to you? You don't remember anything. Now drink this." Jerry handed him a bottle of vodka. It was about a third full. "And John, I'm sorry."

Micah spent more and more time away from home. He flew off to either New York or Los Angeles nearly every weekend. Cara didn't know what to do with herself. Micah wouldn't allow her to work. He didn't even like her to appear at one of his restaurants without him. Aside from running errands or visiting a salon, she was a virtual prisoner in his—their—home. Micah didn't hesitate to show her off when his business associates were in town. In fact, he expected Cara to be in attendance, looking her best, at her most charming.

Gathering her courage, she mentioned to her husband that she was bored, that she wanted more to do, but he dismissed her complaints and told her to shop. In a testy voice he said, "You reason for *being* are very simple, look beautiful and keep me happy."

In late February Micah left for a four-day business trip to New York. Cara decided to take advantage of his absence to visit John. She stopped by the restaurant first. She hadn't seen him there for weeks and she was concerned. He might be a stoner, but he never missed a shift. She found Jerry at the bar.

"Hey, have you seen John around?"

Jerry's answer surprised her. He shrugged and said, "I need to unpack a delivery in the back."

He left her standing alone at the bar.

Now Cara was really worried. She decided to drive over to John's rental house and find out for herself what was going on.

There was no car in the driveway, but Cara walked up to the front door and knocked. There was no answer. She turned the knob, but the door was locked. She walked around the back and peered through the kitchen window. The kitchen was spotless. There weren't any dishes stacked in the sink. The table sat empty. The countertops were clear of cereal boxes and cans of soup. Even the salt and pepper shakers were missing.

She peeked through John's bedroom windows. The closet door sat ajar, the closet was empty. His bed had been stripped of sheets and quilts. Not a stitch of clothing lay on the floor. John was gone. *Why?* Cara figured John might quit his job as a waiter, but he loved to ski. He wouldn't leave his friends, not in the middle of ski season. What if he'd been in an accident? Nobody had said a word to her, not even Micah.

Cara drove to the ski resort to see if she could locate some of his friends in the ski school. She managed to find one of his friends, Spencer, working behind the counter of the rental shop. She waited for him to finish with a rush of rental returns. At last everybody cleared out and they were alone.

"Hey, Spencer, where's John? I haven't seen him for a couple of weeks. I went by the house and it looks like he's moved out."

Spencer looked like he wanted to shake her. "Oh, like you don't know what happened. Give me a break."

"Don't know what?" Cara asked, confused. "What are you talking about?"

"I mean John got the crap beat out of him in Ogden. Three weeks ago. Got his jaw broke. His parents came out here and took him back to California."

"Jesus." Cara felt sick. "I had no idea. I'm so sorry. Do the police know what happened? Do they know who did this?"

"No, they don't know anything and John can't remember. At least he says he can't remember."

"What on earth was he doing in Ogden?"

Spencer stared at her. "Maybe you should ask your husband."

"Why on earth would I ask my husband?"

Spencer shrugged. "Just saying. . ."

"No, I want an answer. Why would I ask my husband?"

"Are you stupid or are you blind, deaf and dumb? What do you think your husband does, Cara?"

"He owns several restaurants. . .and he has a few clubs. . .and. . ."

"Get real, Cara. I swear you must be an idiot. He sells drugs. He's a fucking drug dealer."

Cara laughed. She couldn't help it. "Yeah right and I'm the president of the United States."

"You think it's funny? Go ahead. Laugh. John's sucking down food with a straw and you're laughing. Don't you get it? John wanted in. He wanted to be a high roller too. Why do you think he invited you to come out here? Do you think he cared about you? He talked about it all the time, how if he could hook you up with his boss, he'd have it made. You were bait. And Welsh took you, didn't he? He took the bait. But Micah Welsh doesn't share. It's a family business. He's not gonna let some punk like John work for him. So John pushed too hard and it landed him in the hospital."

Cara couldn't think of a response. Her mind was reeling. She ran out of the rental shop, slipping and sliding her way to her vehicle, the new four-wheel drive Jeep Micah had bought her as a wedding gift. The Jeep where Cara had hidden a cardboard shoebox filled with mementos of another man.

My god, it all makes sense now, all of it. Everything I've ignored for months. The secrecy, the meetings, the backroom deals, the trips to New York and Los Angeles. Cara pressed her forehead against the steering wheel. *What will I do? What the hell am I going to do?* She pulled out of the parking lot. Driving on autopilot, she turned the car towards the interstate, completely oblivious of the heavy snow coming down.

As the reality of her situation set in, Cara sped up. All she could think about was getting away from Micah. Suddenly her Jeep skidded sideways on the icy road. She'd forgotten to engage the four-wheel drive. When she tried to correct, the vehicle spun completely around and flew off the road.

Cara banged her head on the window, knocking herself senseless. When she finally opened her eyes, she saw someone tugging on the driver's door. She heard the woman speak, but her words were garbled. It sounded like she said, "*An ambulance is on the way.*" Cara wanted to laugh. *Yeah, sure. Call an ambulance. Take me to the hospital because I've overdosed on stupidity. Again.*

"Really Jerry, I'm okay. It's just a bump on the head. I promise you I'm all right."

Jerry helped her up the front steps and across the snow-covered porch. "You were unconscious when that woman found you. It's more than a bump on the head. You probably have a concussion."

"No, I'm okay. I'll be all right. Just get me inside. Micah will be home tomorrow." Cara was feeling a little nauseated, but she didn't want to tell Jerry. She needed some time alone to think, to plan.

"Depends on the snow," Jerry said. "I told him I'd stay with you tonight so I'm staying. How the hell did you lose control like that anyway? There's a reason Mr. Welsh bought you a Jeep."

"I don't know. I don't remember. I guess I forgot to engage the four-wheel drive or something."

"See? You don't remember. You have a concussion. I'm staying." He removed her coat and hung it in the front closet. "C'mon, Red. I'll take you to your room. You want anything? A glass of water? A cup of tea?"

Cara realized she wasn't getting rid of him. "A cup of tea and maybe some crackers," she said.

"All right, you got it. You want some help getting into bed? You want to take a shower or something?"

Cara looked at him. "I don't think Micah would like it if you helped me into the shower."

Jerry laughed. "You got that right. But I can turn it on for you and bring you a stool to sit on or something."

Cara laid a hand on his arm. "Jerry, thanks for your help. You've been great. You've been very nice to me. I appreciate your concern."

Jerry was touched. He'd adored Cara since the day she stepped into the restaurant. He didn't want to see her hurt. She was much too good for the likes of Micah Welsh.

"A shower would be nice," she said.

He walked ahead of her to the bedroom, turned on all the lights and flipped on the shower to let the water heat up. He searched her closet for a bathrobe and grabbed a towel.

"Here," he said, laying everything on the vanity. "You feel sick or like you're gonna pass out, you give a yell. And if I don't hear the water shut off in a reasonable amount of time, I'm coming in no matter what."

Cara gave him a wan smile. "I'm sorry to be so much trouble."

Jerry blushed. "It's no trouble. I'll go make your tea."

He headed to the kitchen and filled up the teakettle. He looked through the cabinets until he found a canister of tea bags. After he turned on the stove, he reached for the phone and dialed the boss. He had to wait while some girl went to retrieve him. Micah was at a night-club in New York with one of their newest clients.

"She's home."

"What the hell was she doing driving in a snowstorm?" Welsh sounded pissed.

"It wasn't snowing when she stopped by the restaurant. It started about twenty minutes later. I guess she was running some errands or something." Jerry didn't mention the fact that she'd asked him about John.

"I don't want her out by herself anymore. She needs to go any-where, you take her. You got it?"

"But boss, I've got the restaurant to run and the. . ."

"Don't give me any fucking excuses. I pay you big bucks. She goes out, you drive her."

"Boss, I'm not sure your wife wants to have an escort all the time."

"She'll do what I tell her to do just like you will. Do I make myself clear?"

"Crystal." Jerry heard a loud female voice close to the phone on the other end. "What time do you get in tomorrow?"

"I don't know. I may stay over a couple more days."

"What do I tell your wife?" It sounded as if Micah had put his hand over the receiver but Jerry was sure he heard female laughter.

"Call a florist for me. Get her some flowers. I'll take care of her when I get back."

The phone went dead. *He didn't even ask if she was hurt, the schmuck. So this is how fast a man like Micah Welsh tires of a woman like Cara. If she were my woman, I'd never tire of her. I'd spend my life making her happy.*

The teakettle whistled. Jerry turned off the stove and got out a mug. He opened the paper wrapping around the tea bag and dropped it into the mug, poured the steaming water over it. He found a package of crackers in one of the cabinets and stacked some on a plate. Then he headed towards the bedroom. The water was still running in the shower so Jerry set the cup of tea and the plate of crackers down on Cara's bedside table. He pulled a chair out from beneath her desk and waited to hear the water shut off. He'd seen plenty of concussions and he'd suffered his fair share when he'd played football. He wanted to be able to hear if she needed anything, or hear the thump if she passed out.

Jerry knew why she'd run her car off the road. She'd found out about John and put two and two together. So she finally woke up. Cara was trying to escape. He'd arranged to have the car towed to a repair shop as soon as possible so Micah wouldn't know that she'd crashed just before reaching the eastbound ramp to the interstate. Somehow, before Welsh got back, he'd have to teach her how to survive. It was the least he could do before he disappeared. He'd been planning to get the hell out anyway. The thing with John had left a bad taste in his mouth. Besides, Welsh was using, a lot, sometimes in front of the employees. That was always the kiss of death. It wouldn't take long before his entire operation would be busted or someone new, someone younger, with a cooler head, would take over. The nephew, yeah, his money was on the nephew before the end of the year.

Cara's head throbbed. She rose from the bed and wandered into the bathroom, intending to look for some aspirin. Suddenly the light switched on behind her and Jerry was there.

"What's wrong? What can I get you?"

She blinked at the brightness. "An aspirin, I just want an aspirin. I didn't mean to wake you."

Jerry stepped around her and opened the medicine cabinet. The aspirin was right in front. For a drug dealer, Welsh sure didn't have much in his own medicine cabinet. He popped open the lid and poured out two tablets. He handed them to Cara and filled a glass with water. "Here."

"Thank you."

Jerry watched her take the aspirin, the delicate muscles in her neck working as she swallowed. Suddenly she began to gag. Quick as a flash, Jerry flipped the toilet lid up and Cara dropped to her knees. He knelt beside her and held her, supporting her while she vomited violently and repeatedly. He wondered if he should take her back to the hospital in Salt Lake. Maybe she'd hit her head harder than they'd thought. At last she stopped gagging and leaned against him, spent. He could feel cold sweat on the exposed skin of her arms. She looked as pale as a ghost in the bathroom light.

Jerry swung her up into his arms, intending to wrap her in a blanket and drive her back to the hospital when she said, "No. Put me down. I want to brush my teeth."

"You're going back to the hospital."

"No, put me down. I need to brush my teeth."

Jerry kept an arm around her waist while she brushed her teeth, twice. When she finished she said, "Put me back to bed. Please."

"Cara, I think. . ."

She didn't let him finish. "I'm all right. I know my name. I know who the president is. I know what day it is. Just put me back to bed."

Jerry carried her to her bed. He laid her down, fluffed up the two pillows behind her and then covered her with the sheet and a heavy quilt. He started to return to the living room when she reached for his arm.

"No," she said. "Stay. Stay with me."

Jerry hesitated for only a moment before he climbed onto the bed beside her. He couldn't help himself, he took her into his arms. She sobbed, every muscle in her body shaking. Jerry held her as tight as he could without hurting her. She clung to him.

Poor kid, she's in way over her head. Getting out is gonna be a bitch.

In a halting voice, Cara's story began to emerge. Jerry learned about her childhood, the repeated assaults by her father's law partner, what happened to her in the psych hospital after she'd been caught with Rick, her father's sudden death and her mother's depression. He learned about the attack by a drug dealer that nearly killed her when she was seventeen. Her voice sounded raw, like bloody hamburger meat, but once she'd cracked open the door, she couldn't seem to close it again.

She told him about her dashed hopes for a career as an artist. Last of all, she talked about her former fiancé, James, and their plans, and what Ezra Payne had done to destroy her life. Now things made sense. Jerry understood what he'd seen in her eyes the night he'd met her. He knew why she'd remained passive while Micah shaped her into whatever form he fancied.

Jerry held onto her, rubbing her back and her neck, sliding his fingers through her curls to massage her scalp. He wished he could go back in time and kill all those people for her. He would do that for Cara.

"Jerry." Cara lifted her head. "Jerry, make love to me. Please. Make love to me."

As Jerry's hand moved to cup her cheek, she turned her mouth to his palm and kissed it.

"Red, I don't know if that's a good idea."

"Because you're afraid of what Micah might do to you?"

"No, Red, because I'm afraid of what he might do to you."

"He won't know. I promise you he'll never know." Cara paused. "I need-I need to know if I can feel. I need to feel again Jerry. Please. I don't want to be fucked. I want you to make love to me. Please."

Jerry couldn't say no to her. God help them both, he couldn't say no.

For the next four days Jerry worked hard at the restaurant. He wanted the place to be perfect for Welsh's return. He contacted the buyers, arranged for the shipments, made sure every '*t*' was crossed and every '*i*' dotted. He let nothing slip and he left nothing out of place, calling Micah daily with an update on the business and Cara's condition. As instructed, he called a florist and filled their ranch home with flowers from Micah.

He spent every night with Cara, making love to her. He didn't deserve her, he knew that, but he didn't care. Cara came alive in his arms and he savored each minute with her. He knew he'd remember her for the rest of his life. His only goal now was to keep her alive.

On their last night together he told Cara what he planned to do. She was the only person in the entire world he trusted. He tried to convince her to come with him, but she refused. She knew what he was afraid to admit, that her presence would endanger him.

"Red," he said. "You have to do something for me."

"What?"

"Get out."

Cara was quiet for a few moments. "I'll try. I will. I just don't know how yet. I can't do what you're doing. I don't have those kinds of connections."

"You have to be very careful. Don't give him any reason to be suspicious."

"I never do." She laughed.

"It's not a laughing matter." Jerry gave her shoulders a little shake. "He'll kill you, or worse."

"Worse?"

"Yeah, just ask his last wife. Listen to me, never, never go to the police. You got it? Never go to the police."

"His last wife? Micah has an ex-wife? What-what happened to her?"

"You don't want to know," said Jerry. "You don't even know she exists. And another thing, he's using. Cocaine. That will make his behavior erratic. Be prepared. Promise me, be prepared."

He handed her a manila envelope. He'd already shown her the contents. "Wear rubber gloves. Transfer everything into a plastic bag. Hide the bag. Then burn the envelope."

Cara reached for the package. Her hands trembled.

Jerry set the envelope aside and took her hands in his. He looked her straight in the eye. "Crawl if you have to. Beg if you have to. If he tells you to suck some asshole's dick then you suck his dick. And you act like it's the best thing you ever tasted. Do you hear me? Do whatever you have to do to survive. He can't touch you sweetheart. He can't really touch you, not in here." Jerry placed a big hand over her heart. "None of them can touch you. None of them has ever touched you. Not that pervert neighbor, not those jerks in the hospital, not that monster Ezra Payne and not Micah Welsh. You are still you, Cara. Inside, you are still Cara. I see you. Do you understand me? I see who you truly are."

Tears filled her eyes and Cara clung to him. Jerry laid her down and made love to her as if it was the last time he would ever make love to a woman. For all he knew, it was.

Chapter 23

Cara lifted the loaded pistol. The handgun felt heavier than she'd expected. Jerry had left it with her. It was the gun Jerry kept beneath the bar. It was registered to Micah. He'd pulled it out of his jacket pocket first thing this morning.

"Do you know how to fire a weapon?"

"I can fire a rifle, but I've never used a handgun."

So he'd shown her how to release the safety, how to hold it with one hand and steady that hand with the other one. He'd told her to aim for the torso and to fire multiple times.

"Can you do this? Can you kill a man?"

Cara had nodded. He'd instructed her to use it only as a last resort and then disappear because Micah's family would come after her.

"Wipe my prints off it. Keep it loaded and hide it where he'll never find it."

He'd already told her where Micah hid his other loaded pistol--locked in a desk drawer in his office.

Micah's plane wasn't scheduled to land until just after midnight and since Jerry wouldn't be there to pick him up, she'd have plenty of warning. Micah would call her to come get him, unless he decided to take a taxi. But Cara knew he wouldn't call a taxi because he would want a scapegoat for Jerry's failure to meet his plane, and that scapegoat would be her.

She had time.

She called the auto repair shop to find out if her car was ready. Jerry had ordered them to put a rush on it. When the manager told her they had finished the repairs, she very sweetly asked if someone could drive it out to Micah's ranch since she was stranded there without a vehicle. Of course the manager agreed. Anything for Micah Welsh's wife.

Cara drove the mechanic back to his shop. Afterward she stopped by a local salon to have her hair trimmed and her nails done, swinging by the state-run liquor store to purchase a bottle of Micah's favorite scotch.

She stripped the sheets from their bed and laundered everything including her robe and all the towels. While the linens washed, she tidied the bathroom and the kitchen, removing any evidence of Jerry's presence. The cleaning service Micah had insisted upon hiring had already been by earlier in the week so the house still looked more or less pristine.

When the sheets were dry Cara remade the bed, turning down her side and lying on it for a few moments, rolling around and around. She tossed her silk nightgown carelessly at the bottom of the bed so it would appear as if she'd taken it off in a hurry. Finally, she retrieved the cardboard shoebox containing James' letters from under the back seat of her Jeep. She opened the box and moved the letters aside. She wrapped the gun in a kitchen towel and put it in the box. She quickly closed the lid.

Cara was determined not to think of James. She refused to bring a single memory of him into the mess she'd made of her life. Her time with James was sacrosanct, off limits. She wouldn't allow Micah to sully it.

Finally Cara pulled on a pair of rubber cleaning gloves and got a plastic bag from the garage. She opened the manila envelope, dropped its contents into the bag and tied the bag shut. She tossed the envelope into the fire burning in the fireplace, watching until it had turned to ashes.

Cara knew exactly where she'd hide the shoebox and the plastic bag. Spending so much time alone on the ranch worked to her advantage. She'd explored nearly every inch of the place. There was a crawl space beneath the redwood deck in the back. It could be accessed by a removable screen. Cara had discovered it when she heard some yowling one day and found a feral cat trapped beneath the deck. She'd pried off the screen and set the cat free. As far as Cara could tell, there was no reason for Micah to ever look under there. He didn't do yard work. A grounds crew mowed, trimmed, fertilized and planted in the spring, summer and fall, and in the winter a man kept the long driveway to the ranch clear of snow. Cara shoveled the front walk, the porch and the deck herself.

Cara walked out onto the back deck and down the steps. The night was dark, and other than a single lamp in her bedroom on the far side of the house, the lights were off. Her eyes adjusted quickly to the dark. She dropped to her knees in the snow and reached for the screen. She set the box beneath the deck just to the left of the small opening. She set the plastic bag just to the right. Then she replaced the screen.

The last thing she did was to sweep the deck and the surrounding walkways clean of snow, piling the fluffy white Utah powder over the imprints she'd left next to the crawlspace. Cara removed her gloves and stuffed them into the bottom of the trash bin. Who would think twice about an old pair of rubber gloves?

Cara flipped on the kitchen light and made herself a turkey sandwich. She poured herself a glass of white wine, grabbed her sandwich and sat down with a magazine, waiting. She realized she would have to seduce Micah soon. He hadn't touched her in a month, and in a rare pique of defiance she'd stopped using her birth control pills.

When she and Jerry had made love that first night she'd been in mid-cycle and she knew she'd been ovulating. There was no doubt in her mind that she'd gotten pregnant. If Micah found out, he might kill her. He'd certainly kill her child. Cara wouldn't lose another child. Not this time. This time she'd be smart. She'd try to stay one step ahead of him. She'd follow Jerry's instructions to the letter, no matter how Micah degraded her.

Cara had awakened from her long slumber. *It's about time. I deserved that bump on the head. Something had to knock some sense into me.* Cara snorted. Who was she kidding? It was much more than the car accident. It was John. It was lying in Jerry's arms. Jerry, who spelled things out clearly and didn't put up with any of her self-pitying bullshit. Oh, she might have figured things out eventually, come to her senses one day, but by then it would have been too late. By then she'd be one of Micah's casualties. Things were about to get a whole lot worse, Jerry had said as much and Cara couldn't deny the fear she felt. But she was back. She inhabited her body again. This time, she planned to do her best to stay there.

At ten-thirty p.m., as the waiters and busboys were standing around the bar chatting up the hostess, cashing in their tips, Jerry put in a call to Cara.

"Mrs. Welsh? It's Jerry from the restaurant."

"Yes Jerry, how are you? How was your night?"

"Good. It was good. We were busy. I just called to let you know I'm leaving shortly to pick up your husband. I believe his plane is arriving on time. I should have him home no later than one, one-thirty."

"Thank you, Jerry. Drive safely."

"Will do."

Jerry hung up the phone, asking the waiters to finish up so he could get to the airport. At least six people overheard his conversation with Cara.

Jerry paid out the tips and the waiters and busboys trickled out the front door, following the new hostess. He locked it behind them. He went to check on the kitchen staff. The cooks had gone home. Only the dishwasher remained. Jerry reminded the young man that he would be locking up early so he could get to the airport to pick up the boss. The boy nodded his understanding.

Jerry checked the backroom. The place was empty. All the customers and staff had gone. He'd had the boss's okay to close the club at ten since he wouldn't be there to keep an eye on things. Jerry went up to Micah's office to make certain everything was in its proper place. He turned off the lights and locked the door. By the time he returned to the kitchen, the dishwasher had finished up. Jerry took a look at the parking lot. The boy's car was gone.

Jerry walked through the restaurant one last time, checking and rechecking. He locked the cash into the safe just like he did every night. He made sure the two deadbolts on the door in the rear of the supply room were locked, the door that led to another room where shipments of cocaine and heroin were stored briefly before they were sent on. Park City was merely a way station. Nobody suspected hard drugs in Utah and the boss liked the isolation—at least he used to like the isolation.

Jerry turned out the lights, double-checked the front door, pulled on his wool overcoat and stepped out the back door. He locked it behind him. He'd parked his car in the same spot he parked every day. The night was quiet, the air cold and crisp. He'd deliberately worn his

Boston Celtics jersey tonight, joking with some of the waiters about the team's playoff prospects.

To all intents and purposes, his rental house was the same as it had always been, as if he expected to return tonight. He'd left the porch light on, clothes in the dryer, dishes soaking in the sink and leftovers in the fridge. He hadn't touched any of the money in his account in the small savings bank in Park City. It didn't matter. He'd already stashed most of his cash in a bank in Tijuana in his cousin's name. Aside from his wallet and keys Jerry brought two items with him, an old blue blanket he'd kept in his trunk for years and a hunting knife stashed in his spare tire compartment. He deliberately hadn't washed his car in months and his license plate was filthy. Now all he had to do was get the hell out of Park City and stay under the speed limit.

If it was at all possible, he would have brought Cara with him, but that would get her killed. He didn't doubt that. Someday he'd check on her, make sure she was all right. Over the past week, he'd learned that Cara was a lot tougher than he'd thought. Jerry was counting on her to be a survivor because she was on her own. He'd done as much for her as he dared.

"Hello?" Cara made her voice sound hoarse, raspy, as if she'd been awakened from a deep sleep.

"Where the hell is he?" Micah was furious.

"Sorry, what? Micah? What is it?"

"That fuck, Jerry! Where the hell is he? I've been waiting here for thirty goddamn minutes."

"Where. . .? Where are you?"

"Where the hell do you think I am? I'm at the airport you idiot. Where's Jerry?"

"I don't know. He called me about ten thirty and said he was leaving to get you."

"Shit. Fine. I'll deal with him tomorrow. Get your ass down here now and pick me up. I'm fucking freezing."

The phone clicked off. Despite the knowledge that she was playing with fire, Cara smiled. *Dear God,* she prayed, *let Jerry get away. Let him get far, far away.*

Micah had screamed at her all the way back to Park City. He'd even insisted she drive by Jerry's house at three a.m. so he could, "Beat the fucking son of a bitch to a bloody pulp," but no one answered the door. There was no car in the drive. The porch light was on. Micah had walked around to the back of the house. When he'd returned to the Jeep, he was silent. Cara thought he'd seemed pensive, anxious.

She'd kept her mouth shut all the way home and let him rant. Now she spoke up. "I'm a little worried something may have happened. Maybe he got in an accident. Maybe you should check the hospitals in Salt Lake."

"Shut up and let me think."

Cara could hear the tension in his voice. He probably thought Jerry had gone to the police.

"Don't go home yet," he said. "I want to swing by the restaurant first."

"But it's late. . ."

"Didn't I tell you to shut up?" He looked at her with disdain. "Fucking stupid bitch."

Cara swallowed hard and made a U-turn, heading back to the restaurant.

"Slow down," Micah said as they approached the building.

Except for a light above the bar that remained on all day and all night, the restaurant was dark and quiet, the parking lot empty.

"Pull around back, right up to the back door." Micah got out and fished for his keys. "Wait here."

Cara watched him unlock the back door and disappear inside. She knew he wouldn't find a single thing out of place.

She blew out a sigh of relief. Just sitting close to Micah in the vehicle made her want to retch. She knew she was about to degrade herself and she hated the necessity. Then she remembered Jerry's word. *Survive.* That was her only job, to survive until she could get away from Micah.

Micah reappeared fifteen minutes later. He climbed into the Jeep, he seemed calmer now.

"Everything okay?"

"Maybe you're right," Micah said. "I'll have one of the boys call the hospitals tomorrow. I'm too beat to do anything tonight. Let's go home."

Cara drove out to the ranch as fast as she dared. She didn't want to get picked up for speeding, but neither did she want to be cooped up in the car with Micah. She helped him carry his bags into the bedroom.

Micah flipped off his shoes, tossing them onto the floor. He sat on the edge of the bed and began to unbutton his shirt.

Cara meekly picked up his shoes and put them away, turning back to help him with his shirt.

"So what did you do while I was gone? You miss me?"

She realized he'd already forgotten about her accident. "I missed you terribly. You were away a long time. Can you stay home for a while?"

Micah shrugged the shirt off his shoulders and stood up. He began to remove his trousers. "I don't know. Depends. I've got to figure out where the hell Jerry is."

"I'm sure there's a logical explanation. Maybe his car broke down."

Micah looked at her, suspicion in his eyes. "Maybe his car broke down? You see anything on the highway when you were coming to pick me up?"

Cara realized she'd made a mistake. She had to remember to let Micah devise his own answers. She shrugged, picked up his clothes and headed to the closet.

"I don't know. I wasn't really paying attention. I was sound asleep when you called. I think I could have passed an elephant and not seen it."

"Fuck!"

"What?"

"If something happened to Jerry, that means I have to open the restaurant. Fuck! Fuck! Fuck! Goddamn it!"

"Is there anything I can do?"

"Yeah, you can mind your own business." Micah waved her off. "I gotta make a phone call."

Micah stalked out of the room towards his study, wearing only his boxers. Cara nearly cried with relief when he disappeared down the hallway. Her legs were shaking. Cara took advantage of his absence to get ready for bed. She prayed for the strength to get through this one night.

When Micah reappeared, Cara pretended to be asleep. He flipped on all the lights, making as much noise as he could. She kept her eyes closed and buried her face into the pillow. When he came to bed, he lifted her gown. He spread her legs and entered her from behind, pounding into her until he climaxed with a grunt. He pulled out of her, turned over and fell asleep. Cara's unresponsiveness didn't seem to bother him.

Cara wondered how long things had been like this. How long had she been one of the walking dead? She ignored a wave of nausea. At least they'd had sex. Now she wouldn't have to explain the pregnancy itself, just why she'd stopped taking the Pill in the first place.

"Hey boss, the sheriff's here. It's something about Jerry." It was the new manager his nephew had sent up from the club in Los Angeles.

Micah's stomach clenched. He'd been on edge since Jerry vanished. He hadn't been willing to risk a call to the police, so he'd been forced to wait for the other shoe to drop. Now it had. Over the past few months, he'd toyed with the idea of making New York his permanent base of operations, but his nephew had advised him to stay put. He said he'd get one of his own men up there as soon as possible. He'd put things in perspective for Micah, saying Jerry obviously hadn't gone to the police or the Feds. If he had, they'd already be out of business.

The question remained though, where had Jerry gone?

Micah had stopped by Jerry's house late one night, broken a window in the kitchen door and let himself in. From what he could tell nothing was missing. Jerry's shirts and slacks still hung in his closet. His favorite cowboy boots had been tossed casually at the bottom of the bed. Suitcases were stacked neatly in the garage. Christ, there were clothes in the dryer and dishes in the sink. The man even had leftover pizza in the fridge. As he'd snooped through Jerry's belongings, the hair on the back of Micah's neck had begun to rise. He was beginning to think that Jerry's disappearance had nothing to do with Jerry and everything to do with himself. And now the sheriff wanted to speak with him.

Micah didn't want the sheriff in his office unless it was absolutely necessary. He took a moment to gather his wits. He straightened his suit. He walked down the stairs to meet the man in the lobby of the restaurant.

Jerry's car was found on May Day. A sheriff's deputy discovered it on a dead-end dirt road near Wells, Nevada. It had been stripped. The trunk was open and the deputy peered inside. He noticed a couple of things, a torn stained Boston Celtics jersey and an old blanket, also stained with what appeared to be blood. He radioed in for assistance.

A wider search revealed a bloody hunting knife and a wallet. They were half buried beneath a clump of bushes, about two hundred yards from the car. The wallet was empty. Because of recent rains, it was difficult to tell how long the car had been there or if any other cars had been by. Fortunately the registration was still wedged in the driver's side sun visor. The vehicle was registered to one Jeremiah Mitchell of Park City, Utah.

Micah burst through the front door. "Cara," he yelled. "Cara, get in here."

"Yes, Micah?" Cara walked in from the deck. They'd had a late spring snowstorm and she'd been sweeping the deck clean.

"I need to fly to Los Angeles. Get my things packed."

Cara removed her jacket and headed toward the hall closet.

"Didn't you hear me? He grabbed her arm, jerking her around to face him. "I said I'm leaving for Los Angeles and I need you to pack my things now."

"Micah, you're hurting me. I will. I'll pack your things. I was just going to hang up my coat."

"Fuck your coat. Get my stuff packed." He shoved her toward the bedroom.

Cara stumbled into the bedroom and dragged Micah's luggage out of the closet. She hung his favorite suits, shirts and the matching ties in the hanging bag. She opened his suitcase, packing his boxers, his tee shirts, his socks and his belts.

She neatly packed all his toiletries in his leather toiletry bag, stashing his shaving kit into a corner of the leather suitcase. Her movements were slow and deliberate. Her back still ached from the previous day when Micah had knocked her against the kitchen table. Her legs were sore and stiff from his kicks.

Micah came out of the bathroom. "Jesus Christ. Aren't you finished yet? What the hell is wrong with you?" He shoved her away from his luggage. He held up a pair of socks. "I hate these fucking socks. You know that. Why would you pack these socks? Just to piss me off? Is that what you're trying to do? Piss me off?"

Cara backed away. She knew what was coming.

"Don't walk away from me. What? Are you afraid of me? Are you afraid of me Cara? Huh? Are you afraid of me? Get your ass over here. Get over here and get me some different socks."

Cara looked straight ahead, trying her best to stay out of reach, but she knew it was hopeless. Micah lunged for her as she wove her way to the dresser. He grabbed her and slammed her against the closet door, knocking the wind out of her. Cara struggled to catch her breath, knowing any show of fear would make it worse.

"What the hell is wrong with you? Look at you. You look like shit. I don't know what I ever saw in you. You make me sick."

"Then divorce me," Cara whispered.

Micah laughed. "Like fuck I'll divorce you. Like fuck. I'll kill you first."

He began to pull at her clothes, ripping them.

"Micah, stop. Micah, please. . ."

He slapped her. "Shut up."

Cara gathered herself. "Micah, I'm pregnant."

Micah did stop then and he snickered. "You can't be pregnant. You're on the Pill."

"No, I'm not. I wanted to have your baby so I stopped taking it in January. I love you Micah. I want your child." She filled her voice with phony tears.

"This is a joke," he said, dropping her. "You're making this up."

"No Micah, it's true. I'm pregnant with your child. I saw a doctor yesterday. The baby's due in late November."

Micah stared at her, disgust in his eyes. "Get rid of it," he said. "Take care of it while I'm gone. If you don't, I will. And my way won't be as pleasant."

Cara looked at him in silence, her heart pounding. "No," she said. "I love you and I love this baby already. I won't end the pregnancy. I think it's a boy," she added.

Micah clenched a fist. Cara stood as still as a stone, holding her breath. She wouldn't run; running would him even more violent. The phone rang. Micah glared at her for what seemed like an eternity. At last he said, "I have to take this call," and he left the room.

Cara nearly fell to her knees, but she forced herself to remain upright. She walked to the bed to finish packing Micah's clothes.

"I think it's a good thing," Micah's nephew said. "A child adds some respectability, you know? It is Utah after all. Besides, this keeps her tied to you. You understand? You can control her through the kid. A woman like Cara would keep her mouth shut to protect her child. Yeah, this could be a very good thing."

Micah sat in an oversized leather chair in his nephew's study, nursing a drink. He considered the advice. His nephew was a cool customer. To all appearances, he was squeaky clean. He had a wife and two children. His wife was pregnant with a third. As far as Micah knew the young man didn't drink, didn't smoke, never sampled their product and he wasn't a womanizer. If he had a weakness, Micah hadn't yet discovered it.

Micah sipped his scotch, wondering what a son of his would look like. He'd be handsome, a lady-killer like his old man. His nephew had a good point. A kid would be an excellent way to control Cara and he could teach his son the business. Come to think of it, if he didn't have a son his nephew would end up running the entire show. Micah realized his nephew might not be as happy about a kid as he seemed.

Micah tossed back his scotch. He rose and poured himself another. "Maybe you're right," he said. "Might not be such a bad idea." He moved the subject around to what was really bothering him. "What about Jerry Mitchell? You think it's a message from one of our competitors, a warning?"

Micah's nephew shrugged. "Maybe, maybe not. Seems to me that if it was, they'd have left him out in the open. Made sure somebody found him months ago. There hasn't been a whisper of any trouble. Yeah, there are a couple schmucks who style themselves hotshots, but I don't think they'd go so far."

"So you think this was random? A robbery?"

"No, I think it was somebody out for Mitchell. What did he do before he hooked up with you?"

"I don't know. A little bookmaking in California, worked the border area. He was a good manager. Like I told you before, everything was on the up and up when I got back from New York."

"What did the cops have to say?"

"They showed around the bloody Boston Celtics jersey they found in the trunk of his car. Everyone said he was wearing it that night. Nothing's missing from his house. Even his money is still in the bank. The cops asked how to contact his family. I had no idea. For all I know he had no family, at least nobody he ever mentioned. They asked for his social security number. I had that on file. Of course they asked me why I had never reported him missing. I told them that I'd just assumed he'd moved on. That it was one of those things. I decided a little honesty was the best policy. I told them I was pissed off at him for leaving me in the lurch so I didn't bother to look for him."

"They bought it?"

"No reason not to. I wasn't even around that night. I was on a plane. They interviewed Cara and she backed me up. She told them I called her from the airport mad as hell because it was after midnight and I was stuck there waiting for him."

Micah's nephew laughed. "She does have her uses. Even a cop can tell there isn't a dishonest bone in that woman's body. She's good cover for you."

"True," said Micah. "There is that."

His nephew set down his glass of orange juice. "You want to check out the new shipment? It's unusually potent stuff. We should be able to cut it and increase our profits. According to a man I trust a little goes a long way. You're welcome to try it. See what you think."

Micah finished his scotch and nodded his agreement. A little cocaine would be nice right now. He'd been careful about using since Jerry's disappearance. Micah wondered if he should give Cara a call, just in case she'd decided to do as he told her and end the pregnancy. He shrugged. If she did, she did. He'd know in a week.

Cara called her mother to give her the news about the baby. She hadn't spoken with her in over a month. She decided she needed to tell her, share her news, feel a connection with someone, someone who would care if she disappeared.

Her mother was happy for her, in a guarded sort of way. She begged Cara to come for a visit. They hadn't seen each other in over a year. Cara declined. She allowed her mother to hear the remorse she felt.

Micah would never allow Cara to leave, but she didn't tell her mother that. When her mother offered to come there, Cara hedged. She didn't want to expose her mother to any danger.

As Jerry had predicted, Micah's behavior was becoming more erratic. She could sense that he barely managed to keep himself under control even on his good days. On a bad day he was capable of anything. He'd said as much when she'd uttered the words, "Then divorce me."

"I'm fine, mom," Cara said. "Maybe I'll fly back to Iowa at the end of the summer." She knew full well that any such visit was unlikely.

Before she could stop herself, Cara asked, "Mom, um, how. . .? How are. . .? Have you heard from. . .?"

She stopped James' name from leaving her mouth. What would happen if he knew about her situation? Would he fly to her rescue? Or would he shrug and say, "Well, that's Cara for you." She suspected the latter and she couldn't say she'd blame him after the way she'd treated him.

God, she was hardheaded. Look what it took to wake her up, a monster named Micah Welsh, her husband.

Instead she asked, "How's Phil? How's the weather?"

Before she hung up, Cara said, I love you, mom."

She meant them, the four little words. It felt good to say them aloud. The way Micah was behaving she might never have another opportunity to tell her mother how she really felt.

Louise Jackson called Will. She'd promised to do so whenever she heard from Cara.

"Cara's pregnant," she said. "But something's not right."

"Pregnant?" Will had a hard time getting past the word. He vividly remembered her last pregnancy.

"Yes, she's about two and a half months along, but I'm worried. I haven't seen her in over a year and when I ask about a visit, she says no."

"I wouldn't worry. I think she's avoiding us. She made it clear she wanted a clean break. Did she ask about James? Or me?"

"No, but I got the feeling that she wanted to."

"What gave you that impression?"

"There was a moment when she started to ask a question, but then she hesitated and she asked about Phil instead. I got the distinct feeling she was going to ask about James. She never talks about her husband, you know, Micah."

"What does he do again?"

"Honest to god, I'm not sure. That's another thing she doesn't talk about."

"Did she say anything else?"

"Not much. She told me she loves me."

That gave Will pause. Cara wasn't sentimental or affectionate where her mother was concerned.

"Well," he said. "She's pregnant. That can make a woman emotional."

Louise said, "Will, not Cara. I can count the times Cara's said she loves me on one hand, on half a hand. There's something wrong. I'm going to try to see her this summer. Phil has a two-week vacation coming up in August. We can take a drive out to Utah."

"Don't you think you should ask her first?"

"I'll let her know when we're on our way. She's my daughter. It's her first child and I've never even met her husband."

"All right then, just keep in touch and let me know if she calls again."

"Are you going to tell James?"

"No," said Will. "He's got a new girlfriend. He seems pretty serious about this one."

"It's a darn shame," she said. "James and Cara were meant for each other."

"You don't have to tell me. Goodbye, Mrs. Jackson."

Will hung up the phone and stood in silence. He hoped Cara wasn't in trouble. If she was there wasn't much any of them could do. He didn't plan to tell James about her pregnancy. That would be cruel. He didn't even plan to mention the call unless James specifically asked.

James was just starting to pull out of his melancholy. He'd nearly completed his cardiology fellowship and he'd accepted a *locum tenens* position at a family practice clinic in northern Minnesota, in Grand Marais. He was scheduled to start in a couple weeks. Three, four months ago James had begun dating again. He'd recently hooked up with a real looker, a society babe. Jennifer Bates. She worked as a part-time fashion model and a features' editor for some magazine. Will had met her a few weeks ago when he'd been out to the East Coast.

There was no question that Jennifer was beautiful and brainy. But she wasn't Cara. Will had found her to be somewhat superficial. She was the country club type, but if she made James happy then what Will thought of her didn't matter, so he'd kept his opinion to himself. James deserved some happiness.

Will was the one who found himself at loose ends. He'd decided to stay on in Iowa City and continue his work in cancer research. He had no shortage of dates, but not one of the women he went out with was what he was looking for. He was looking for someone like Cara, someone complicated and creative, a woman who came with a little angst, but who possessed a quirky sense of humor. He wanted a woman who wouldn't worry about her hair or how her butt looked when she was in bed with him.

Maybe it was his age. Will was beginning to feel like he should get serious. Fall in love with some woman, marry, and start a family. Serial dating just didn't cut it anymore. He wondered if there was a woman out there for him.

Louise Jackson had nailed it when she said James and Cara were meant for each other. That worried him. Look what had happened to them. They'd both suffered and Cara had compounded the tragedy by refusing to turn to the man who loved her. Will understood her reasons, but that didn't make the situation any more acceptable.

He was surprised at how philosophical he'd become over the past year and a half. Maybe it was the shock of seeing Cara like that, broken and bloody. He'd always blithely assumed that life would work out, that love would work out. That if you screwed up a second chance would be waiting for you right around the bend. If there was one thing Cara and James had taught him, it was that he couldn't take love for granted. Sometimes you didn't get a second chance.

Chapter 24

August 13, 1978

Cara drove to the restaurant. She needed to talk to Micah, but she was terrified of his reaction. She wanted to have the conversation in a public place. There might be consequences to pay later, but perhaps she could mitigate the worst of it. The past couple of months had been relatively quiet. A good part of the reason was that Micah wasn't home much. If he did come home he ignored her, that is he ignored her when he wasn't yelling about what a fat pig she'd become. Cara always did her best to look contrite, reassuring him that after the baby was born she'd get her figure back quickly. The only good thing about his disgust was that he had no interest in sex—at least in sex with her.

Micah's words were ironic. She'd just been to the doctor and he was concerned about the fact that Cara was underweight. She'd only gained ten pounds in five months. The doctor believed her when she claimed her morning sickness hadn't abated. The truth was somewhat different. When Micah was anywhere near Cara became incapable of eating. Just the thought that he might show up at home kept her out of the kitchen. It was as if she lost the ability to swallow the instant he walked through the door.

Cara knew she needed to eat for her baby. She tried. As soon as Micah left for the restaurant or one of his clubs, and she was absolutely certain he wouldn't be back, she'd prepare herself a well-balanced meal and force herself to eat it. She took her prenatal vitamins and her iron tablets religiously. It was only when Micah was out of town that Cara managed to relax enough to eat like a normal pregnant woman should.

Cara couldn't help it. When she opened the door to the restaurant her eyes automatically sought out Jerry. She kept expecting to see him behind the bar.

This new manager was cold and calculating. She had to be careful around him. He didn't miss much. His name was Brian. Cara didn't know his last name.

She said, "Hi. I need to speak with Micah. Is he in?"

"He's up in his office. I'll let him know you're here."

"Thanks."

Cara sat down to wait. After a few moments Brian returned. Cara couldn't miss the odd look on his face.

"Mr. Welsh says to go on up."

Cara rose from her chair. She had been hoping she'd be able to say what she had come to say in front of an audience. She didn't relish the idea of being alone with Micah.

She climbed the stairs to Micah's office. The door was closed. She knocked, as was her custom, before entering. At first, the sight that greeted her didn't register. Then Cara began to focus. Micah sat on the edge of his desk, eyes narrowed, grimacing. His fly was open, and one of the new cocktail waitresses—what was her name? Natalie?—knelt before him, her hand on him, her mouth around his erection. She was giving him a blowjob. Cara let out an involuntary gasp and reached behind her for the door.

"Stay," Micah gritted out through clenched teeth. "Watch and see how a real woman gives a man head. Maybe you can learn something."

Natalie pulled her mouth away long enough to giggle, then she returned her attention to Micah. Cara ignored Micah's words and grasped the doorknob.

"Stay, bitch, or I'll fucking kill you."

Cara removed her hand from the knob and faced Micah. She forced herself to watch, her face a bloodless mask, as Micah tugged at the young woman's top and toyed with her breasts. Finally, Natalie, or whatever her name was, brought him to climax. As he groaned his release, he shut his eyes.

Cara was grateful that he did or he would have seen the pure hatred written all over her face. By the time he opened his eyes again she had managed to compose herself. Micah patted the woman on the head.

"Thank you," he said. "You are much better than that piece of ice over there." He pointed at Cara.

Cara didn't respond. Standing there, watching the show, she'd come to a crucial decision. She couldn't wait any longer. Next week, she would either be gone or she would be dead. The young woman pulled down her top and straightened her skirt. She flounced toward the door. Cara moved out of her way. She even opened the door and held it for her. She left it open. She waited for Micah to zip his trousers.

"You enjoy that?"

"It appeared you did," Cara replied, before she could stop herself.

"Damn right I did. That girl knows how to make a man feel like a man, unlike some people." Micah frowned at her. "What the fuck do you want?"

"I came by to let you know that my mother and her husband will be in town next week. My mother is coming by to see me. We haven't been together in almost two years."

"Oh, hell no! Hell no. I don't want her in my house."

"Micah, please, I'm talking about my mother. She only plans to spend a day or two. I'm pregnant. When a woman is pregnant she wants to see her mother. Please Micah. You won't have to do anything."

Recognizing the expression on Micah's face, Cara braced herself. Whatever he planned to do was going to hurt. She wrapped her arms protectively around her swelling abdomen. Suddenly, there was a body behind her.

"Boss," Brian's voice came from over her shoulder. "Boss, we need you downstairs, now. There's a problem with one of the deliveries."

Micah gave her a shove as he passed by. "We'll finish this conversation later."

Cara waited until she heard their footsteps fade away before she crumpled into a chair. She didn't know how much more of this she could take, but she had to make it another week at least. Until her mother and Phil could get here. She wanted witnesses. If she was going to die she wanted someone to know she was dead. She refused to vanish.

Cara remembered what Jerry had said, "Don't call the police."

She hadn't, so far. Over the past few months, she'd devised a plan. It was risky and it could get her killed, but then anything she did or didn't do could get her killed. The police were essential, but not yet. She couldn't call them yet. She prayed for the sake of her baby that she could survive one more week, just one more week.

Cara looked around. She realized she was alone in the office. It was the first time she'd ever been alone in Micah's office. This might be the only opportunity she'd have to help herself. She tip-toed to the desk. Micah kept a pad of expensive linen notepaper next to his phone. Cara tore off the top piece. She folded it and slid it into her purse, listening as she did so for the sound of footsteps.

She quickly checked the desk drawers to see if they were locked. They weren't. She found the gun Jerry had told her about. It was shoved into the back of a drawer beneath a file. She emptied it of bullets, dropping them into her purse too. She wiped the gun clean with her skirt, then returned it to its original location and shut the drawer, wiping the desk clean as well. She didn't want to leave any fingerprints.

Cara returned to the restaurant. She made a point of chatting with the busboys as they set up for the dinner crowd. Micah and Brian were nowhere in sight.

She climbed into her car and drove towards the ranch, eyes on her rearview mirror. Nobody followed her. Micah was too self-absorbed to even consider the possibility that she might have a working brain.

Cara stopped her Jeep on the bridge over the creek near their property. She dug the bullets out of her purse and tossed them over the side of the bridge into the water below. Once they'd plopped beneath the surface they were no more visible than the little pebbles.

She hoped Micah wouldn't check to see if the gun was loaded. He had no reason to. He had no idea she knew about it. Besides, Brian probably kept another gun stowed beneath the bar. Micah would expect Brian to act as enforcer just as he'd expected Jerry to. Brandishing a gun around would attract unwanted attention. Micah wasn't that stupid. The only person Micah might actually use the gun on would be her.

Chapter 25

August 21, 1978

Dread settled in the pit of her stomach. Cara knew she had to approach Micah now. Her mother and Phil would arrive in Salt Lake City today, in the late afternoon. Phil planned to attend a two-day conference and Cara's mother was insisting upon staying with her. Micah seemed to have entirely forgotten their previous conversation about her mother's visit. Cara hadn't brought the subject up again. Now she had to tell him. She couldn't risk surprising him. She didn't want to endanger her mother.

She woke up early. While Micah slept, she took a quick shower, did her hair and applied a little make up. She dressed in her prettiest silk nightgown and robe. Cara stepped outside onto the deck. The sun was already up and the redwood planks felt warm beneath her bare feet. Birds sang in the pines and the breeze ruffled her hair. It was a lovely morning. Cara rubbed her belly, feeling the baby kick against her palm, and she smiled. It would be nice to relax and enjoy the pregnancy, but she didn't have the luxury.

Cara returned to the kitchen. She retrieved the can of frozen orange juice she'd left in the fridge overnight to thaw, poured it into a glass pitcher and added water, then stirred it and returned it to the fridge. She filled the coffee maker and switched it on, making sure the coffee was strong; the way Micah liked it. She set the table with two placemats, determined to try to eat some breakfast with him even if she threw it up later. Micah had always like omelets. Cara had eggs, tomatoes, green onions and white cheddar cheese. Perhaps if she took the time to make him a special breakfast, she could improve his mood.

As she stood beside the counter slicing tomatoes, Micah walked into the kitchen.

"Good morning."

Her greeting went unacknowledged. He opened the refrigerator door.

"I was hoping you might have time for breakfast today."

He reached for the glass pitcher of orange juice.

"Why?" He looked at her suspiciously as he opened a cabinet and grabbed a juice glass.

Cara hesitated. This wasn't an auspicious beginning. "I-I wanted to remind you that my mother is coming today. We talked about this last week."

"And I said 'No' last week, as I recall."

"But Micah, she's on her way. She'll be here this afternoon. She's going to spend a couple of nights with us. It's important. She wants to see. . . She wants to see how well I'm doing and I. . ." Cara didn't get to finish the remainder of her sentence.

Micah slammed the glass onto the countertop, breaking it. Slivers of glass flew all over the kitchen. Cara jerked out of the way, but she was too late. One of the larger pieces sliced into her forearm. She grabbed for a kitchen towel to try to stop the bleeding.

"Fucking bitch," Micah hissed. "Look what you made me do."

"I'm sorry Micah. . . I'm sorry. . ." Cara stammered. She began to pick up pieces of glass with one hand while trying not to step on any with her bare feet.

When she least expected it, Micah charged her like a prizefighter coming out of his corner. He wrapped his hands around her upper arms, squeezing until she cried out in pain. He forced her onto her knees in the middle of the glass-covered floor.

"Pick it up," he yelled. "Pick it all up." He let go of her with one hand and reached back for the glass pitcher full of orange juice. He held it above his head and then let it drop. Despite his iron grip on her arm Cara managed to duck. The heavy pitcher missed her head, but it glanced off her left shoulder. Cara grunted with pain as the pitcher crashed to the floor beside her, shattering into a million pieces and splattering everything in the kitchen with juice.

"Look what you did." Micah laughed. "Look what you did now. Damn, you're clumsy. Better clean it up before your mother gets here. Wouldn't want her to know what a slob you are." As he stalked out of the kitchen, he called out, "Don't wait up sweetheart, I'm going to be late." Then he stopped. "Oh and Cara, one more thing, if you're thinking of leaving with your mother, think again. I'll kill you. I will fucking hunt you down like a dog and kill you both."

Cara knelt on the floor, still as a stone. Her shoulder had gone numb and she wondered if something was broken. She knew from past experience that both her upper arms sported red handprints. The handprints would become purple bruises within the hour. The towel she'd grabbed had fallen away and blood ran down the side of her arm. It dripped into the pool of juice on the floor. Her robe was soaked and sticky, glistening with a thousand tiny fragments of glass. Cara sensed that if she tried to move, she'd merely grind the glass beneath her into her knees and lower legs. So she stayed. She stayed until she heard Micah finish in the shower. She stayed until she heard him walk down the hallway. She listened to his laughter at the sight of her still on her knees. She knelt there until he closed the door leading to the garage and she heard his car drive away.

Cara closed her eyes and took a deep breath, shaking the glass from her robe. She placed both hands on her belly, cradling the child within her. "It won't happen," she whispered. "I promise you he won't kill us."

"Mrs. Welsh, my nurse tells me you've had an accident with a sliding glass door?"

"Yes, Dr. Smith. I walked right into it. I'm just clumsy, I guess."

The doctor asked Cara to remove her gown so he could examine her shoulder. She hesitated. He would see all the bruises.

"Mrs. Welsh, I understand you may be a bit shy, but I do need to examine your shoulder and check for other cuts. We're going to have to stitch that slice on your forearm and I can already see that I may have to dig some glass out of your knees."

Cara thought quickly. Doctors were sworn to keep anything their patients told them confidential. If she told him not to say anything, he wouldn't, but he would chart everything she told him. That could work to her advantage.

Cara slowly slipped the gown from her shoulders. She heard Dr. Smith's quick intake of breath. He stared at her in silence.

"Mrs. Welsh, Cara, you didn't run into a glass door, did you?"

Cara began to retch. The doctor fetched an emesis basin and he held it for her while she threw up. She apologized for being so much trouble.

"It's okay," he said, setting the basin aside. "You're not any trouble. You're safe here, Cara. You can tell me what happened."

Cara dropped her defenses. He was right. For an hour at least, she was safe. Dr. Smith held her hand and listened. She didn't say a word about Micah's business or his drug use. She simply chronicled the episodes of physical abuse, starting with the events of this morning and working backward. Finally, exhausted, she agreed to let him examine her. Dr. Smith made a detailed note of each and every one of her injuries. Her shoulder was badly bruised, but not broken. The bruises on her upper arms matched Micah's handprints exactly. Dr. Smith numbed her forearm and closed the laceration with eight stitches. Then he numbed both knees and dug out several large slivers of glass. At last, he told Cara she could get dressed.

By the time he returned, Cara had dressed and composed herself. She sat on the edge of the exam table.

"Cara, I think you know what I'm going to say."

She nodded.

"You are being abused. Your husband is abusing you. It's illegal. You do have recourse." He handed her a pamphlet from the Center for Domestic Violence in Salt Lake City.

Cara took the pamphlet from his hand, setting it aside. The Center for Domestic Violence in Salt Lake City wouldn't be of any help to her.

"Thank you Dr. Smith, but this isn't a solution."

"I don't understand. They have counselors. They can help you find a lawyer. They have a safe house where you can stay."

"Salt Lake City isn't far enough. I'd have to go to the moon to get away from Micah Welsh. This morning he told me. . . He told me that if I left him he'd hunt me down like a dog and kill me. That's what he said. My baby would die too."

"Then you need to call the Sheriff's Department. Or you need to let me call the Sheriff's Department for you."

"No." Cara gripped his arm. "No, that's the last thing I can do right now. He'd get out. You know they wouldn't hold him for long. He'd get out and he'd come after me. I can't take the risk. I can't risk my child. Please don't call the Sheriff's Department. I'm begging you. Please."

"Mrs. Welsh, every single day you stay in that house you put your child at risk."

"I know, Dr. Smith. God help me, I know. But if I try to leave right now, if I go to a shelter, my husband will kill me. I swear to you. He will kill me."

"Then we're at an impasse."

Cara thought for a moment. "I'll sign a release. You can keep it in my chart. In the event that I. . ." She took a deep breath. "In the event that I disappear, or if I'm found dead, you can give your notes to the Sheriff's Department. I'll agree to that."

"Mrs. Welsh, Cara, I hope to God it doesn't come to that."

"That's as much as I can do for the moment."

"No, there's one more thing you can do."

"What's that?"

"You can come in every week. If your husband asks, tell him there's a problem with the pregnancy and you need to see me every week. And let him know when your appointments are. Maybe we can get him to control himself a little bit if he knows I'll be examining you, that if he bruises you, I'll see it."

"Thank you," said Cara. "I'll do that. Thank you so much."

Dr. Smith rose from his stool. "I'll get you some of my letterhead and you can write the note. I'd like my nurse to witness it if you don't mind. She's completely trustworthy. She won't divulge your confidence. In the meantime, try to ice that shoulder and take it easy on those knees."

Cara nodded. It had been a great relief to tell someone. Now if she disappeared or was killed someone would do something about it. The police would have a suspect. If she was dead, she'd no longer have to worry about what Micah or his nephew would do to her when the police discovered their real occupation.

"Oh my darling, look at you! Look at you! Why, you barely look pregnant." Cara winced as her mother hugged her. Her shoulder hurt like hell.

Cara kissed her mother on the cheek. "I am so happy to see you. I really am, Mom. I'm so glad you came." She turned to Phil and gave him a hug. "You both look great. You look happy," she said, meaning it.

"And as usual, you look too thin," said her mother. "Don't you know you need to eat for two?"

Cara took her mother's hand and gave it a squeeze. "I try, Mom, trust me. I try."

Cara had driven down to Salt Lake City after her doctor's appointment to meet her mother and Phil at their hotel near Temple Square.

"I'm anxious to meet this mysterious son-in-law of mine," said her mother.

Cara laughed, nervous. She was afraid to bring her mother into the situation, but she was afraid not to. Before she and her mother left Phil, she wrote down the phone number of his hotel and his room number and stuck it in her purse, giving him a slip of paper with her phone number and address on it. She also gave him Dr. Smith's office number. Phil looked at her quizzically.

"Just to be on the safe side," Cara said.

Cara's mother seemed to enjoy the drive back to Park City. She exclaimed over the beauty of the mountains. "I haven't been on such a scenic vacation in twenty-five years."

Eventually the conversation got around to Cara's pregnancy, her husband and her marriage. Cara's answers were noncommittal at first, but as they approached the turn off into town, she felt her mother deserved some honesty.

"Mom, I'm going to tell you something and I want you to listen carefully."

"Is it the baby? Or is it something else? Is it your husband?"

Cara took her eyes off the road for a moment to glance at her mother. "Yes, Mom, it's my husband. It's Micah. I'm leaving him."

"I wondered," said her mother, her voice soft. "I'm not surprised. To tell you the truth, I've been wondering for a while what was going on. When are you leaving?"

"Tomorrow, I'm leaving Micah tomorrow. This is important, Mom, really important. Whatever happens tonight and tomorrow, whatever you see, whatever you hear, don't interfere. Do you understand what I'm saying?"

"Cara, if he's hurting you. . .? Cara, I can't just stand by and do nothing. I can't do that."

"Yes, you can and you will. Mom, Micah can be a charming man. He can also be a nightmare. I want you to pretend you are delighted to meet him. I can't promise you he'll be on his best behavior, but I think it will be okay, and tomorrow we'll leave."

"Why can't you leave tonight? Why don't we turn around right now and go back to the hotel. Phil can take care of everything. Phil can handle the divorce."

"No, Mom, he can't. This is Utah. Phil isn't licensed to practice in Utah. Even if Micah would give me a divorce, I can't risk letting him get his hands on my child. Not under any circumstances. You have to trust me on this, Mom. Can you do that?" Cara saw her mom nod slightly.

"Why? Why do you need me?" Her voice trembled.

"I need you with me because I think Micah will behave himself in front of you. But if this is too much, if you can't do this, tell me now and I'll drive you back to the hotel. I won't be mad at you, I won't be upset with you, and I won't blame you. I'll figure out a way to do this on my own."

"No," said her mother, determination creeping into her voice. "I'll do this. I wasn't there for you, honey. I wasn't there for you for so many years. All those times you needed me and I didn't protect you like a mother should. You're just trying to protect your child. I can do this for you. You need me. I will do this."

Cara's eyes filled with tears. She reached over and took her mother's hand. "I love you, Mom. I don't know how to thank you."

"You can thank me by getting out us out of this."

"I will, Mom. I promise I will get us out of this."

The ranch house was dark when they arrived. Cara breathed a sigh of relief. She hoped Micah had kept his word and stayed late at the restaurant, but when she opened the garage door she saw Micah's car parked in the other slot. Cara's heart began to pound. This could be bad. This could be very bad.

Cara grabbed her mom's overnight case.

"Stay behind me," she said.

The two women walked into the kitchen. Cara turned on the overhead lights. She'd cleaned up all traces of Micah's abusive behavior. The kitchen was spotless.

"Micah? Micah? We're home. Micah, are you here?" Cara's stomach churned. The baby was kicking like mad. She laid a protective hand across her belly. "Stay here, mom."

Cara walked through the house, turning on lights as she went. She found Micah in his study. He sat in the dark, two lines of cocaine on the desk in front of him. He'd never before brought drugs into their home. Cara turned on a reading lamp and approached him. She noted the open bottle of scotch, the pale face, and the dark circles beneath his eyes. He was very drunk.

"Micah, I'm home. My mom's here."

"Get rid of her." Micah slurred his words. "Don't want her here."

"I'm going to get her settled in the guest room and make some sandwiches. Are you hungry? I'll make you whatever you want."

"Get me a drink," he mumbled. "I want a drink."

Cara stayed on the far side of the desk. She reached for the bottle of scotch and filled his empty glass. He grabbed her hand as she moved to set the bottle down. His palm was clammy against hers.

"Don't leave me," Micah said. "Don't leave me. I don't wanna be alone. I can't be alone." He sounded like a frightened child.

Cara said, "I'm just going to help my mom unpack and then I'll make us all something to eat. I'm not going anywhere. I promise. I'm not leaving you."

"You swear? You swear on your life?"

"I swear, Micah. I swear on my life that I won't leave you."

"Ever? You'll never leave me?"

"I will never, ever leave you. I promise." Cara took a chance and walked around the desk. She moved behind him and put her arms around him, kissing the side of his neck. "I'll never leave you, Micah, never. Now I'm going to get you something to eat."

Cara gently disengaged herself and left the room. To say she felt surprise was an understatement. She was completely unprepared for this Micah. Drunk out of his mind, pitiful, sad, and lost, but seeing him like this didn't change her plans. She would do what she had to do just as she knew he would do what he had to do.

By morning this Micah would be gone. He would be replaced by the vicious, brutal, manipulative, unpredictable beast she had come to know over the past year. By morning, the man who had threatened to hunt her down and kill her like a dog would be back.

Cara escorted her mother to the guestroom. She gave her a quick tour and she told her she would bring her some supper. She instructed her mother to keep the door locked and sleep in her clothes. As Cara turned to leave the room her mother stopped her. She put her arms around Cara and embraced her.

Cara leaned against her mother, gathering strength from the older woman's astonishing courage. Tempting as it was to cry on her shoulder, Cara couldn't do it. She had to be strong for both of them right now.

With one ear tuned toward Micah's study, Cara prepared chicken salad sandwiches and cut up some fruit. She poured two glasses of milk, one for her mother and one for herself. She took a tray of food to her mother's room and kissed her good night, reassuring her once more that it would be okay. Nothing would happen tonight.

She looked in on Micah. The cocaine was gone, as were another few ounces of the scotch. She brought him a plate of food and a glass of water. He didn't seem to notice when she set it down on the desk in front of him.

Cara sat down at the kitchen table to eat. She didn't have an appetite, but she hadn't eaten all day. That was irresponsible of her. Her baby deserved better. She forced herself to finish two sandwiches, an entire orange and a handful of grapes. She drank two glasses of milk.

Cara cleaned the kitchen, deciding that no matter how she dreaded it, she should get ready for bed. She was tired. Her shoulder hurt, her arms and her knees were sore.

Cara was desperate for sleep, but she knew Micah could rouse from his stupor at any time. She had to be ready.

Cara was in the throes of a nightmare. It seemed so real. She could feel Ezra Payne's hands around her throat, hard, relentless, squeezing the life from her. Her eyes flew open and she was suddenly wide awake. A hulking shape straddled her. His hands were wrapped around her throat. It was Micah.

Cara fought, clawing at his face, at his eyes, at any part of Micah she could reach. Abruptly, he stopped and rolled away. Cara threw herself in the opposite direction, choking, gasping for air. She flew out of bed and backed towards the door, prepared to run but Micah got there before her.

"Don't leave. I won't let you leave me."

Cara could tell he was still very drunk.

"I'm not leaving." Cara held a hand to her throat. "I'm just going to check on my mother. She's in the next room, Micah. Remember?"

"Why is your mother here?"

Cara kept her voice low, calm, sweet. "She's here to meet you, Micah. You're my husband. She's here to meet you and see all you've done for me. Everything you've done for me."

"Yes, I have done a lot for you, haven't I? I've given you everything, haven't I?" Micah's voice grew louder. "And look how you repay me. Look at you. Look how fat you're getting. How ugly. You won't even fuck me. You won't even fuck your own husband."

Cara watched his hands clench into fists. She swallowed hard. She had to make this convincing. "Of course I will. Of course I want to make love to you, Micah." She reached for one of his hands with both of hers and held it, opening his closed fist, tugging him towards the bed. "Come Micah. Come here. Let me do the work. Let me love you."

After a brief moment of resistance, Micah followed. She sensed he was close to tears. Cara didn't care. She hardened herself. Right now she had to give the performance of her life. She remembered Jerry's words, "If he tells you to suck some asshole's dick then you suck his dick. And you act like it's the best thing you ever tasted." Cara did that and more. She did whatever she had to do.

Cara pretended to be asleep until she heard Micah get into the shower. It seemed he intended to go into the restaurant today. She prayed that was the case. Her entire plan depended upon it. But if he didn't, she'd find another way. She'd shoot him in cold blood if necessary. Cara hoped it wouldn't come to that, but she couldn't lie to herself. It might.

The water shut off. Cara turned her head away and closed her eyes. The bathroom door opened.

"Get out of bed and make me some breakfast you fucking lazy bitch."

Cara felt a foot against her bottom. He gave her a hard shove. The beast was back.

She rose from the bed, her body stiff and sore. She knew if she looked into a mirror, she'd see new bruises on her neck. She reached for her nightgown and robe, this time she added slippers. Cara walked past her mother's door. Micah was still in the bathroom, shaving. Cara knocked softly. Her mother opened the door a crack. Cara could tell from the look on her mom's face that the new bruises were bad.

"Oh, Cara." Her mother's eyes filled with tears.

"Make sure you have everything ready to go and then come into the kitchen," Cara whispered. "Remember, it's just a normal day."

Her mother nodded. Cara could see her fear. She was sorry she had to involve her, but things had deteriorated to the point where she knew if there were no witnesses Micah would kill her. She would simply disappear.

But killing two people? One of whom had a lawyer husband staying in a hotel in Salt Lake City? Micah wouldn't do it. He'd wait for a better opportunity.

Maybe he'd hint to his nephew that Cara was a threat and let his nephew's people do it, someone like Brian. Cara shuddered. Brian wouldn't just kill her. He would make her suffer first. He struck her as that kind of guy.

Cara held her hand steady as she made the coffee and poured three glasses of orange juice. She set the juice on the table and cut up some strawberries and bananas. She got out eggs and a loaf of bread. Her mother joined her and the two women chatted together in normal voices. They made small talk about the weather, Phil, his practice and the conference in Salt Lake. Within a few minutes Micah joined them.

"Mrs. Jackson," he said, taking her hand. "I'm delighted to meet you at last. Now I know where Cara gets her unusual looks."

"Oh please." Cara's mother laughed. She acted her most gracious self. "Aren't you charming? Call me Louise. After all, we are related."

Cara noted that her mother didn't flinch. She was so proud of her.

"Darling, you made breakfast," said Micah. "I'm so sorry, but I won't be able to eat with you ladies. I have to get to the restaurant. We've had an early delivery. I'm certain I'll be able to make it home for lunch though. You'll be here, of course. I'd love to join you. Especially since you. . ." He looked directly at Cara's mother, "will be leaving tomorrow. I'd like to spend as much time with you as possible."

"We'll be here," said Cara. "I want to show my mom around the property."

Cara's mother said, "From what I can see it's beautiful."

"Yes it is," said Micah. "The ranch is very isolated. I prefer the isolation. So does my wife. Oh Cara, I almost forgot. I can't find my car keys, so I'm going to borrow your car. I grabbed your keys out of your purse. I hope you don't mind, but I just don't have the time to look. Maybe you can find them for me?"

Cara took a breath. She had to ask because he would expect her to ask. "Why don't you just pull the extra key to your car off my key ring?"

"That's too much trouble, darling. You're staying around here anyway and I'll be back in a few hours. I'm sure my keys will turn up by then." He leaned over to kiss Cara on the cheek. "Goodbye, Louise, it's very nice to meet you."

"You too," said Cara's mother. "Perhaps I can whip up my famous lasagna for supper tonight?"

"That would be delightful." Micah opened the door to the garage. The two women watched in silence as it shut behind him.

Cara rushed to grab her mother before she fell down. She helped her to a seat.

"He's so handsome," she said. "He's so beautiful. My god, he looks like James. How can he be such an awful man? How can someone so charming do such bad things to you?"

Cara knelt beside her mother, wrapping her arms around her waist. "I know, Mom, I know. For a long time I asked myself the same question. I don't ask it anymore. I don't care anymore why he does the things he does, I just need to make sure he can never hurt my child."

Cara's mother reached down and laid her hand over Cara's swelling abdomen. The baby kicked right at that moment and her mother smiled. "It's a boy."

"How do you know?"

"He just told me."

Cara laughed.

"Well, I'm glad to see you can still laugh," said her mother.

"Sometimes," said Cara. "But now we have to get moving. I want you to call Phil. Let him know what's going on. Tell him we'll meet him at the hotel. Get your bag. I have to do a couple things. It won't take me long."

"But how will we get to Salt Lake City? Micah took your keys."

"I have an extra key, a valet key, for both cars. Micah forgot about them. We should be able to get out of here in his car." Cara wanted to reassure her mom, but the truth was she knew the valet key wouldn't help. Micah was probably parked just down the road, waiting to see if they'd try to walk into town. She couldn't call a cab. There was no taxi service in Park City. The confrontation was not only inevitable; a confrontation with Micah was essential.

Cara hurried to her room to get cleaned up and run a comb through her hair. She dressed in loose slacks and a knit top, and slipped on her running shoes. Finally, she went out onto the back porch and retrieved the cardboard box, making sure to replace the screen covering the crawl space. Cara carried the box into the kitchen where her mother waited, overnight case in one hand, her purse in the other.

"Is that what I think it is?"

"Yes." Cara reached into the box and pulled out James' letters. They were tied together with twine. "Take these." She handed them to her mom. "Put them in your bag. I want you to keep them safe for me."

"Cara. . ."

"Just do it Mom. Please."

Louise reached for the bundle of letters and stuffed them into her purse. Cara removed the gun and set it on the kitchen counter while she fished beneath the silverware tray for the extra key, then she grabbed the gun and her purse.

"Did you talk to Phil?"

"Yes. I explained everything to him. If we're not there in one hour he's calling the police."

"That's perfect," said Cara. "Let's go."

Cara's mother didn't hesitate. She tossed the overnight bag into the back seat of Micah's car, and climbed into the passenger seat. Cara opened the garage door, checking to see if Micah was anywhere in sight. She didn't see anything suspicious.

She discarded the empty cardboard box in the garbage can. Nobody would think a thing about an old cardboard box. Cara climbed behind the wheel, put the gun in the glove compartment and stuck the key in the ignition. She turned it. Nothing happened. She turned the key again, still nothing.

"What's wrong?"

Cara jumped out of the car and threw open the hood. She fished around the engine compartment for a few minutes.

"Damn."

"What?" Her mother was by her side, staring at the engine.

"He removed the distributor. He must have done it last night. The car won't start."

"What are we going to do, Cara?"

At that moment, the phone rang.

"I have to answer it," said Cara. "It's Micah." She ran for the kitchen, her mother trailing behind.

Cara took a deep breath before she picked up the receiver. She had to control herself. She had to sound calm.

"Hello?"

"You're leaving me, aren't you?"

"Don't be silly, Micah. We're having coffee and then we're going for a walk."

"You're leaving me." Cara heard something in his voice she'd never heard before. Death. She heard death in his voice.

"No, Micah, we're. . ."

He'd already hung up.

Her mother began to panic. "What are we going to do?"

"Call the sheriff."

Cara dialed 9-1-1.

"9-1-1 operator."

Cara attempted to keep her voice even. "My name is Cara Welsh. I live in the ranch at the end of— yes, yes that's the place. My husband is Micah Welsh. He's been beating me. Yesterday he threatened to kill me and my mother. I'm pregnant. I'm trying to get away from him, but he's on his way home. He's going to try to stop me. He's going to try to kill me. Please send a patrol car. Please send someone to help me. Please send someone now."

"Is your husband there ma'am?"

"Not yet. He's on his way home. He knows I'm leaving and he's on his way home. His office is only fifteen minutes away. He'll be here soon. Please send someone. Please."

"Is he in the act of assaulting you?'

Cara's voice rose. She yelled into the phone, "No, he's not assaulting me! He's coming home to kill me! He'll kill me and he'll kill my mother! Get someone out here! Get someone out here now!"

"I'm sorry ma'am, but if he's not in the act of assaulting you, there's nothing we can do."

"What are you talking about?" Cara screamed into the receiver. "He's coming home to kill me! You have to get someone out here now! Get someone out here now! He's going to kill me! He's going to kill my mother! He'll kill my baby!"

Cara dropped the phone. She leaned back against the closest cabinet, panting. She couldn't breathe. It felt like there was an elephant sitting on her. Micah was coming home. She was a dead woman. She and her mother were both dead.

Cara grabbed her mother and dragged her out the back door. Her mother still clutched her purse. "Look there." Cara pointed at a grove of trees. "Do you see that path through the trees? Do you see it?"

"Yes," her mother said, her voice trembling.

"That path leads to another ranch. It leads to our closest neighbor's house. Go. You won't get lost. Just stay on the path. It's about half a mile. You can do this. You can do this, Mom."

"I can't leave you. I can't leave you here."

"You have to. You have to get help. Go get help. The sheriff will come. I swear they'll send someone."

"What if they don't?"

"Then you'll know what happened. You'll be able to tell them what happened. Tell them the gun is Micah's. Tell them I got it from his desk drawer. Do you understand what I'm saying?"

Her mother nodded. "What about the baby? Come with me."

"Mom, I'm begging you. Go. Go now."

She gave her mom a shove in the direction of the trees, watching until she vanished from sight. Cara listened for sirens, but she heard only the wind. She ran up the steps and across the deck. She'd left the gun in the car. She retrieved it from the glove compartment. She had some time. If he'd called from the restaurant, even if he sped out to the ranch, she had a little time. The front of the house, that's where she'd have to wait for him, in front, so the Sheriff's deputies could see everything.

They'd come. They had to come.

Cara surveyed the front yard. She could wait by the shed on the side of the house, but it was a little too exposed. There was a large grove of Aspens down by the creek, but she didn't think she could get there before Micah drove by. It would have to be the evergreen shrubs beside the front porch. They were thick and would provide her with cover. Cara looked at her feet. If Micah looked down, he might see her black running shoes. Cara slipped them off and tossed them onto the front porch.

She wondered if she should close the garage door, but decided she'd leave it open and hope the sight of his car with the hood up and both doors open would distract him. Cara said her trigger word, *James*. She prepared to meet her fate.

She crouched in the bushes. Her heartbeat slowed. Her breathing became regular. She felt the baby flutter within her and she laid a protective hand over her abdomen.

A car flew down the graveled drive. It had to be Micah. Cara clicked off the safety just as Jerry had shown her.

Chapter 26

Goddamn bitch! Goddamn mother fucking cunt! How dare she do this? How dare she think she could leave him? Cara was his. She belonged to him. He would see her dead before he let her go.

Micah was speeding and the Jeep swerved as he hit the gravel drive. He overcorrected, and when he did the pistol slid off the passenger seat. It clanked against the car door. The gun didn't have a safety. Micah cursed and tried to reach for it, nearly losing control of the car again. He left it where it was. He'd have to get it when he stopped. It was her fault. It was all her fault.

Micah saw the open garage door. She'd tried to leave. He knew it. Goddamn her, he knew it. He pulled up behind his own car, not that she could go anywhere without the distributor. He'd removed it last night as his insurance policy. The hood of his car was up. So she'd figured it out, had she? The smart little shit.

"Damn, this is going to be fun."

Micah felt himself getting a hard-on. Maybe he wouldn't kill her. Maybe he would just teach her a lesson. Make sure she understood once and for all that he was the boss. He climbed out of the Jeep and walked around to the passenger side. He grabbed for the gun before it could drop out of the car.

"Cara," he called. "I'm home for lunch." He walked through the garage into the kitchen.

Cara waited for Micah to come back outside. She'd seen the gun in his hand. She prayed he hadn't realized the chamber was empty and reloaded it. She heard Micah yell her name, but Cara tuned him out. She was listening to the approaching sirens.

Thank God.

She heard sirens and they were getting louder. Micah needed to come out of the house now. The timing was critical. Cara called Micah's name. He came running out onto the porch and down the front steps. He stopped in the grass fifteen feet from her, looking around like a wild man, looking for her. She stepped out from behind the bushes and approached him on bare feet. Safely out of reach, she stopped.

"Micah, turn around."

Micah pivoted. Cara pointed her gun at his chest. Her hands were steady.

He laughed, incredulous. "You're going to shoot me?"

Looking beyond Micah, Cara saw two sheriff's cars swerve into their driveway.

"Yes, I'm going to shoot you."

Micah raised his gun and pointed it at her face. "Checkmate," he said. "I'll splatter that pretty face of yours all over the yard."

"Maybe."

"Don't play with me bitch. I can take you down in a heartbeat."

"I'm not playing."

Cara watched as four sheriff's deputies climbed out of their vehicles, guns drawn. Two went right and two went left, flanking them.

"Mr. and Mrs. Welsh, lower your weapons," one of the deputies called out. "Lower your weapons and we can help you work this out. We don't want anyone to get hurt."

Micah waved his gun around, baiting her. Cara didn't flinch. She didn't move a muscle.

"Mr. and Mrs. Welsh, listen to me. Lower your weapons. I'm ordering you to lower your weapons."

Micah winked at her. "I'll lower mine if you lower yours. I'm so hard already I could burst" His grin was positively evil.

Cara kept her face blank. Her heart pounded. Terror threatened to knock her legs right out from under her. If she'd guessed wrong, she would die. Her baby would die with her. She no longer hated Micah for the abuse she'd suffered at his hands, but neither did she pity him for what she was about to do. She prayed it would work.

She called out to the officers, "I'm dropping my gun."

"That's right." Micah laughed, his gun still pointed at her. "Ladies first."

Eyes locked on Micah's face, Cara lowered her hands, tossing her gun far enough that he couldn't reach it.

She hissed three words, just loud enough for him to hear. "It's Jerry's baby."

Cara watched, fascinated, as Micah's angelic face contorted and he bellowed like a raging bull. He pulled the trigger.

Cara dropped to the ground, rolling into a ball, wrapping her arms about her unborn child. She heard the report of three, maybe four shots, and then a thud when Micah fell a few feet from her.

Cara couldn't look at him, so she closed her eyes.

It seemed as if an eternity passed before someone reached her. A voice repeated her name, but she was unable to respond. Friendly hands helped her to her feet, but her legs refused to hold her. Strong arms lifted her.

"We need an ambulance. I think she's in shock."

I'm not in shock. I'm just very, very tired.

Frederick Escobar, Micah's nephew, sat in the waiting room. He balanced a crystal vase filled with lilies on his lap. He'd decided to forego roses. That had been his uncle's favorite flower.

He'd wanted to speak with Cara the day he flew in, but he'd been told she couldn't have any visitors. She'd gone into premature labor and the doctors were doing their best to stop it.

When he'd received the phone call from Brian, he hadn't been all that surprised. His uncle had been disintegrating for months now. Frederick had known it was just a matter of time before the man fell apart. He'd warned his mother about it. That's why they'd decided to send Brian to Park City in the first place, to keep a close eye on the business and have someone, someone who could stay one step ahead of Micah.

Unfortunately, even Brian hadn't seen this coming. Nobody had, except perhaps Cara. Brian was meticulous about cleaning up his uncle's messes. The police found nothing suspicious at the restaurant.

Frederick had been asked to identify the body. The experience was unpleasant. Micah had been shot three times, twice in the back and once in the abdomen. Any one of the shots by itself would have been fatal.

He'd been told by the officers involved that Cara had dropped her gun as ordered. His uncle had not. Instead, he'd pointed the gun at her and pulled the trigger. The deputies had no way of knowing when they fired that Micah's gun wasn't loaded

Frederick wondered why Micah had brought an unloaded gun. It seemed odd, but then Micah had become very unpredictable. Perhaps he'd just wanted to scare Cara, but he'd lost his head. Or maybe he'd forgotten the gun wasn't loaded.

Frederick rubbed his temple. He could have intervened, he supposed, if it had suited him. Perhaps he should have, perhaps not. He doubted she realized it, but Cara had done them a favor. His uncle had become a huge liability. He felt some sympathy for her, but all the same, he needed to find out how much she knew. He suspected Cara was quite innocent, in which case he'd certainly provide for her and the child. But if she intended to go to the police unfortunately something would have to be done about her as well.

She hadn't said anything yet. As far as the sheriff in Park City was concerned, this was a case of domestic violence, pure and simple. Even Cara's physician had given a statement to the police attesting to the cause of the bruises and the recent injuries she'd sustained. The cause was Micah.

His uncle had been the reason he'd gotten into the business in the first place. Frederick owned a chain of furniture stores. He imported much of his merchandise from overseas. His import business, his stores and warehouses were the perfect cover. The additional money allowed him to support his family and his widowed mother in style. His mother had encouraged him to form a partnership with his uncle. She'd always doted on her younger brother and she'd hoped Frederick would have a stabilizing influence on him. Unfortunately that hadn't been the case.

Cara's mother entered the waiting room. "She says she'll see you, but please keep your visit short."

"Thank you."

Cara was propped up in bed, her face pale, her auburn curls tucked behind her ears. The greenish-yellow color of resolving bruises wrapped around her graceful neck and extended down her arms.

Even here, in this sterile colorless hospital setting, even pregnant and wearing a shapeless hospital gown, she was quite possibly the loveliest woman he had ever seen.

From the moment he'd met her, he'd understood Micah's attraction to her. Frederick was happily married. He and his wife had two daughters and she'd given birth to a son just six weeks ago. He was devoted to his wife, but never the less, he could imagine keeping Cara for himself, maybe set her up in Cabo or Puerto Vallarta, Mazatlan, possibly. Just so he could have her once in a great while. *Once in a great while.* It was tempting. She was tempting. If nothing else, it might make for a good compromise. Might keep her quiet.

He set the flowers down on her bedside table.

"Cara," he said, taking her hand, "I'm sorry."

"Thank you, Frederick."

"Had I known, I might have been able to help."

"I doubt it," she replied. "Micah could be quite single-minded."

"Yes."

"Please sit with me for a few moments."

Frederick pulled a chair up to the side of the bed. He cleared his throat. "I think you should know that all of Micah's assets are in my name but. . ."

Cara held up a hand. "I assumed as much. It's all right. I don't want anything of Micah's."

"Let me finish," Frederick said. "It's my responsibility to see that you and your child, Micah's child, are taken care of. You'll be provided for."

"There's no need," said Cara. She was blunt. "This isn't Micah's baby. There's no need for you to provide for me."

Frederick prided himself on his control, but he couldn't hide the shock he felt at hearing her words. He looked at her as if she'd lost her mind. What the hell? She'd cheated on Micah? Was she suicidal?"

"Then that's why he. . .?"

"No." Cara said. "Micah didn't know. He thought this was his child. Micah came after me because I was leaving him. I planned to leave with my mother. He wouldn't allow it. He wouldn't give me a divorce."

"Whose? Whose child? Whose? Jerry's? This is Jerry's child."

Cara didn't deny it. She looked directly into Frederick's eyes. He saw tears on her long lashes. "Yes," she said. "This is Jerry's child."

"Micah. . .? He killed Jerry, didn't he?"

"I believe so," said Cara. "But if he did it wasn't because of me. He didn't know anything about our affair. If he killed Jerry, it was because of you."

Frederick's mouth fell open. "Me?"

"Before he disappeared, Jerry told me Micah had ordered him to kill you, to kill you and your family. Micah paid him. . ." Cara fought for control. Her bottom lip trembled. "Micah gave him a lot of money to do it. Right before Micah left for Los Angeles Jerry told him he wouldn't do it. He tried to give the money back."

"But you said Micah called you from the airport when Jerry didn't arrive, that you picked him up."

"I lied. God help me, I lied. I was afraid of what Micah would do to me if I told the police the truth. He did call from the airport, but he didn't ask me to pick him up. Micah didn't come home at all that night. When he showed up in the morning he climbed straight into the shower. His clothes were in a paper bag and he burned them in the fireplace. I'm so sorry. I couldn't tell you. Micah was out of control." She wiped at the tears with the back of her hand. "You're the only other person who knows."

Frederick sat back in his chair, stunned. Unbelievable, absolutely unbelievable, but it was the only thing that made sense. He'd always found Jerry's disappearance suspicious.

Could Micah have killed the man because he screwed his wife?

Frederick dismissed the thought instantly. Micah would have killed Cara first; then he'd have gone after Jerry.

"Why? Why would he ask Jerry to do something like that?"

"I don't know." Cara reached for his hand. "I don't know. But Jerry gave me the money. He told me to use it to get away from Micah. I think he knew what might happen to him."

"How did Micah get home that morning?"

"I don't know that either, but someone must have brought him home."

"Where's the money?"

"Under the deck, in the back of the house," said Cara. "Down the steps and to the right is a crawl space. There's a screen. Pull it off. The money's in a plastic bag just to the right of the opening. I didn't touch it. Jerry told me to hide it so I hid it."

"Why didn't you use it to get away from Micah?"

Cara looked at him, her hazel eyes enormous. "Do you really think I would have been able to get away from Micah? Hide from Micah? A pregnant woman? Where would I go? I don't even have a passport." She squeezed his hand. "It's blood money. I didn't want it. I don't want anything from you. I just want to go home."

Frederick returned to his hotel room and he made a phone call. He'd sweated through his shirt, so he took a shower and changed into fresh clothes. Then he ordered room service and he waited. At midnight the phone rang.

"I've got it."

"How much?"

"Two hundred thousand and a note."

"A note?"

"Yeah, your address written in Welsh's handwriting on Welsh's fancy stationary. What do you want me to do with it?"

"Pack it up and deliver it to my mother. Tonight. Send someone you trust."

"Will do."

"Did you find anything else?"

"Not a thing."

"Nothing that might tell us who helped Micah with that little job?"

"No."

"Brian, Cara Welsh is going home with her mother. I don't want anyone interfering. Make sure everyone understands she's off limits."

"Got it."

Chapter 27

June 1979

The baby scooted across the polished wood floor, heading straight for the stairs. Cara reached him before he could get into trouble. She swung him up onto her hip.

"You would head right for the stairs, you little munchkin. I need to get the gate from the car."

Jeremy grinned at her; rubbing his tongue along the edges of his two bottom teeth.

He was a big, handsome baby, with dark brown curly hair, bright blue eyes and a ready smile. He was pretty, but no one would mistake her son for a girl. He was all boy, physically precocious, already crawling at seven months. Over the past week he'd been trying to pull himself up on furniture. Cara smiled. She wouldn't be surprised if he was walking in another six weeks, and then she would never be able to take her eyes off him.

"He's a handful," said her mother, reaching for the baby. "Are you sure you want to do this?"

"Absolutely," said Cara. "This is what I want. Besides, you and Phil are only two hours away. Don't worry, Mom, you'll see plenty of him."

Her mother brushed her lips over Jeremy's soft head. "It has been nice having you and the baby around. I'm going to miss you."

"I'll miss you too, but this is exactly what I want."

"When do your classes start?"

"Two weeks."

"Are you sure you can handle this? You'll be working as a teaching assistant at the same time you're trying to study, and you'll have this little guy to take care of. It's an awful lot of responsibility."

"Piece of cake, Mom. Piece of cake."

"Yes." Her mother bounced the baby up and down on her hip. "I guess you're right."

They didn't talk much about it, but it was always there, what had happened in Utah nine months before. Cara didn't have words enough to thank her mom for what she'd done for her. For everything she'd done.

Her mother had lied to the police without hesitation. It was just one lie, one little lie, but that lie had been critically important. She said she'd seen Cara get the gun from Micah's desk. It had been imperative to remove any niggling doubt in the minds of the police or Micah's nephew about what had actually happened. If there was any question about premeditation, it could have proved fatal for all of them.

"So how does Iowa City look to you?" asked Phil, entering the front door, a big box in his arms.

"Perfect," said Cara. "Incredibly, indescribably, wonderfully, amazingly, perfectly perfect."

"Do I hear someone talking about me?"

"Will!" Cara leaped past Phil and landed in her friend's arms.

Will stumbled back a few paces to steady himself, laughing at Cara's antics as she practically climbed on top of him.

"And to think, I wasn't sure of my reception."

"How did you know?" Cara asked, disentangling herself, her cheeks pink with embarrassment.

"A little bird told me." Will glanced over at Louise. "Will he let me hold him?"

"Jeremy? He loves guys, especially tall guys. Go for it."

Jeremy stared up at Will from the safety of his grandmother's hip. He stuck two fingers in his mouth.

"He's teething," said Louise.

Will squared his shoulders. "Well, let's give this a try. It's been a while since I did my pediatric rotation."

Jeremy went right into his arms.

Cara said, "This is your Uncle Will. He's a funny guy. He'll play cars with you. He likes cars." Cara retrieved a big red fire engine and a yellow pickup truck from the toy box she'd shoved into the living room. Jeremy wiggled in Will's arms.

"I guess that's my cue to sit on the floor," said Will.

"I guess it is." Cara sat down with them, leaning her head against Will's shoulder for just a moment. "I'm glad to see you," she said. "I really am. Right now I have to finish unpacking, but don't go anywhere. We have a lot of catching up to do. Okay?"

Jeremy thrust the fire engine onto Will's lap. He laughed. "I suspect we firemen will be busy for a while."

Summer flew by and turned into fall while Cara compiled research for her Master's thesis. She finally gave in to temptation and returned to painting. Because she no longer possessed the fine dexterity in her fingers she'd once had, she was forced to explore new avenues, new media and different techniques. If anything, her abstracts became more experimental, increasingly adventurous. The colors she used were bolder now, more assertive.

By October, she was ready for her first showing. Her job as a teaching assistant kept her very busy, as did her son, but because of Jeremy, Cara was easily recognized by students and professors alike. Her son was such a flirt that Cara had no shortage of female students willing to babysit.

Will helped out too, and Jeremy adored him. Cara treasured his friendship, but more and more she'd noticed Will watching her, and she was becoming increasingly concerned that he wanted more than a friendship. She knew she'd have to speak with him soon. She loved spending time with him, but their relationship would never be anything other than a close friendship. Cara had known true love with James yet she'd run from him. She didn't expect to find it again.

She and Will never spoke of James. Cara didn't ask a single question about him, because she preferred not to know what he was doing or who he was seeing. She refused to allow herself to dream of what might have been. There was only now, and now she was happy. She loved her son more than life itself. She had plenty to occupy her time—school and work and painting. She and her mother had grown very close, something Cara could never have imagined, and she'd begun to think of Phil as a father. He'd certainly become a grandfather to Jeremy in every sense of the word.

When she lay in bed alone late at night, Cara often found herself mulling over the events of the past few years. She apologized to Micah out loud, her whole being sad for him. He'd died. She'd lived. She wished Micah hadn't forced her hand, but the irony didn't escape her. Micah had accomplished what years of therapy had failed to do, forced her to grow a backbone.

After apologizing to Micah, Cara always thanked Jerry for his help, for giving her a son. She wished she could tell him what a wonderful child Jeremy was, but that was impossible. She had no idea where Jerry was or how to reach him, and she would rather die than put either Jerry or her son at risk.

Cara and Will spent Jeremy's first birthday with her mother and Phil. It was on the drive home, with Jeremy asleep in his car seat in the back, that she spelled things out for Will.

"Does this have anything to do with your feelings for James?" he asked.

"Yes and no."

"How much *yes* and how much *no?*"

Cara sighed. "Yes, because I still have feelings for James despite the fact that I don't expect to see him again. No, because you are my friend and I want to keep it that way. I don't want to become lovers, Will, and that has nothing to do with James. I'm sorry."

Will gave her a crooked grin. "Do you anticipate a time, maybe in the not too distant future, when you might want to become lovers? Because I'm willing to wait for you."

"Oh Will. I love you, I do, but. . ."

"Not in that way."

"Yeah," she answered ruefully. "Not in *that* way."

"Well, that sucks."

"It does, doesn't it? I'm sorry."

"Don't be sorry. Give me a chance. One night in your bed, that's all I'm asking, just one night. C'mon Cara. You've really bruised my ego here. It may take me years to recover from this."

Cara laughed. "No nights in my bed and I'm sure you'll recover quickly." She reached over and laid her hand on his. "You are one of the most wonderful men I know. You're very cute, you're tall, you're a doctor. You are considerate and kind. . ."

"Don't forget extremely intelligent and witty. I'm quite witty."

Cara laughed again. "Yes, that too."

"So what do we do now? Now that I've shown you how vulnerable I am and you've broken my heart?"

"We don't do anything different. We stay friends. We stay really good friends who don't have sex. Will, you're my best friend. I cherish you. You have to know that. I cherish you."

"Cherish is good." Will poked her leg with his fingertip. "I can go with cherish."

"Incorrigible," grumbled Cara.

"That too. I can go with incorrigible."

"Seriously Will, I don't know what I'd do without your friendship."

Will pulled his car up to the curb in front of Cara's house. "Look, I'll always be here for you. I want you to know that."

"I know." Cara leaned over the console and kissed him on the cheek. Together they got Jeremy out of the car without waking him. Will unlocked the front door and held it open for her."You want me to come up with you?"

"No, I'm fine." She kept her voice to a whisper. "Thanks for bringing in the car seat. I can get him to bed. Goodnight, Will."

Cara climbed the stairs, Jeremy cradled in her arms. He slept soundly, his little belly full of pizza, birthday cake and ice cream. He'd had a big day playing in her mother's backyard. She doubted he'd even wake up for his bedtime bottle. She managed to get his clothes off and change his diaper without waking him.

She zipped him into his flannel sleeper and turned him onto his stomach, covering him with his favorite quilt. She watched Jeremy's little fist reach for the edge of the quilt and he pulled it towards his face. He always slept with the soft quilt nestled against his cheek.

God, Cara loved this child. She ran her palm down his back. He meant everything to her. She turned out the light and started down the stairs. She had a few papers left to grade before class on Monday.

Just as she reached the bottom of the stairs, Cara heard a soft knock on the door. Will. The man had a hard time taking no for an answer. She flipped open the door.

"Will, I already told. . ."

Jerry stood there beneath the porch light. Cara clicked off the light and grabbed him by the shirt. She hauled the big man inside and shut the door behind him, flipping the deadbolt.

"Jerry. . . Jerry. . ." Cara stammered. She buried her face in his chest and began to cry.

Jerry wrapped his arms around her and held on tight. After a few minutes he backed up a step and lifted her chin. He examined her with a critical eye.

"Looking good, Red, looking good. Just wanted to see for myself. I had to make sure you're okay. Why the hell are you crying?"

"Because I'm so happy to see you. Because of everything you did for me. Because. . ." Cara burst into tears again. "Are you safe? Is it safe for you to be here?"

"I wouldn't be here if it wasn't."

"How long can you stay?"

"I'd like to be gone before dawn. I wouldn't want any of your neighbors to catch you with a strange man." He chucked her under the chin.

"Come on then. Let's not waste any time. Come upstairs and see your son."

"He's mine, huh?" Jerry asked, his face breaking into a huge grin. "I wondered."

"Yes, he's yours. I'm glad he's yours."

Cara led Jerry up the steps. They stood side by side over Jeremy's crib.

"Can I wake him up? Can I hold him?"

"Of course," said Cara. "It's okay. He's an easy baby. It won't bother him. It's his birthday today."

Jerry hoisted his son out of the crib, bringing the quilt with him. The big man cradled the baby like an expert.

"My cousin in South America has a couple of kids," he explained.

Cara suggested they bring Jeremy to her room where Jerry could stretch out on the bed with him. She lay down with him, the baby between them.

When Jerry removed the quilt to have a good look at his son, Jeremy began to whimper and he opened his eyes. Still sleepy, he looked at his mother first; then he turned toward the big stranger lying next to him. Cara watched his eyes grow wide with surprise. He grinned his silly baby grin and poked Jerry in the chin.

"Tuck. . ." he said.

"He means truck," said Cara. "He wants to play."

Jeremy wiggled his way down to the bottom of the bed and stood up, ready to head downstairs.

"No, baby, Mommy will bring your toys up here. This is Jerry, he's your. . ." she looked at Jerry.

"His friend," Jerry said. "I'm your friend, Jeremy. And your mommy's friend too."

Cara went downstairs and returned with as many of Jeremy's toys as she could carry. She left the two of them alone on the floor of her bedroom, playing a game of horsy. She went into the kitchen and made a plate of sandwiches for Jerry and got out a box of animal crackers for Jeremy. She grabbed a couple of sodas and warmed a baby bottle of milk and carried everything upstairs. Then she walked back downstairs and sat at the kitchen table, grading papers for over an hour while they played.

She smiled as she heard Jerry change a dirty diaper. Finally he came downstairs, alone. He flopped onto her couch.

"I put him back to bed," he said, patting the cushion next to him. "C'mere, Red."

Cara came to him. She nestled into his broad chest and he wrapped an arm around her.

"So where's the schmuck from North Carolina?"

Cara laughed out loud. "In Minnesota."

"When's he coming down here?"

"He's not," said Cara. "I haven't spoken with him."

"What is he, some kind of idiot?"

"No, I am. Remember?"

Jerry wagged his finger at her. "Uh-uh. None of that. I never want to hear those words come out of your mouth again. You're smart and you're tough, Red. You protected my kid when I couldn't. I can never thank you enough for that."

"You thanked me in advance," said Cara. "Everything you told me, everything you warned me about, happened. I mean, it wasn't exact, but it happened like you thought it would. The baby. . . The baby made me more determined. It wasn't just me anymore. I had to think about my child. I couldn't bring my child into that world."

"It was bad, wasn't it?"

"Yes Jerry." She buried her head deeper into his shoulder. "It was very bad."

"I'm sorry, Red. I'm sorry." He leaned over and pressed his lips against her curls.

The two sat in silence for a while, comfortable, like old friends.

Cara asked, "What are you doing back in the States?"

"I had to see for myself that you were okay. I read the newspaper accounts. I heard about the baby. I wanted to know. I had to see him at least once."

"He looks like you, I think—the hair, the eyes. He's going to be tall too. You know he was walking at eight months. I guess running is more like it. He was standing in his playpen one day in the backyard while I mowed the grass. I looked over just in time to see him throw up his arms and race across the playpen. He hasn't stopped running since."

Jerry laughed. "Don't let him play football," he said, "too many injuries. He should stick with track and field or baseball. If he's really tall, he can play basketball."

"Yes sir." Cara smiled up at him. "No football. Baseball. Track and field. Basketball if he's really tall. Got it."

Jerry drew his fingers along the side of Cara's face, tucking a loose strand of hair behind her ear. "He looks like you, Red. He's pretty, like you."

"He's a good baby, Jerry," said Cara, yawning. "He's a lovely child." She put her feet up and wiggled under Jerry's arm, making herself more comfortable.

"You rest. I'll stay for a while. Go ahead, relax. Where did you say that Minnesota boy is?"

"Hmm? Oh," Cara said, with another yawn, "Grand Marais."

Cara woke up on the couch, alone with a kink in her neck. She reached down and found that a blanket had been thrown over her. She still wore her clothes from the night before. Upstairs the baby fussed in his crib. Jerry was gone.

The last thing Cara remembered before falling asleep was feeling completely at ease, safely cocooned in Jerry's strong arms. Tears stung her eyes at the thought that she might never see him again, that he wouldn't get to watch his son grow up. Worse, she knew Jerry wanted to be here.

A lot of guys would be happy to get off the hook. Jerry wasn't one of those guys. But he didn't have a choice in the matter, nor did she. They had to protect each other and their son. Cara stretched to relieve some of the stiffness in her body. At least Jerry knew now that he had a son. And now she knew that he knew how to find her.

After a big morning kiss, Cara lifted Jeremy from his crib. She managed to convince him to hold still long enough for her to change his wet diaper. As soon as she'd finished, he squirmed away and toddled off to slide down the stairs on his stomach. Cara supervised despite the fact that her son had become quite adept at going up and down stairs by himself.

To describe her son as *a handful* didn't do him justice. He was a mini hurricane. Cara helped him into his high chair, dropping a few Cheerios onto the tray and handing him a bottle of apple juice.

As she scrambled some eggs for the two of them, she realized that she missed a man. One man in particular. She missed James. Damn him. She missed James.

Chapter 28

December 1979

James paced back and forth over the rug in his office, restless. What the hell was he still doing in Grand Marais? He reminded himself that he had it all. He should be grateful. A beautiful woman named Jennifer Bates counted the days until he moved to New York. Her father's well-established cardiology practice with its gorgeously appointed offices was waiting for him on Manhattan's Upper East Side. The last time he'd spoken to Jennifer, she'd told him she was already looking for a three-bedroom apartment with a view. So, he asked himself again, what the hell was he doing in Grand Marais? He should have left a year ago. Jennifer had wanted to get married a year ago, but he'd stayed on.

For what? The cross county skiing? Kayaking in the Boundary Waters? The hellacious mosquitoes? The babies he wasn't even trained to deliver? The kids with strep throat? The bad roads in the winter, the cold, the snow, the ice storms? Why was he still here? He had a life waiting for him and a woman who made no bones about the fact that she wanted him.

So what if Jennifer was, well, a socialite? What was wrong with that? At least she wasn't complicated. He'd had complicated. It hadn't worked out very well.

James asked himself a fourth time. Why the hell was he wasting his time in Grand Marais? He stopped in front of the window, watching the big fat flakes of snow swirl around the old brick building. He'd stayed because of one word.

Cara.

Will had told him she'd moved back to Iowa City. His friend had even said, blunt as always, that he thought he was in love with her. James had been tempted to jump in his truck, race down to Iowa City and punch Will's lights out when he heard those words, but instead he'd kept his distance.

He loved Cara, goddamn her, he loved her, but he couldn't stand the thought of being hurt like that again. He couldn't go through that kind of hell ever again. He couldn't watch her fall apart. He couldn't sit by, helpless, while she destroyed herself again and destroyed him in the process. So he wished Will the best. Fuck it. He'd go to New York in the spring. He and Jennifer would set a date, he'd move into his nice, spacious, well-appointed suite of offices and he'd learn to play fucking golf.

James hated golf.

James tossed his stethoscope on the desk and ripped off his lab coat. He'd seen his last patient. He decided to forget the stack of charts on his desk and go home early, maybe put on his skis and head out into the fresh snow. Clear his head.

Jennifer had been begging him to come to New York for Christmas. He'd told her no. He'd already volunteered to take calls so the regular docs could have the holiday off. Maybe he should reconsider. Peter would probably agree to work for him. James figured the man could use the extra money. Christmas was expensive when you had four kids.

James decided he'd talk to him about it tomorrow. He stalked to the door of his office and threw it open. His receptionist let out a startled shriek, nearly falling on top of him. James caught her and set her back on her feet.

"S-S-Sorry, Dr. Mackie, I wasn't expecting you to open the door like that. I was just coming to knock."

"Don't worry, Marie. No harm done. Do you need something?"

"There's another patient, a walk-in."

James stopped himself from rolling his eyes. "I'm leaving for the day. Wayne can see him."

"But he specifically asked for you. He said he has chest pain and he wants to see Dr. Mackie. He heard you're a cardiologist."

James snorted. The guy probably had a bad case of indigestion. He was about to tell Marie to let Wayne handle it anyway when he suddenly reconsidered. Why not? Why not practice what he'd trained for?

Maybe diagnosing a good old-fashioned heart attack was exactly what he needed today.

"Did you put him in an exam room?"

"Uh, no. The gentleman says he wants to speak with you first, in your, uh, office."

"Why? Put him in an exam room and let him know I'll be right with him."

"Um. . ." Marie hesitated. "He's, uh, he's kinda big."

James couldn't help but smile. "You get a name?"

"No, uh, he just says he has a broken heart and only you can fix it."

James burst out laughing. "I'm sure he's fine. Show him into my office then."

James backtracked and bent over his desk to retrieve his stethoscope. Someone cleared his throat from the doorway. James cast a glance over his shoulder. Marie hadn't exaggerated. The gentleman was quite tall, at least six-four and he was a good two hundred thirty, two hundred forty pounds. He was powerfully built. He looked like he was made of solid muscle. Like a linebacker. He was a good looking man even though his nose appeared to have been broken a time or two.

"I'm Dr. Mackie," James said, extending his hand towards the gentleman. "What can I do for you?"

The big man came forward and shook his hand firmly. He shut the office door behind him. "I'm Jeremiah Mitchell," he said, "and I'd like to talk to you."

Chapter 29

Christmas Day 1979

"Thanks Mom, you are a life saver."

"Ten days with my grandson is no hardship," said Cara's mother, as she took Jeremy's little hand. "I wish you'd let me keep him more often. Phil and I love to have him visit."

"I may take you up on that once I start pulling everything together," Cara said. "Right now I've got a lot of research to do and this is the perfect time. Things are quiet and I'll have the library and the art building all to myself."

Her mother nudged her towards the door. "You better get going, sweetie. It looks like it may snow again."

"Listen Mom, all his bottles are in the fridge. I stuck his cereal and his snacks in your pantry. His diapers, his snowsuit, his warm clothes and his stuffed animals are in his room and I put all his cars out on your sun porch. Oh, and his quilt is already in the crib. If you need anything call me, and I can bring it by. And I can pick him up early if he gets to be too much."

Cara's mother smiled at her. "I know it's hard to leave him, but he'll be fine. I promise I'll call if we need anything."

"Mom, I haven't been separated from him for more than one night since he was born. It feels really strange already."

"He'll do fine and so will you. Now go, before you get stuck here."

Cara lifted Jeremy into her arms and held him tight. She kissed his rosebud mouth and told him to be good for his grandma and grandpa.

He gave her a solemn look. "Mommy bye-bye?"

"Yes, baby, Mommy's going bye-bye, but I'll see you in a few days. I love you baby."

Cara handed Jeremy to her mother. She threw on her jacket and ran to the car before she started crying in front of him. She wasn't sure her apron strings could stretch for ten long days, but she had work to do and her mother had been kind enough to offer to watch Jeremy. Cara figured if she worked constantly she could get a significant portion of her research organized, and then she could pick him up early. The thought gave her a little comfort.

As Cara hit the Interstate, the snowfall grew heavier. She didn't mind driving in snow as long as the visibility was still good. Besides, the gray skies and the drifting flakes matched her mood. She was feeling nostalgic and a little melancholy. It was almost like one of those nagging feelings she got when something was about to happen, something unexpected.

Cara shook it off. It was just that she was leaving Jeremy. That's all it was. She tried to look on the bright side. She could get a tremendous amount done in ten days. Then she'd have more time for him.

James waited in his pickup. He'd parked in front of Cara's house. So far, he hadn't seen any sign of her and the snowfall was heavy and he was getting cold. He hoped she hadn't decided to stay on at her mother's, but he wouldn't blame her if she did. If she didn't show up in another hour, he'd head over to Will's apartment and crash with him.

He grinned when he remembered Will's threat. "*You hurt her and I'll break every bone in your body.*" James had laughed uproariously.

"What's so funny?" Will had asked. "I'm dead serious."

James had laughed even harder. "I heard something very similar just last week from someone a lot bigger and a lot tougher than you."

"Who?"

"Oh, just a patient who came to me with chest pain."

"Mack, you're not making any sense." James had sworn he could hear Will rolling his eyes over the phone. "Look, if you're going to do this then get your ass down here. Cara's spending Christmas with her mother and she's leaving Jeremy there for ten days so she can get some research done. If you want to try to work things out with her, now is the time."

"When will she be back in Iowa City?"

"She's coming home Christmas Day."

So James had begged Peter to take Christmas for him and he'd kissed the job in New York and Jennifer goodbye forever.

But he had no choice. Cara was the only woman he wanted. There was no substitute. She was the real thing.

Jeremiah Mitchell had laid it all out for him, the entire awful story. James had been floored. He'd had no idea.

Ever since the day he'd learned Cara was married, he'd avoided asking a single question about her. Even his friend, Will, hadn't told him she had a child. He'd only told James she'd left her husband and returned to Iowa City.

But Jeremiah Mitchell knew the entire story. James had hung on the man's every word. A lot of what he heard made him sick, but it also made him see Cara in a new light.

James spent hours kicking himself over the fact that none of them knew. None of them had been there for her. She'd had to figure out how to survive all on her own.

Mitchell hadn't been able to disguise his admiration for Cara. He hadn't even tried. The fact that the big man was willing to allow James to raise his son, that he encouraged him to do so, had James shaking his head in disbelief.

James tried and failed to feel any jealousy over the fact that the man had slept with Cara and fathered her child. Instead, James thanked him for helping Cara to stay alive.

Jesus, he'd wanted to hug the guy.

Mitchell had said, "If I thought there was a chance for me, if I thought I could keep her for myself, I would. I would move heaven and earth to take Cara and my son away with me. But I can't."

"Why can't you?" James wanted to know. He'd really wanted to know.

Mitchell shot James a look so intense James took a few steps back

"I would never do that to her. She'd be staring over her shoulder every minute of every day. I want Cara to live a normal life. I want my son to live a normal life. Besides, here's the kicker, she'll never feel about me the way she feels about you."

"But why would you want another man to raise your son?"

"Cara loves you. If a woman like Cara loves you, that's good enough for me."

James blurted out, "But you love her too."

The big man shrugged. He stood up and walked to the door, then he'd turned and his smile was wicked. "Hey Doc, you fuck with her and I'll break every bone in your body." Just before he disappeared down the hallway, he said, "You know, it's a strange thing. You look so much like Micah Welsh the two of you could be brothers."

Jesus. He left James speechless.

And now here he was, sitting in an ice cold truck, praying the love of his life would drive around that damn corner.

James had no intention of fucking with Cara. James wanted her. Just like Jeremiah Mitchell, if there was a chance for him, James was willing to move heaven and earth to have her.

The muffled sound of her tires on the snow covered street made Cara drowsy. The snow was really coming down. It was a good night for doing nothing. Maybe she'd cut herself some slack, forgo the work and instead curl up with a mug of hot chocolate and a good book.

When she came around the corner, she noticed a brown pickup parked in front of her house. That woke her up. For just an instant she hesitated, took her foot off the accelerator and the car slowed, almost to a stop. What if. . .? What if someone had followed Jerry, and. . .?

James stepped out of the truck.

Cara's breath caught in her throat. It had been nearly three years since she'd seen him, yet her heart pounded out a fantastical rhythm and her knees felt weak. He hadn't changed at all. He was still the most beautiful man she'd ever seen. Cara's hands shook so bad she didn't trust herself to pull into the driveway, so she parked right behind his pickup. She turned off the headlights and the ignition and sat there, not entirely certain she could get out of the car.

But James was waiting for her.

Cara waited until her heart stopped its flutter. At last she opened the driver's door and climbed out. She approached James with slow, cautious steps.

"Hello."

"Hello, Cara," James said, his breath frosting the air about his head. The familiar warmth of his voice brought tears to her eyes.

"Are you here to tell me, to tell me you're marrying Jennifer?"

"No."

"Then why are you here?"

James took a step towards her. "I'm here to say I'm sorry, to tell you that I've been a fool. I don't want to marry Jennifer. I don't love Jennifer. I love you. I've always loved you and I always will. I'm here to beg you to take me back." He extended his hand. "Will you take me back?"

Cara stood in silence for a moment, watching the snowflakes drift in the space between them. At last she took his hand, grasping it in both of hers. She raised his hand to her cheek and held it there, closing her eyes, savoring the feel of his rough palm against her skin.

She opened her eyes and looked into his, challenging him. "Maybe," she said. She saw James raise an eyebrow. "I have a son. We're a package deal."

"I know," said James. "Jeremy."

"I'm not the same person I was three years ago, James."

"Neither am I."

Cara laughed. The sound was sweet music to his ears. It had been far too long since he'd heard that musical laugh.

James stepped a foot closer to Cara. He raised his other hand to trace the delicate line of her jaw. He brushed his thumb over her lips. They felt soft and full, exactly as he remembered them.

"I want you," he said at last. "I want to be a father to your son. I want to be in your life and I want you in mine. Every part of me wants you. Even my bones ache with wanting you."

"Your bones ache, huh?" Cara laughed again. "Then why are you standing there? Come here and kiss me."

James closed the distance in a heartbeat. One of his arms slid beneath Cara's jacket to wrap around her waist, the other he twined in her curls as he gathered her close. His lips touched hers.

"Yes," Cara murmured against his mouth. "Yes, James. Come back to me."

THE END

J. R. Barrett has lived many lives, but the one central theme of each is her writing. She's written prose and poetry since she was a child. Her grandmother was a playwright, an uncle a noted journalist, another uncle wrote college textbooks, and her father acted as an advisor to the Iowa Supreme Court. She's had articles published in various medical and nursing magazines and poetry published in various literary journals.

Julia and her family live on the West Coast with an entire food chain of animals.

Contact the author:

Website: Julia Barrett's World
http://juliarachelbarrett.net/
Twitter: @JuliaRBarrett

Made in the USA
Columbia, SC
13 April 2022